Sometimes When We Say Good-bye

Haley R. Grayson

Magic Valley Publishers

Published by Magic Valley Publishers

ISBN 0-9716681-0-8

Cover design by Matt Gonzalez
Cover photo by Terri Cash

Manufactured in the United States of America.

First Edition

Dedicated to the Kyle in my life . . . .
He knows who he is

Acknowledgements

*A very special thank you to Laurie,
for her resourceful suggestions, and
to Colleen, for her painstaking help*

Sometimes When We Say Good-bye

Chapter One

Beth knew it was her turn to email Susan. *It's hard during the day to find a few quiet uninterrupted minutes to sit at the computer and try to string together a sentence or two that conveys all the thoughts and feelings that I want to share. I am so grateful that you have been there for me, Susan. I hope I have been there for you too.* Although the two sisters had always been close, lately it seemed that they both needed someone to talk to and confide in. When she confided in Susan about her own situation, it had been such a great relief for both of them to finally have someone to talk to. Susan, who had moved north to another state two and a half years earlier, had been deeply involved with a married man for the past eighteen months. She had been enduring her own private hell. She finally confessed that the man that she had been seeing was married. *He sounded so wonderful, I was so happy for you. I know that you were devastated when you found out that he was married.* Susan had misunderstood a conversation between herself and her boyfriend and thought that he was a widower.

"I never would have gotten involved with him if I knew he was married," Susan had remarked. "When I finally found out, I was already in love with him." *I know she would have walked away had she known. I know how much harder it makes it for her that he is unavailable.* Over the past week, they had been emailing or talking daily on the phone.

Beth, at age forty-five, had found modest success in her business life as an accountant. Although she found it frightfully boring, she was good at her work, and, as the owner of her own firm she had the freedom to come and go as she pleased. *Sometimes, it seems like I'm on auto-pilot, my hands are doing the work, doing it well, thoroughly and neatly, yet my mind is simultaneously a great distance away. I feel that I even hold conversations that way, half listening, getting the point, yet missing all of the detail, because I'm somehow just not there.*

She turned to study herself in the bathroom mirror. Beth was looking at the image of a woman with clear skin, shoulder length auburn hair and green eyes that twinkled when she smiled. *I have never been beautiful, or stopped traffic on the street, but there is an attractive quality about me. I think it's more about me as a whole person than it is just about my eyes or mouth. My energy is what I think that people - men - find most attractive.* Although she had filled out a few of her curves when she was pregnant with her son Jacen, she worked out regularly practicing Taekwondo, a Korean martial art, and was in good shape. After splashing her face with cool water and running a brush through her hair, she stopped by the kitchenette, fixed a cup of hot Chi

Spice tea with cream, then walked into her office to answer Susan's last email.

"I don't know what I am going to do," confided Beth in her email to Susan. "I feel like I am at a crossroad in my life. Change is scary. I don't want to hurt the people that I love. I don't feel content in my marriage, and I'm not sure why. I don't think I want out, but there is not any feeling of real togetherness anymore. I feel very lonely. Is there really a problem? Or, is the lack of satisfaction my own shortcoming and I just need to get over it? Remember the song "Is That All There Is?" that was so popular in the sixties or seventies? I feel like that song. Too many questions, huh! Is this what menopause is all about? God, I hope not!"

Beth had been married for fifteen years. It was amazing how dramatically people could change over time. Ethan had been spontaneous and flamboyant, loved women, and was a passionate and imaginative lover. She had fallen madly in love and had married him after a nine-month courtship. Gradually he became withdrawn and the two of them drifted into seemingly separate lives. Where they once embraced adventure together, their lives now were reduced to bickering and monotony. The spontaneity that Beth adored had been replaced with cynicism, and his desire for Beth seemed to be way down on his list of priorities. *Where did all the passion go? Where was I when it all went away? Why didn't I see it happening? It had to be all around me. Why didn't I do something about it? My life seems to be in layers. Each layer leading to the next, all separate yet all joined together. Like an onion, layer upon layer.   There are no simple answers or simple questions.   Everything is there, the passion, the love, the adventure, the hurt, the promises, the expectations, the disappointments, the past, the present and the future.*   She had stayed in her marriage hoping that her relationship with her husband would improve. Always the eternal optimist, she believed time after time that things would change between them and he would live up to his promises to her. Each time she would have faith in him, only to be disappointed again.

Beth was rambling on in her email to Susan. This was not unusual for her. Sometimes she would start a short note and four paragraphs later she was still typing away. She glanced at her watch, "Guess I better close for the time being and get some work done. Will write later when I get a chance."   She closed the email and pressed the 'send' button.

It was a warm summer afternoon, blue-gray city sky and sunshine. Beth, in black slacks, black heeled sandals and a bright sunny yellow waist length jacket, had no idea how warm it was outside, as she was in her air conditioned office.   Her private office was comfortable; she had a reception/secretary area, a conference room and the "war" room, or work room, that contained the FAX machine, copier and filing cabinets. Something about spending her days in an artificially controlled environment really bothered her. *I would rather be working outside in the yard,* thought Beth. She wanted to feel the day, hot or cold, humid or dry. She was drawing a parallel between her life and her days in her air-conditioned office. *I really should try to get some of this paperwork done*, Beth sighed quietly to herself.

Beth and Ethan's fourteen year old son Jacen, spent his afternoons in the office doing homework during the school year, handling the filing and chatting on the Internet. Jacen was now as tall as Beth, with dark brown hair, expressive brown eyes and copious freckles that covered his cheeks and the bridge of his nose. He had unlimited imagination, always storytelling and role-playing. He was convinced that he and his mom had a special bond between them that could never be broken. *I wonder what kinds of adventures are happening in the Star Wars world today,* Beth thought. She and Jacen had an excellent relationship, and Beth would do anything to avoid hurting him and their relationship with each other.

Beth realized that it was time to start closing up the office for the evening. *Another boring workday under my belt,* she thought. As she turned off equipment, closed blinds, locked doors and rinsed out coffee cups, she started the process of getting Jacen out the door.

"Jacen, time to log off," said Beth, "we need to get ready to go work out."

"Okay, I will be off in a second," he said in his off-handed way as he continued typing.

Jacen spent too much of his time, in his mom's opinion, chatting in a Star Wars role-playing chat-room. It was always a fight to get him to log off, especially if he was in the middle of an imaginative battle. Beth had threatened to bar him from any chat-room activity if she continued to have to fight with him to get him off of the computer. He was trying to be cooperative to keep his mom from making good on her threat.

Five minutes later Beth again asked Jacen to log off the Internet. With a huff, Jacen logged off and started putting his things away, getting ready to call it a day.

"Mom, I couldn't just quit in the middle of a battle," remarked Jacen. "What would all my friends think?"

"Friends? You don't have any idea who any of these people are. They could be little old ladies, as far as you know. Anyway, when I tell you it is time to go, you need to say your good-bye's and get logged off."

"Okay," said Jacen, in a voice meant to pacify his mother.

Finally logged off, Jacen brought in Taekwondo uniforms for both himself and his mom to change into. A 'dobok' is a cotton pajama-like two-piece uniform with elastic at the waistband in the pants, and a V-neck top with long wide sleeves. Beth was wearing a dobok that was all black and Jacen was wearing a white top with black pants. Beth, Ethan and Jacen started taking Taekwondo when Jacen was five. Taekwondo had been an important aspect of their lives, as the philosophy is based on success by a series of baby steps. After a couple of years, Ethan had looked elsewhere for a place to train, experimenting with several other martial art styles. Although he had trained with Beth and Jacen on and off, there had been no consistency. Both Beth and Jacen had told him in the beginning that they missed having him be part of their training, but after a while they just accepted his absence and trained on their own. The training had been excellent for Beth and Jacen. Both had earned the rank of second degree black belt.

As the air conditioning was turned off along with the lights, Beth locked the door and she and Jacen walked into the parking lot to their car. Five minutes later, they were at the local YMCA, home of their Taekwondo School.

Tonight's class consisted of an hour of kicking and punching, plus they also did some shadow sparring involving light contact with their opponent. After an excellent workout, Beth walked into the now deserted shower. She let the stream of hot water pound against her body soothing the tired muscles. *God, the hot water feels good,* she thought. She and Jacen were ready to finish off their day and head home. Their usual stops included dropping off the mail and doing grocery shopping, if needed. Many evenings they also stopped at the local video store to pick up a movie for the evening. On this night, they needed to drop the mail, but already had a video at home that still had not been watched.

"Can we make cookies tonight when we get home?" asked Jacen.

"Do we have all of the stuff? I don't want to have to go to the store, but if we have everything we can make a small batch, okay?"

"We should have everything," replied Jacen, "we bought chocolate chips last time we went to the store."

What a great kid, I am the luckiest mom on the planet, thought Beth. "Okay, you'll make the dough, right?" Beth and Jacen had this cookie thing down pat. Jacen made the cookie dough while Beth was making dinner, then after dinner, Beth did the baking. Their cookies were made from a standard cookie recipe that they had modified just enough so they could call it their very own. Jacen was proud of his cookies.

"Yes Mother, I always make the dough," he said matter-of-factly. "I got dibs on licking the bowl." *I think the dough is his favorite part, actually I like the dough too.*

"Your dad will have a fit!"

Ethan always hated when Jacen and Beth ate the cookie dough before it was baked. He was sure that they would both get stomach worms, or would die, or something equally unpleasant. They both took a finger full of dough here and there, just to do a taste test, when he wasn't looking.

Being mother to Jacen was the highlight of Beth's life. While her relationship with Ethan had grown distant over the years, she had come to realize that motherhood was her most important role. *Jacen is growing up and becoming an independent young man. There will be such a void in my life when he no longer needs me.* At the moment, Beth was the kingpin on which her family revolved. The direction that her life takes in the future may be dramatically altered by choices she now makes.

On this warm balmy September night while driving home, Jacen was listening to the oldies station on the radio and chattering to Beth about his Star Wars chat-room adventures today. Beth seemed a little preoccupied as her mind drifted back to last week, to the phone call that lead to her current situation.

***

What is it about Kyle that is so special? Beth thought to herself. *Why am I so drawn to him and will it ever go away? Do I really want it to go away?* she wondered. Over the past couple of months, she had felt an urge to call Kyle, a very special person in her past. It was a familiar urge, one that she had experienced many times in her life. She made several phone calls to his work number, but he had not been available. Each time she was told that he was not in, she felt slightly relieved, yet always disappointed. Kyle had always been glad to hear from her in the past, as she had always been glad to hear from him whenever he called her. On this Thursday, at about 2:00 in the afternoon he answered the call.

"Hi, Kyle? This is . ."

"Hey Beth, I know who you are. I still recognize your voice," replied Kyle, as though he had been expecting her call. He didn't even seem surprised. She fantasized that maybe he had been thinking of her too.

"How are you? I was just thinking about you and decided to call and say hi. I have actually called a few times over the past couple of months, but you have never been in."

"Why didn't you leave a message? I would have called you back," said Kyle. *I wasn't sure that you would be glad to hear from me and was afraid that you wouldn't call me back,* she thought.

"I don't know, I guess I wasn't sure if it would be okay if you got a personal call at work, but I'm glad that I caught you in today. You sound good. How is life treating you?" asked Beth. *I am short of breath,* she thought incredulously.

"Can't complain too much, no one listens much anyway," he sighed. "It is the usual routine for me, work, work, work, fish a little now and then, nothing too exciting, I'm afraid. How about you? Been to the mountains lately?"

"Actually, yes, I go almost every weekend. Been doing a lot of work on the place and still enjoy a motorcycle ride now and then. Jacen is now fourteen and is riding the bike that I had when I was his age. Do you remember?" *I wonder if he remembers that time in his life as clearly as I remember. I wonder if he still thinks of me as I think of him, after all these years.*

"Oh yes, I sure do. You were a vision on that bike! Bet you still are. I would love to get up there but I don't have a truck. I am stuck in this lease on a car that I don't even like."

"What kind of car?"

"A little Nissan."

"Oh," she replied with a little giggle, "you're right, you would tear that car up on our road." *I miss seeing you up there,* she thought.

"I'm envious and would love to get up there one of these days," he replied. "My next vehicle will definitely be some kind of truck."

"You still visit me in my dreams sometimes, you know. You did about a month ago. I guess that's really why I called. It's nice to hear your voice."

"You sound good too. I'm glad that you called, I've missed you.   I hate to cut this short, but I need to get to a meeting. Do you have an email address?"

"I've missed you too.   You have a very special place in my heart still, even after thirty years. Yes, I have an email address."

After the brief phone conversation, they exchanged email addresses and promised to email each other. Beth got off the phone, trembling with the old familiar feeling of longing that she had felt many times over the past thirty years. Somewhat confused over her reaction to the phone call, she pulled up her email and jotted Kyle a quick note.

~

EMAIL
TO: klm@qmail.com
FROM: beth0711@qmail.com
RE: Hello

Hi Kyle,
Just wanted to make sure that I had the right email address. It was nice to hear your voice today. It has been a long time. Write back when you get a chance. –
b

~

Chapter Two

After Kyle hung up the phone, he sat there for a minute trying to organize his thoughts and feelings. *Beth, you always do this to me*, he thought. Normally, very in control of his emotions, Kyle always experienced a moment of panic when he talked to her. All the bottled-up emotion hidden very deep inside came bubbling up to consume him, like a bottle of coke that had been shaken very well, then someone popped the top.

He was slightly annoyed at his own reaction. Not having dared to actually drop his guard that had protected him so well to see if his feelings had changed, he really thought that maybe after thirty years he might have finally gotten over her. Actually, he was trying to fool himself. He smiled an amused smile at the absurdity of one trying to fool oneself. *You still think of her everyday, you stupid idiot*, he silently chided to himself. *She says that she calls when I visit her in her dreams. Babe, you are always in my dreams!*

While trying to develop an organized plan of action, a single brick falls from the wall that he so emphatically keeps around him. A single memory tumbles out, the day he first met Beth. As the memory starts to take control, he takes the briefest second to feel, really feel, before stuffing the memory back in and shoving the brick firmly in place. If he never allows himself to experience his memories, he never has to feel the pain associated with them. He also will not have to acknowledge his loss or his part in creating the loss. High towering walls, thick and strong, this is his way.

Later he will realize that his perception of what love feels like is based on his memories of being with Beth. Oh this day, however, without knowing why, in his heart he knew that he would write to her and would eventually see her. He also knew, with startling clarity, that she would create for him an opening in his wall that would allow him to feel the joy of being complete and the pain of knowing what cannot be.

Kyle jotted a quick email to her, telling her how nice it was to hear her voice. He told her that he has thought of her often, yes, even after thirty years. He questioned the wisdom of continued correspondence knowing the feelings that would surface and the desires that could never be fulfilled. Although he expressed his concerns to her in his email, he knew how Beth would react . . . . full steam ahead, passion pouring from her very soul and her usual exuberant deep-seated belief that love will conquer all.

Chapter Three

Beth and Jacen were singing "This Magic Moment," by Jay and the Americans, playing on the oldies radio station, when she realized that her freeway off-ramp was coming up and she needed to negotiate a lane change.

The line that goes "This magic moment when your lips are close to mine" reminded her of a magic moment in her life, the day that she first met Kyle.

***

Beth Collins, at age 15, was impulsive and outgoing, with a gentle way about her. Always the eternal optimist, she had boundless energy and a passion for life. Her long, fine auburn hair complimented large green eyes and a sprinkle of freckles across her high cheekbones. This fateful afternoon, Memorial Day weekend, her life was to change in ways that she would never have been able to foresee. Beth and her sister Susan, who was two years younger, had been sitting inside their cabin in the mountains working on a sign painting project. Beth had finished her "Private Property" sign and was ready to lay it out to dry. *I'm ready to get out into the fresh air,* she thought to herself.

"Sis, lets go for a motorcycle ride and get outside for a while," said Beth as she got up to stretch her legs.

***

Kyle Montero, six months older than Beth, was conservative, self-assured and extremely stubborn. He was solidly built with large brown eyes and short brown hair streaked with red highlights. Kyle's family struggled with the directions that they were given to find the Utell's new family weekend property. His family lived across the street, in the city, from the Utell's.

"This is out in the middle of nowhere!" exclaimed Kyle's dad as he finally spotted the Utell's trailer. Nestled in the foothills of the San Bernardino Mountains, about fifteen miles down an unmarked dirt road, they finally arrived. The property was in a shallow valley with a bright blue sky and pure clean mountain air scented with pine, juniper and sage. As Kyle's dad made the final turn into the Utell's property, two girls, around his age, riding side by side on small motorcycles passed them on the road. The bikes were screaming as the two girls flew by, hair billowing out behind them. Kyle was fascinated and watched them until they turned a corner and rode out of sight. He looked back to where he first saw them, momentarily unsure of what he just saw. *A vision*, he thought to himself.

"I'm sure I saw two girls on motorcycles when we drove in. Who are they?" Kyle asked Merrill as soon as he saw him. Merrill Utell was a year younger than Kyle. Although they lived across the street from each other, they had different friends and were not close.

"Oh, that's Beth and her sister Susan. They have the cabin down the road a bit. We can walk down and I'll introduce you," explained Merrill. "Don't get your hopes up though, I have been trying to get their phone number ever since we bought this place."

"Why didn't you tell me about them before? I would have talked my dad into coming up here long before now. I'll get a phone number, you just watch."

"I've got a quarter bet that you won't have their phone number by the end of the weekend."

Kyle, in jeans and a light green striped tee-shirt, exclaimed, as he pointed a finger at Merrill, "You're on!"

Beth saw Kyle's family arrive as she and Susan took off on their motorcycles. *I wonder who that is?* she thought. They did not get many visitors in their neck of the woods. She and Susan took a short ride, smoothly riding side by side on the one lane dirt road, moving in tandem, anticipating and compensating for each move that the other made. They took the roads fast but very much in control.

"I don't want to be gone too long," yelled Beth over

the noise of the engines, "let's find out who that was that just drove in." Beth pointed to a spot to turn around. Both girls made the turn easily and a few minutes later were flying back toward their cabin.

Fifteen minutes later Merrill was introducing Kyle to Beth and Susan. Standing next to her motorcycle with cheeks flushed with the excitement of an exhilarating motorcycle ride, Beth met Kyle. *Why am I feeling so warm all of a sudden?* thought Beth. *Look at the way he is smiling at me. I am actually flustered. I can't believe this.* Kyle's first thought was that Beth was a vision face to face, as well as riding into the horizon on a motorcycle. He was completely intrigued with her and all at once realized how beautiful the valley was, how blue the sky, and how much he was going to enjoy this weekend. His family was planning on staying through until Monday and Kyle already sensed that something special was happening.

Beth had known Merrill for the past four months, seeing him on an occasional weekend when both families were at their property for the weekend. *He's a little strange,* Beth had thought when she first met him. Merrill was a round faced, brown skinned boy with shiny black hair and a dimpled smile. He was a very nice person but there was no romantic interest. Merrill was a very unusual sort. Not the brightest bulb in the room, but he had a heart of gold.

Over the next couple of hours, Beth learned that Kyle's family lived in Anaheim, a town about thirty miles from where she lived. He was starting the tenth grade too and would be going to a Catholic High School. He planned on trying out for the track team. *I can picture him running track,* Beth thought to herself. His family had a camper and dune buggy and did a lot of camping. They were considering buying some land in this valley next to Merrill's family.

"We've only had our place for a little less than a year. I love it here. We used to go camping a lot too, but I like coming here better. Camping is fun, but there is so much to explore out here." Beth threw her arms out wide to dramatically show the whole valley. "This whole area used to be used for mining gold and there are still gold mines all over. Susan and I've found a couple of mining shafts. I'll have to show you." *I feel like I'm rambling on, but just can't help it.* "There are even a few miners still around. Lots of characters in these hills." Kyle couldn't take his eyes off of her, the way she used her hands when she talked, he couldn't help smiling.

Sitting out in front of Beth and Susan's cabin drinking grape soda, Kyle finally asked Beth how long she had been riding a motorcycle.

"Oh, about a year, this actually is my second bike." *I love the way he keeps smiling at me. It's like I'm the only person on the planet.* "Hop on, I'll take you for a ride," giggled Beth as she stood and brushed the dirt off her jeans. Beth was wearing faded Levi blue jeans, with patches over the knees of a deep red and yellow paisley pattern and a yellow button up lightweight flannel shirt. She was already anticipating how close he would be sitting behind her.

How could Kyle say no? Why would he even consider saying no? Beth started up the bike and Kyle climbed on behind her. *His hands feel so warm on my waist.* They did not go far. Down the road a bit the road made a sharp left turn. Smoothly, Beth downshifted and continued left to another sharp turn, which was in slippery sand. *I really want to impress him,* she thought to herself. Beth had obviously handled the bike in sand before, because, with the confidence of an experienced rider, she negotiated the road until they came to the final left turn which would complete the loop and take them back to the cabin. Unfortunately, the bike stalled. *Oh man,* she thought, *I can't believe the plug has fouled now, of all times. Fortunately, it won't be too embarrassing. At least I know what the problem is and it should only take a couple of minutes to have it fixed.* As Kyle climbed off and was about to offer to help push the bike back to the cabin, Beth reached under the seat and pulled out the small tool pouch.

"This will just take minute," Beth remarked. To Kyle's astonishment, she removed the spark plug, cleaned it and re-installed it. The bike started on the first kick. "Spark plug fouls a lot on this bike," explained Beth, as she gestured for Kyle to hop back on. Kyle, speechless, climbed back on the bike as they took off on the straightaway that led back to the cabin. Grinning from ear to ear when they stopped in front of the cabin, he got off the bike.

"Merrill went back home, his mom called you guys for dinner. He told me to send you home when you got back," said Susan.

"Thanks, well, I guess I'll see you later. Beth, thanks for the ride, I'll take you for a ride in our dune buggy one of these days." Beth had never ridden in a dune buggy, but saw their's when they pulled in earlier that day.

"Sounds fun." *Maybe this weekend?* thought Beth with a smile.

***

"So, where did you two go?" asked Susan, as they started walking toward the cabin.

"Just for a short ride around the loop. The bike stalled and I had to clean the plug, so that is why we were gone so long."

"He's cute and I think he likes you." *I really like him too,* thought Beth.

"He is cute, huh. I think I may have scared him a little on the bike when we went through the sandy part," giggled Beth.

"Let's go see what we're having for dinner."

***

Later that evening, Merrill and Kyle knocked on the cabin door asking Beth and Susan if they wanted to come over and roast marshmallows over the campfire. The girls grabbed a sweatshirt and headed out the door. After the sun went down behind the mountain, the air cooled off to comfortable sweatshirt weather. As the four walked over to Merrill's place guided only by starlight, Kyle took Beth's hand in his. *I was hoping that he liked me. There is something special about him. I'm afraid that if I look at him it might spoil the moment, or he might let go.* She just enjoyed the feel of his hand holding hers, walking side by side in the starlight.

The mountain sky was magnificent at night. Without smog or city lights to interfere, the inky blackness of the sky was lit with billions of stars. Kyle never imagined that there could be so many stars in the sky. He and Beth sat on the ground beside a roaring campfire with Susan and Merrill. Kyle's parents were sitting with Merrill's parents in folding chairs just outside the trailer door. Beth and Susan were introduced to Kyle's parents.

"Hey, I'll get the coat hangers and we can make marshmallow roasters," said Merrill, as he got up to get the hangers. Merrill's mom got out a bag of marshmallows as they each started un-twisting their coat hangers and bending them into the perfect marshmallow roasting tool.

"You said there are some gold miners still around, didn't you, Beth?" asked Kyle, as he carefully placed a marshmallow on the end of his roaster. He put the marshmallow far enough above the flame, turning it constantly so it wouldn't burn, but would roast to a golden brown.

"Yeah, the guy who has the mining claim where we get water, his name is Sonny and he has several claims. You'll meet him. He has more stories to tell than anyone else does on this mountain. At least that I know of," remarked Beth. She put her marshmallow on her roaster and stuck it directly into the flame. It immediately caught fire and she took it out of the fire, blew it out and ate it. *Look how carefully he roasts his marshmallow,* thought

Beth. *It takes forever that way.*

Beth took another marshmallow and put it on her hanger and again, thrust it directly into the flames. Again, it immediately caught fire, as she blew it out, Kyle looked at her raising his eyebrows.

"Do you roast your marshmallows that way on purpose?" asked Kyle. His first marshmallow was not even done yet and Beth was just popping the second one in her mouth.

"Yeah, it takes to long to roast them the way you do. They're great this way, you should try it." She was getting ready to put on a third one. "Three is my limit though, then I am marshmallowed out." She then noticed that Susan and Merrill were also still on their first one. "Sorry, but patience is not one of my strong points," giggled Beth, as she was ready to eat her third marshmallow. Kyle was just eating his first golden brown marshmallow while she had already eaten her fill.

***

The feeling of when Kyle first took my hand that night, a simple enough gesture, is still very vivid in my mind, remembered Beth. *Even after all this time, I can bring out that memory and it is almost as real now as it was then. The connection, the electricity, I don't understand what it was. Maybe it had to do with cosmic energy, or the beauty of the stars above, or maybe at the exact time that Kyle took my hand, there was a shooting star that created some invisible link between us. Maybe it simply was the moment that we fell in love.*

By the end of the evening he had his arm around her shoulders and by the end of the weekend, they had exchanged phone numbers and addresses and had both promised to write.

Chapter Four

Four days after they met, Beth got her first letter from Kyle. *I knew he would write,* thought Beth. Actually, she had hoped and prayed that he would write. It was written the same day that he left to go home from the mountains. She had also written her first letter to Kyle telling him how much fun she had over the weekend and how glad she was that they had met. *I want to tell him that he was all that I've thought about ever since that first night when he held my hand. I want to tell him how I prayed that he would not let it go and that I was so glad when he held my hand again the next day.* She found herself babbling on about some of the places she wanted to show him, how uneventful it was after he and his family left, and how she hoped he would be back.

Kyle's letter was written on blue lined notebook paper with elegant cursive that graced the page like a work of art. *He has beautiful handwriting,* she thought. The two page hand written note told of how she had been "heavy on his mind" and that he had great news, his parents had signed the papers to buy a piece of land across the road and up the hill from her cabin. *Another of her prayers had been answered.* They would be neighbors. He went on to describe his dad's feelings about the dirt road and his plans to bring a pick and shovel and fill in some of the larger holes. *How funny,* she thought, *about his dad's comment on the dirt road. That road is my favorite part of the long trek to get to the cabin. Once we hit the dirt road, it's like the trip is finally over and I'm home. Now I have another reason to love my valley. It's where I met Kyle.*

Beth and Kyle wrote frequent letters to each other over the next couple of weeks. The letters told of their daily activities and each got a snapshot of the other's life. Both Kyle and Beth had strong family ties with loving parents in middle income, happy homes. Neither of them wanted for anything, yet were taught the economic value of hard work. Although Kyle's family was more involved in the church than Beth's, both families demonstrated strong moral character and wanted health and happiness for their children.

Two weeks later, on a Friday night, Kyle called and asked Beth if she would be home on Saturday, so he could ride his bike over to see her. *I have missed him so much.* She was thrilled that he wanted to see her. She had actually planned to be at her friend Tracy's house, so they arranged to meet there. She had told Tracy all about Kyle, so this would also give them a chance to meet. Beth had not seen

Kyle since that first weekend. *I am so anxious to see him,* she thought. Saturday morning crawled by, but finally it was eleven AM and she was at Tracy's house. Kyle was expected around noon.

"I thought I would die waiting a whole night and morning," Beth confided to Tracy. Patience was definitely not her strength.

"What's he like?" asked Tracy. Beth and Tracy had been best friends during junior high school. They had first met in choir class in the seventh grade. They both sang and played the guitar a little, and discovered music in a very personal way that year. With Tracy singing lead and Beth adding harmony, they spent countless hours practicing at either Beth's or Tracy's house, to learn new songs and prepare themselves for life in the music industry. They played in school concerts, local talent shows and charity events. In the summer between junior high school and high school, Tracy's parents divorced and she moved with her mom to a condo complex in another school district. Tracy would be going to a different high school. A few inches taller than Beth at 5'4", Tracy had long dark hair and expressive brown eyes. She had a very pretty smile and a winning personality. Tracy had a sister that was five years older therefore, she had a much more worldly view of her teenage years. Although Tracy had moved, she and Beth were still best friends. Tracy had made a lot of friends in her new neighborhood. There were a lot of divorced parents and single mothers, so the kids spent a lot of time on their own. Unlike Beth's house, where there was always parental presence, Tracy's house was a gathering place for all of the neighborhood kids while her mom was at work.

"Well, I only actually met him that one weekend, but he was very sweet and he has been writing to me almost every day. *I now believe in love at first sight.* I can't believe that he is going to be here in a little while. Can I use your curlers when you're done?" They were in Tracy's room using each other's makeup, talking girl talk and doing what teenage girls do. Beth didn't take the time to curl her hair at home that morning, in her anticipation to get to Tracy's.

"Sure, they're already hot, go ahead and use them. What school will he be going to?"

"It's a Catholic high school, but I can't remember the name of it. He told me that he has a bunch of friends that are going there too. He's going to try out for the track team."

Kyle got there a few minutes after noon, after the long ride of about 20 miles. *He looks a little different. I wonder if I look different to him too. I hope I look as good to him as he looks to me*, thought Beth nervously. She had changed clothes at least a dozen times that morning. She finally settled on the usual blue jeans and a scooped neck blouse that had little puffy sleeves, was light green cotton with small pink flowers. She had gotten compliments on this blouse before because it was the same color green as her eyes.

This day was to mark another milestone for Beth. She and Kyle sat in Tracy's living room all afternoon, stereo blaring, talking and drinking Pepsi. Tracy and some of the other kids were baking a cake for someone's birthday, Beth did not really care whose birthday it was.

She was deliriously happy and later couldn't even recall who was there that day. She would only remember sitting hand in hand with Kyle, the birthday cake with the awful purple frosting, and their first kiss.

About four PM, Beth walked with Kyle to the corner. *I don't want him to go,* thought Beth. But, it was time as he had a long ride home.

"I'll write soon," he promised. "I can't wait until we are both at the mountains again." *I wonder if he will kiss me goodbye.* She remembered being kissed one time in junior high school by a guy she had a crush on. He had pushed his tongue into her mouth and almost choked her. It was awful. As this memory briefly passed through her mind, Kyle took her hand and pulled her gently into his arms and leaned down and tenderly kissed her lips.

***

Beth has the memory of that first kiss locked away along with so many special memories with Kyle. There is this special little place in her heart that can never belong to anyone else. Most of the time, this place is locked up tight. Occasionally throughout her life, she unlocks the room, takes out each memory, examines it, re-lives it, and tries to figure out why it is there. Sometimes she will add a few new memories to her collection, then lock them all away, until next time. Although she has gone through this ritual many times through her life, she had no idea that Kyle performed the same ritual.

On this evening as she pulls into her driveway, she

takes an extra moment, using the excuse to Jacen that she wants to hear the end of the song that is playing, to re-live that first kiss.

***

As soon as our lips touched, I felt like I was tumbling through space and that this kiss would last forever and never last long enough, all at the same time. I wanted to stay in his arms and kiss him forever, I remember thinking, as I put my arms around his neck and enthusiastically kissed him back. His kiss was gentle, yet firm, tender, yet passionate. How can a kiss feel fresh and inexperienced, yet have the power to create a memory for a lifetime? I had weak knees and butterflies in my stomach, and felt a new feeling of a power beyond understanding, that I knew would bind me always to Kyle.

***

Beth's memory of the first time that Kyle kissed her still caused the butterfly feeling. *How can it feel so real thirty years later?* she mused to herself, as she locked up the car and went inside. With dinner to fix, dishes to do, a movie to watch with Jacen, and cookies to bake, she was not able to have time for her own thoughts until she was ready for bed. This was not unusual for a working mom. *With my heart wide open, I feel compelled to examine each special memory, feel the joy while I can, before the pain comes crashing down and I frantically scramble to push all the memories away and slam the door, locking it up tight.*

Beth lay in bed that night remembering.

***

That summer passed like a whirlwind. Beth lived for her weekends in the mountains and her letters and phone calls during the week. She and Kyle launched into an adventure of learning about one another, understanding and trusting each other and building a bond that would last their whole lives. Through their letters to each other, they poured out all of the feelings in their hearts.

On weekends, they explored the mountains by motorcycle, dune buggy and on foot. Kyle's family had a Volkswagen dune buggy, painted green, that seated four. His dad would occasionally let him take it to explore the countryside. Beth and Susan had their Yamaha 80 trail motorcycles and Merrill had a Honda 50 motorcycle. Kyle rode behind Beth when they went for a motorcycle ride. Beth and Susan also had use of a Ford Galaxy that had the back cut off so it had the configuration of a pickup, without being a truck. Although it was ugly, it ran great. The group used the Ford to pick up old cans and haul rocks for home improvement projects that seemed to always be going on at the Collins property, and for hauling water.

The water source for the valley was an artesian well that flowed about three miles away. Beth's family had built a tower with a 1000-gallon tank on top that fed the cabin. In order to get the water from the well to the tower, it had to be hauled by a 300-gallon tank on a trailer that was towed by the modified Ford Galaxy. One of Beth's chores each weekend was to get a load of water. It was then pumped into the main tank with a gas-powered pump. It took about two hours to fill the tank on the trailer. Many times Kyle would go with her to get water. This gave them two uninterrupted hours to explore the mining claim where the well was, or sit and talk. Kyle, a very physical person, was always touching her with his arm around her or holding her hand or kissing her. He could never get enough of her, nor she of him.

***

When Beth recalls the memories of that summer, she can only remember happy times, bright color, dramatic sky, star filled nights, quick, sweet kisses, deep meaningful kisses, and laughter. In her mind's eye, she pictures the way Kyle's face would light up when he would look at her, the special glances that were just for her to see, and his eyes, those unforgettable eyes. It was like looking into his soul. At that time in his life, his heart had never been broken or bruised, therefore, it was wide open and the depth of his feelings could be read in his eyes.

***

The last week before school started, Kyle and his family went out of state on a camping trip to another piece of property that they owned. Kyle wrote her every day. In one of his letters he wrote how he carved their names into a tree on their property, with a heart around it, knowing it would be there forever. It was in that letter that he first told her that he loved her. These were happy days for both Beth and Kyle; their only problem was not having enough hours in the day to spend with each other.

As the summer came to an end and school started, she and Kyle continued writing to each other every day. Beth would start her letter every morning in her first period class and share her day with Kyle. They devised a plan to talk to each other occasionally after school. Beth would go to a phone booth off campus and, at a specified time, would call a phone booth collect that was next to Kyle's school. He would answer and accept the call and they would talk until they had to get home.

Kyle and Beth had found love that was both sweet and true. Even they had no idea of the magnitude of their feelings, having nothing with which to compare them to. All they knew was that they were happy and had grown to trust and believe in each other. Their passion for life and each other was becoming overwhelming. Both were consumed with feelings that they didn't know what to do with. Because they believed they would always be together, they discussed becoming lovers and both believed they were ready.

The beauty of spring was in full bloom, with hills carpeted in lavender and yellow flowers. The cactus plants were ablaze with red and pink blossoms and the pines and juniper bright green with tender new growth. Kyle and Beth marveled at the magnificence of the valley that they had begin to think of as their own. It was a warm weekend in early May and the stage was set for love. Kyle knew of an abandoned cabin where he and Beth could be together.

Chapter Five

Both families had arrived in the valley about nine AM on Saturday morning. Kyle's dad had bought a mobile home and had it brought out to their newly purchased property so they had a comfortable place to stay. Beth and Kyle spent the day together doing the usual chores, getting water and collecting rocks. They went for a dune buggy ride in the afternoon with Susan, exploring some of the back roads. *I love feeling my hair blowing in the wind and being able to look at everything without having to pay attention to the road,* thought Beth. They were around either his family or hers all day, so they did not have much of a chance to talk privately.

Later that night, after she and Susan were in bed, Beth heard a small pebble hit the bunk house window. *I know I heard something,* she thought. *There,* she heard it again. She and Susan had their own bunkhouse that was separate from the cabin because the cabin had only one bedroom. The two girls had decorated their bunkhouse with comic strip newspaper shellacked to the walls giving the room a very festive and colorful look.

Beth lifted her head off the pillow and looked out her window. Kyle was there gesturing quietly for her to come out. Susan was already asleep so she slipped out of her sleeping bag and soundlessly went outside. Clad in flannel pajamas and slippers, she and Kyle walked down the road, arm in arm in the moonlight, until they were away from her place.

"Babe, I want to make love to you, but I want you to be sure about this," he whispered as he held her and brushed his lips over her neck. "I will never hurt you and will always love you." *I believe him and want him too.* Still warm from her sleeping bag, Beth cuddled closer into his arms and kissed him long and deep. He held her close pressing his body hard against her running his hands along her back and up over the curve of her breast. *I love him,* she knew, *and he loves me too.*

"Lets plan on going to the cabin tomorrow," Kyle said as he walked her back to the bunkhouse.

Moaning softly, she whispered "I love you, Kyle, and I'm sure about this."

Smiling, Kyle said, "Night Babe, see you in the morning." He kissed her gently and watched as she turned and walked the length of the lane between him and the bunkhouse. He waited until she quietly opened the bunk house door before turning and heading back down the road toward his place

***

Their first time together became Beth's most cherished memory. This is the fragile memory that exposes every vulnerability and insecurity and demands the most trust. This one event in every girl's life paints the picture of how she views herself, lives her life, handles intimacy, and is able to give and receive love. The stage was set, it was a beautiful warm spring day, and she was desperately in love.

***

The cabin was very small. It was built on a mining claim and had been the home of one of the miners who lived in the mountains. The miner had left the valley for health reasons several years before, and had recently died. The cabin had been kept intact, as the miner had always planned on coming back to the mountains. After he died, the house had been cleaned out the by the miner's son and the few items of value had been taken.

The cabin consisted of a small living room with an old wood-burning stove on a slab floor. The wood stove was used for both cooking and heat. There was a basin that drained to the outside, but no running water. Water was usually kept in a five-gallon jug on a counter top next to the basin. A cupboard with a couple of mis-matched dishes, an old jelly jar for a glass, a kettle on top of the wood stove and a broken towel rack completed the kitchen conveniences. In the center of the room was an old table with one chair that had been painted blue, in another century. On the other side of the room was a small single bed, complete with mattress, covered with a badly stained, off white bed spread. At one time, there was an outhouse, but it had since blown over and the only thing left was the seat and the pit.

The mining claim had recently been abandoned. The cabin had not been occupied for some time, but since it had been closed up it was, although dusty, relatively clean. Kyle and Beth had found the cabin one afternoon while exploring and had asked Sonny about it. He had told them the whole story while Beth was getting water. "Sounds perfect," remarked Beth when Kyle suggested that they go there to be alone.

On Sunday morning, plans were made to go on a motorcycle ride together that afternoon.

"Susan, Kyle and I want to go alone this afternoon, so when I suggest that we go for a bike ride, say that you don't really feel like it, okay?" *I can't believe this is really going to happen. I'm nervous and excited,* she realized. *I wonder how Kyle is feeling.*

"Sure," said Susan. "Where are you going to go?"

"Oh, I am not sure yet, but we hardly ever get any time alone and we just want to be together." *I can't tell her. She would never understand. She can't know how much I love him or how important this is to me.*

***

After lunch, Kyle finally could break away and Beth announced that she and Kyle were going to go on a motorcycle ride.   After riding to the cabin on Beth's motorcycle, they parked in the back so the bike could not be seen from the road, and went inside. *I am shaking all over and my knees feel like Jell-O, I hope he doesn't notice.* Kyle, trembling slightly, took her in his arms and kissed her tenderly. "Are you sure about this?"

"Yes," she said, "I love you, and I will love you forever."

"I will love you forever too, Babe," he murmured softly in her ear as he held her close, feeling every softness and curve of her body pressed against his. He walked her over to the tiny bed and sat down pulling her next to him. *I love you with all my heart,* she thought, as he lay down beside her and began kissing her neck and opening her blouse to caress her bare skin.

Although their lovemaking was clumsy, as expected for two inexperienced in the art of love, their passion for each other was certainly real. Beth remembered not being quite sure if they even got it right, but the tenderness and trust between them heightened exponentially that day. As they lay in each other's arms, laughing, touching and exploring the wonder of each other, a permanent thread, never to be broken, not by time nor distance, was being formed.   Neither realized the bittersweet gift that was bestowed upon them that day.

"You are so beautiful," Kyle whispered, "I could spend a lifetime just looking at you." He lay next to her on one elbow looking at her face, her breasts and her body that he had just claimed as his own. He gently kissed her rosy nipple, "but if we don't get going soon, our families are going to send out a search party, and that would not be pretty."

Beth giggled, his kisses tickled. "I don't want to go, let's just stay here forever." Kyle, the voice of reason, stroked her thigh and told her that he did not want to go either, but it was time.

On the ride back to drop Kyle off, Beth rode on the back of the motorcycle, something she rarely did. On this day, however, she was completely content and clung to him, resting her cheek on his back with her arms wrapped tightly around his waist. *I have never been so happy,* she thought.

* * *

Beth fell asleep that night, warm, engulfed in her memories of being loved so completely and remembering what it felt like to love someone with her heart, body, and soul. She dreamt of Kyle, his touch, his smell, and woke the next morning longing for him as she had not longed for anyone in a long, long time.

Chapter Six

Beth awoke alone in her bed. Ethan had gotten up early and was already gone. It seemed to Beth that lately, whenever she was going to bed in the evening, Ethan had some reason to get up and whenever she was getting up, he went in to take a nap. She seemed to be alone whenever she fell asleep and was alone again when she awoke in the morning. *I hate sleeping by myself. I want to cuddle, I want to lay in bed and talk and be playful. I want our bed to be a place of refuge, to recharge, to have our private time with each other. I hate the feeling of rejection, of being unwanted. I start out my day sad, and have to build from there. I want to start out my day happy and soar from there!*

Jacen was still asleep. She threw on a thick pink

bathrobe and went into his room to get him up. It was time to start getting ready for school. As usual, Jacen was curled up in his bed with his covers a tangled mess over his lean long legged body. Mornings were usually a hectic time for Beth, struggling to get Jacen ready for school and getting herself ready for work. Beth busied herself making Jacen's lunch, being sure that all of his homework was secure in his backpack, reminding him of the day's important events and appointments, and being sure that he got some sort of breakfast before they left for the day.

In a melancholy mood that morning, Beth took her shower, made a cup of her favorite Licorice Spice tea, and proceeded to get ready for work. She realized that she was only partly in the present. Her mind seemed to be locked in the past. Kyle was again in her dreams last night. She couldn't shake the feeling of longing. *Am I longing for Kyle? Or, for the feeling of being completely loved and whole again. I remember how it felt, the happiness, the lack of stress, the harmony between two people, the laughter between us. Will I ever have that again? Does anyone ever get to actually live with these feelings for a lifetime? I have so many questions.*

I remember when Ethan and I were first were married. He used to surprise me every weekend with some kind of outing. He would go through the newspaper calendar section, and clip out some events that he thought sounded interesting. He would tell me what time to be ready and how to dress, casual, warm, comfortable shoes, whatever was appropriate. Then would load me up in the car and take off to some unknown destination. He would never tell me where we were going. Almost without exception, he would get lost saying something like, "I know there used to be a shopping center here . . . I wonder when it became a gas station?" We would laugh. I would tease him and sometimes we would finally get to the original destination, once in a while on time, more often than not late, but happy. Sometimes, we would never get there at all, but find something else along the way and get sidetracked. But, we always had fun. We always enjoyed each other. I can't remember the last time we did this.

On her way to her office, Beth wondered if Kyle would answer her email. She had sent him an email the day she called him and he had responded right away. He had sent her one too. Although the email was short and somewhat impersonal, writing to him had seemed so natural for her that she found herself wanting to write to him again. Later that day, she had written a longer email telling him about her day and her dreams of him and that she had thought of him so much over the years. She seemed to fall into her old habit of writing; her thoughts flowed through her fingers and onto the screen. The familiar habit of writing to Kyle felt good, seemed to give her hope and she knew she had a lot in her heart to tell him. *I wonder if he will write me back? I wonder if he wants to know what is in my heart? I wonder if he is happy? I wonder . . . I wonder . . . . .*

Beth seemed to have a million questions for Kyle, questions for his heart and feelings, to his daily life, to details about his family and work. She wanted to know everything; she wanted to feel some of the extraordinary things that she remembered feeling once upon a time . . . .

Chapter Seven

Kyle earned the privilege of a driver's license when he turned sixteen. Although he did not have a car to drive, occasionally he was able to get permission to drive the family VW, which was painted the same green as their dune buggy. Although he came to visit Beth as much as he could, he was not able to use the car not very often.

One Saturday afternoon, just before the end of tenth grade, Kyle got permission to use the VW, and he and his friend Ray drove over to see Beth and Susan. *I am finally going to get to meet Ray, who Kyle has written about so much in his letters.* Ray was a little taller than Kyle, about 5'10," had dark brown hair, brown eyes and was always smiling. His smile lit up his entire face, centering in his eyes. Ray was enchanted with Susan. The four of them spent the afternoon in the Collins family room playing pool and listening to music. Beth thought, *I'm glad he brought Ray. He seems to really like Susan.*

Kyle and Beth lived only for each other these days. *I am happy as long as I can touch him,* thought Beth. It did not matter if there were a hundred other people in the room, or only two, they only saw each other. On this day, although they were always either holding hands or arm in arm, they included Susan and Ray in their own private world. Actually, they kept their world very private; they just stepped out of it temporarily to enjoy the company of Susan and Ray.

Ray, in tan cords and a dark red T-shirt, was a riot. He was having a great time and was very interested in impressing Susan. Ray had the four of them laughing the whole afternoon with his quick, witty sense of humor. With the stereo blaring, they played pool, ate ice-cream bars and sat on the back porch and talked. Ray went to the same Catholic High School as Kyle and was on the football team. Susan, who was just thirteen, not to be fourteen until October, was flattered by all of the attention, flattered and just a little nervous. She liked Ray, he was cute, funny, older, and on the football team, but she mostly loved being included and welcomed into her sister's very private life.

Ray managed to get himself invited to the mountains with Kyle's family the next time they went. Susan had promised to take him for a motorcycle ride on the back of her bike, and Ray had every intention of seeing that she kept her promise.

School was finally out and it was an early summer day. The sky was the deep brilliant blue that always seemed to favor the valley. The wild flowers were just starting to lose the freshness of spring, and were beginning to harden to weather the heat of summer. The air was still cool in the morning, warming up during the day and cooling off for a pleasant evening under the stars. Kyle and Beth had not had another opportunity to get away to be alone, but they were as inseparable as always. *I miss the way he touches me when we're alone.*

Kyle's family arrived on Saturday about noon. *I am so glad that Kyle is finally here,* thought Beth. She and Susan had already been at their mountain home for a couple of hours. They knew that Kyle and Ray were coming up for the weekend, and had been keeping an eye out for them. Soon after they saw Kyle's family pull in, they got on their motorcycles and rode by. This was the usual signal. When everything was unpacked, Kyle would walk down the hill and meet them, or if he had permission, would drive the dune buggy down to meet them. Soon, Beth spotted Kyle and Ray walking down the hill toward them.

"Hi Susan," called Ray as they approached the girls on the road. "I came to collect the motorcycle ride you promised me! Hi Beth."

Susan grinned, "You will be taking your life in your hands, but if you are feeling lucky, come on and hop on the back." Ray did not need to be asked twice.

"Hi Babe," said Kyle as he kissed Beth and put his arm around her shoulder. "I guess we are going motorcycle riding." *He smells good,* she thought as she kissed him back. *I have missed him; I can never get enough of him.* He looked at her with an expression that told her everything that she would ever need to know. A smile and she was completely at peace.

"Guess so," said Beth as she smiled back "That is just fine with me." She kicked the starter and on the second kick, the bike roared to life.

Although Susan did not have much experience riding with someone behind her, she was a good rider. Ray hopped on the back of her bike and Kyle on the back of Beth's. They took off down the dirt road and rode for about an hour. Susan did fine with Ray riding behind her. He had the biggest smile on his face that Beth had ever seen when they got back to their cabin. *I think he loved it, look at that smile,* thought Beth

"So, how was it?" Beth asked Ray, as she put her bike on the kickstand.

"Totally bitchin'," replied Ray. Susan beamed. "Can't wait to go again, you will take me again, won't you Susan? Was I an okay passenger?"

Susan laughed, "you did fine. It is a little different when you're riding with someone behind, you don't have quite as much control."

"Susan, you did great," said Beth as she walked over and put her arm around Kyle's waist. He put his arm around her shoulder and gave her a small squeeze as they walked down the road toward Merrill's. His family had just arrived. It was the valley of kids and motorcycles that weekend.

* * *

Beth remembers her life being full of love, sunburned skin, wind blown hair, watermelon and extreme happiness. She and Kyle never fought, always were touching and giving each other looks that were intense with raw emotion. They were so young that their hearts were not tainted with hurt or baggage of failed relationships. They were wide open to feel the full intensity of what love is supposed to feel like. When Beth looks back at what they had, she realizes that they had it all. Their compatibility was complete. Beth, the dreamer, with a soul oozing with passion for life guided completely by emotion, was full of ideals, boundless energy and a love for Kyle that was unending. Beth also had a very logical aspect to her personality. She was hard working, always the first one to pitch in on any project and the last one to quit. She never complained, was bright and convinced that she could do anything she set her mind to. She was a total complement to Kyle's reserved style. He was solid as a rock, was her "voice of reason," and loved her energy as she energized him too. She saw him as her anchor that kept her from floating off into space and he saw her as his balloon that allowed him to soar.

That weekend was a blur of motorcycles coming and going, trips to get water, and campfires under the stars. One near mishap stands out that Beth still thinks about every time she goes to her cabin in the mountains.

***

There is a plant that grows in the desert and the

foothills that city folks rarely have any exposure to. It's an interesting plant, somewhat like a cactus, but having characteristics that are far more sinister than any cactus that ever grew on the face of this good earth. This plant is called a cholla. It grows like a small tree, with branches as thick as the arm of a three-year-old child. Cholla can grow to be quite big, the tallest being about five feet and maybe three or four feet wide. The sinister part of this evil plant is the stickers. The entire plant, all branches from top to bottom, are covered with stickers. These are not just average stickers, these stickers are an inch or two long and have barbs that are shaped like a fishhook, curved to go in smooth and tear as they come out. It seems like the stickers are connected to a spring. When someone even gets close, they appear to jump at you and embed themselves in your skin. Although there is no scientific evidence of a spring mechanism, the locals swear it is so!

It was a typical day in the mountains. Ray had come up with Kyle and the four were planning a motorcycle ride to explore the hills. Ray decided that it was time that he did the driving. He had had endured being driven around by a girl long enough. He had paid close attention and felt it was time for him to take charge of driving Susan around.

"Work the clutch with your left hand and let it out slowly while you give it some gas, here, want me to show you?" instructed Susan. "You're sure you're ready for this?"

"Yeah, yeah, I got it. Hop on, I can handle this," Ray said with a determined look on his face. Determined enough to inspire confidence, in spite of the total lack of experience.

"Practice once or twice, just to get the feel of the bike," suggested Susan.   With total concentration, he started letting out the clutch, stalling the bike on his first attempt. Ray kicked the kick-starter and the bike roared back to life as he reseated himself and, with renewed determination, started working the clutch and gas.   His success, on the second try, impressed even Susan.   Ray stalled it again as he stopped to turn the bike around and come back to pick up Susan.

"Have to pull in the clutch when you stop," she shouted over the sound of the engine that he had just restarted. As he stopped next to her, he pulled in the clutch and smiled as the engine idled smoothly.

"Nothin' to this," he grinned, "Hop on." His smile was infectious, as was his confidence. Susan hopped on the back.

Susan and Ray were speeding along the dirt road, maybe going a little too fast, when they approached a hard left turn that was slippery with loose sand. Kyle was riding Beth on her motorcycle bringing up the rear.

"You need to slow down for this turn," Susan shouted into Ray's ear from her seat behind him.   Too late Ray realized his error, and cringed as he felt the bike start to slide in the sand.   He was going to miss the turn altogether and they were heading straight for a cholla bush. He heard Susan scream, "LOOK OUT . . . ." as they went zooming past the cholla bush, missing it by less than a quarter of an inch, and crashed headlong into the dirt. As they lay in the dirt, the bike on its side with the wheels still turning in the air, both shouted "Are you all right?" at each other in unison. When they realized that no one was hurt, they both burst into uncontrollable fits of laughter, realizing how close they'd come to hitting the cholla bush. Beth and Kyle, who were riding with them, witnessed the scene in wide-eyed horror as they watched Ray dump the bike. Seeing that neither was hurt, they joined the laughter.

Beth still sees this same cholla bush every time she goes to her cabin. She always remembers, with amusement, the day that Ray learned to ride a motorcycle.

***

The beginning of the summer of her sixteenth year marks the year that Beth obtained her freedom. On her sixteenth birthday in July, she went with her mom to the DMV and officially became a licensed driver. *Freedom! Now all I need is a car.* She was thrilled about being able to drive the thirty miles that separated Kyle's home from hers. She laughed as she remembered a time, right after she met Kyle, that she wanted to know where he lived. *I just wanted to be able to picture his house in my mind,* she thought. She talked Tracy, who always did have a crazy side to her anyway, into riding their bicycles to Kyle's house.

"Okay, we can ride our bikes there, but again, why do you want to do this when you know he is not home?" asked Tracy.

I miss him and want to be near something that is

his. I hate when he is gone and I can't see him or talk to him. But what she said was "I just want to see where he lives . . ."

She knew that he was out of town with his family for the weekend. At the time she did not realize just how far away he lived. She looked his address up on a map so she had the directions. It took her and Tracy all day, on a Saturday, to ride there and back. *I had no idea that he lived so far away. On the map, it didn't look that far.* Still laughing to herself, she pictured the bikes that she and Tracy rode. One speed, string ray bikes with banana seats. Not comfortable ten speeds made for distance riding, oh no. Boy, were they sore!

"Beth, you are nuts and my legs are killing me," whined Tracy with a shake of her head and a smile, "and we still have to ride all the way back!"

"I know, I know. My legs are killing me too," she sighed as she looked at his house.

"You must really like this guy."

"Yeah, I really do." *I am in love with him.*

Kyle's house was on a corner. It was painted light green with white trim. *Someone in his family likes green,* thought Beth with a smile. The driveway led to a two-car garage that was attached to the house. It was neat and well kept in a stable middle class neighborhood. *I can almost feel him. This is where he sleeps at night and eats dinner with his parents and gets ready for school in the morning. I don't want to leave.*

"Let's stop and get an ice-cream cone on the way back. I'll buy," said Beth as she turned her bike around to start back. Beth glanced back over her shoulder for one last look.

"You are on! Come on, let's go. We need to be back before it gets dark."

She can almost feel just how tired they were when they got back. *I don't know if I will be able to walk tomorrow. That's going to be interesting to try to explain!* Of course, Tracy's mom never knew why the two of them went to bed so early, or slept so soundly that night.

***

Beth and her dad had been car shopping, so when she started eleventh grade, she would have her own car to drive. She wanted a car that she could take to the mountains and did not cost too much money.

After spending much of the summer looking, they finally settled on a Ford Ranchero that needed engine work. Beth was excited at the prospect of her first car. She and her dad had to tow it home, because it was not running. Beth drove the family Toyota Landcruiser and towed her dad in the Ranchero with a towrope. She remembers how nervous she was towing someone on the street. She had to try not to let the rope jerk or the Ranchero would run into the back of the Landcruiser. *I have never towed anything before except a motorcycle, and that was on a dirt road, nothing like this!*

The body on the Ranchero was straight and the tires were good. The interior was very sad and the color of the outside was ugly beige. She looked over her new/old car with ideas leaping through her mind. It took her and her dad two greasy weekends to get the engine work done.

Beth's dad never treated her, or Susan, like it was a handicap to be female. He taught them how to work on their motorcycles, and expected Beth to do the engine work on her car. *I will probably be the only girl in the eleventh grade that has rebuilt a car engine,* she thought with amusement. Beth learned how the engine was put together and spent a lot of time cleaning parts. *I remember being out in the garage with a smock over my jeans and T-shirt, grease on my face and hands, and curlers in my hair because I was seeing Kyle that night. Mom thought I looked so funny and took my picture. It's still in an album somewhere.*

Her dad taught her well. Throughout her life, she would draw on the knowledge and mechanical ability that her dad taught her during those teenage years. These were good times between her and her dad. They worked well together and Beth pulled her weight regarding the project. Before long, the Ranchero was driveable and Beth had her first car.

Her first trip was to Tracy's house. Beth had been busy during the week with a summer job at her dad's office, so she had not seen Tracy since they bought her car.

"Come on out and I'll take you for a ride," said Beth, in her blue jeans with some grease still under her nails that she had not been able to get out. The old Ranchero runs pretty good. Don't mind the interior, I am going to change it. What color do you think I should paint her?"

"Orange, bright orange," exclaimed Tracy, "you will be the only bright orange truck on the block, maybe in the whole city!" Tracy giggled.

"Orange, I think I like that idea. No one will miss me, that's for sure!"

"Hey, this is very bitchin'," Tracy remarked as she walked around the truck. "Has Kyle seen it yet?"

"No, I want to go by and show him, but you were my first stop."

"Let's go right now! We can surprise him."

"I am wearing my old jeans, I can't surprise him looking like this!"

"Let's go inside and go through my closet. We can find you something to wear and you can use my makeup and curlers. Come on."

Tracy went through her closet and found Beth some clean jeans and a light blue blouse. Beth scrubbed her fingernails once again and got off most of the grease. She freshened her mascara and added a touch of lipstick and they set out for Kyle's house. Of course, she knew where he lived because they had ridden their bikes there one very tiring day!

Beth was a little nervous about just showing up at Kyle's without being expected. *Will he be glad to see me?* She was not sure if it would be okay with him, or even if he would be home.

With the AM radio playing a rock and roll station, they arrived about twenty minutes later. *Much faster in a car*, Beth smiled to herself. Beth got out and went up to Kyle's door and knocked. *Don't know why I am nervous,* thought Beth. Kyle answered the door, and his big smile told her that he was thrilled to see her.

"Beth, where did you come from?" he said as he opened the screen door to invite her in.

"Come out and take a look at the car; I drove over with Tracy." He stepped onto the porch and looked toward the street.

"Got it all done already? I can't believe that," he remarked as he walked out to take a look at her car. He took her hand as he walked down the driveway toward the street.

"It still needs to be painted and the interior done. I think I am going to paint it orange, it was Tracy's idea. What do you think?"

Kyle gave her one of his "I think you are nuts, but I know you will do it anyway" looks and said, "Orange, huh, well, you won't lose your car in a parking lot at least! Orange," he muttered as he shook his head slightly. "Any ideas on the interior?"

"Not yet, bucket seats maybe. I need to price them. The paint job comes first. I think I will have enough money to do the outside by next month. I have been saving my pennies."

"You two want to come in for a while?" asked Kyle as he slipped his arm around Beth's shoulders. She felt the familiar warmth.

"Can't, my parents don't even know that I am here, I was only going over to Tracy's and we decided to drive by and show you the car. We really need to go," explained Beth, "I wanted to see you and say hi."

Kyle cupped her face in his hands and tenderly kissed her on the lips. He whispered that he loved her and was glad she came by and promised to call her to do something next weekend. She hugged him tight, wanting to never let go. When she finally broke the embrace, she smiled and told him she loved him too, and asked when he thought they would be going to the mountains again.

"Probably not for a couple of weeks. I know we will be going in October, probably not until the end of the month, maybe even Halloween. I will let you know for sure so you can see if you can get your family to go at the same time."

"Okay, well at least I have wheels now so I can come and see you more often." She opened the door, slid into the driver's seat and started the engine.

About the time that Beth and Tracy were getting ready to take off, Merrill came out of the house across the street. Beth knew that he and Kyle were neighbors, but did not know which house was his.

"Hi you guys," said Merrill. "Cool wheels. This your car, Beth?"

"Hi Merrill, so that's where you live. Yeah, it looks a little rough, but it runs great."

"Beth and her dad just rebuilt the engine," explained Kyle, with a little pride in his voice. "It sounds really good too."

"Well guys, Tracy and I really do have to go. I don't want to get grounded my first day with a car! Merrill, it was nice to see you, and Kyle, I will talk to you later."

Kyle leaned down and kissed Beth good-bye. He reluctantly let go of her hand, closed her door and stepped back from the car as she pulled away from the curb.

***

As a wonderful summer wound down, Beth, Susan, Kyle and Ray had become very close. Susan and Ray had tried the girlfriend/boyfriend thing, but it was not in the cards. Beth suspected that Ray still had a crush on Susan. Although Susan really liked Ray a lot, and the four of them had a ball whenever they were together, there were no sparks for Susan. Just about every weekend during the summer, the four were together either in the mountains or doing something in the city. The summer was too short and soon it was time for school to start.

Both Kyle and Beth were starting the eleventh grade. They got back into the routine of daily correspondence. Their letters were much more personal, and each expressed the desire to be with the other, and always declared their love. They missed each other terribly and hated being apart.

Kyle and Beth finally had the opportunity to make love again on a cool Halloween night a few months after Beth's sixteenth birthday. Their valley was decorated in fall colors. The trees had the bright yellow, red and orange leaves of autumn. The days were shorter, which gave Kyle and Beth more time to enjoy the starlight. The valley had lost the intense heat of the day, although still warm and comfortable, there was no longer the extreme heat of the summer. Both families were in the mountains for the weekend. Kyle's parents were over at Beth's cabin enjoying the evening playing cards with Beth's parents. Beth, Kyle, Susan and Ray were in the mobile home on Kyle's property, playing board games and telling stories. Kyle had been holding Beth a little tighter than usual, squeezing her hand a little more often and couldn't take his eyes off of her. *I want him to lie next to me and hold me,* thought Beth. The evening was cool and they decided to rekindle the fire outside and roast some marshmallows. After sitting outside under the stars for a while, Kyle took Beth's hand and led her inside. They cuddled together in the darkened front bedroom of the mobilehome. Beth trembled with anticipation as Kyle kissed her and loved her.

"I love you, Beth."

"I love you, Kyle."

Their kisses that night held the passion of two lovers forever bonded. They felt sheltered in each other's arms. *She has captured my soul,* thought Kyle as he kissed her lips and caressed the warmth of her skin. *Her scent and taste is so sweet.* He pressed against her and they were joined as one, floating on a cloud that held them enveloped in warmth. They soared together in perfect harmony, motion meeting motion, feeling the intense vibrations of a roller coaster ride, as well as the gentleness of a small creek daintily flowing down the mountainside. She felt color in every movement, every kiss, hot reds and oranges, then she would breathe and feel cool blues and greens. She felt the high bright yellows and the low deep purple. *This must be heaven,* thought Beth. Together they sailed higher and higher up a magical wave, found the crest and rode the exhilarating ride until the wave broke in a thunder of color and texture that left them breathless with wonder. *I think we got it right this time,* she mused to herself. She was warm and content in his arms wishing the night would never have to end.

***

At daybreak, Beth looked out the bunkhouse window and knew it was going to be a glorious fall day. Although the sun was coming up over the east hills, there were dark brooding clouds full of moisture to the west. The clouds reflected the morning sun painting the sky hot pink and brilliant red. She got out of her bed and went to the door to get a better look. The sunrise was dramatic and, with arms wrapped around her to protect her from the chilly morning air, she looked at the magnificence with awe and wished she were a poet. *I hope Kyle is looking at this too.*

As the day wore on, the heavy clouds covered the valley and it started to sprinkle. Not the pounding, large drops of the summer showers, but light misty drizzle. Beth had been hooking up the water trailer to go get a load of water when Kyle arrived.

"I was just going to get water, wanna go?" asked Beth. Kyle smiled as he watched Beth bend over the trailer hitch, checking to be sure that it was secure.

"Sure, I thought you might be getting ready to go. Looks like I'm here in the nick of time. I was helping my dad change the oil in the truck, or I would have been over sooner."

"Hop in," replied Beth as she brushed some sand off her hands.

When they arrived to fill the tank, Sonny was no where in sight, so Beth and Kyle had the place all to themselves. As they waited for the tank to fill, they hiked up the hill to check on Sonny's latest progress on the gold mining operation. Sonny was convinced that someday he was going to hit the motherlode, and had been setting up his gold mining operation for as long as Beth or Kyle could remember. He was always adding a new piece of equipment that he had either traded for or found. His operation looked like a giant version of the board game Mousetrap, where the marble starts at the top and moves from one gizmo to another. Instead of a marble, he was using rock and sand. As it was being processed, the light material was being moved away from the heavy material, and at the end of the process, there was suppose to be a concentration of gold. So far, neither Kyle nor Beth had actually seen it work all the way from start to finish, but Sonny kept fiddling with it.

As they examined his latest acquisition, the drizzle started again, where a minute ago the sun had been shining. With his arms around her to keep her warm, Beth and Kyle turned to look into the sky. They both exclaimed with a loud "Ahh" at the sight they beheld. A double rainbow, so close they could almost touch it.

"Have you ever seen a double rainbow?" asked Kyle.

"No, have you?"

"No, but this is beautiful!"

"Breathtaking," Beth whispered. "You know how the legend says that there is a pot of gold at the end of a rainbow?"

"Yes?"

"Well, I think that at the end of a double rainbow, you find something even better than a pot of gold, I think you find your soul mate, the one person that God created especially for you. I would find you at the end of my double rainbow, I know that in my heart." He pulled her closer to him and she felt his warm breath in her hair as they stood there watching the double rainbow start to fade.

***

After all this time, Beth still marveled at the perfection of what she had with Kyle. While Tracy had a love/hate relationship with her boyfriend and other friends were always breaking up or fighting, Kyle and Beth enjoyed total harmony. She reflected on how different her life may have been and wondered how long the perfection would have lasted.

Beth remembered exactly when the feeling started. She can still picture Tracy's room, upstairs in the condo where she lived. Her bedroom was painted Navajo White, with dark green carpet and a pile of clothes on the floor. She had a dark green and gold flowered bedspread that was a mess on a bed of white sheets. Posters were tacked up on the walls, and there was only one window and it did not let in very much light. Tracy was burning strawberry incense and the room was a little smoky. There were ashes from the incense on her black chest of drawers.

Beth and Tracy had just come in from being at the local pizza place, with some of the other kids from the condo complex. They were laughing and having a great time until they entered the room. All of a sudden, Beth thought she was going to vomit. *What is this feeling all about?* she thought. *What kind of incense is burning? It smells sickly sweet and awful.* Having always enjoyed excellent health, Beth couldn't understand her sudden urge to vomit. She had never experienced anything like this before. It was all of a sudden, as soon as she smelled the incense, with no warning and no other symptoms. To this day, Beth still blames the strawberry incense for the tragic turn of events that followed.

Chapter Eight

Beth tried not to panic as the next chapter in her life came tumbling forward. She squeezed her eyes tightly shut trying to push away the memories that always cause her so much pain. *How did I endure,* she silently askd herself. *How could Kyle ever know the torment and pain that I lived with at the tender age of sixteen, and still live with so many years later.* Time seemed to fragment, and each piece of the puzzle that she could deal with as a small part, started fitting together into a complete picture that she did not know if she was ready to face. The picture felt like it was shrouded by fog so thick that she hoped she would never have to face the clear facts that shredded her heart, and her life, so many years ago.

I don't know if I will ever be ready for this, but I

have so many questions about my feelings. Why is Kyle still in my dreams? Why do I still feel such intense emotions for him after thirty years? Are these feelings punishment for the terrible sins that I committed? Or was I granted the exquisite gift of true love and managed somehow to ruin it.

And suddenly, the fog lifted and the pain was acute. Beth fought back the tears as she tried to catch her breath. She knew she could no longer hide from her past.

***

After two weeks of alternating between feeling fine, then bouts of nausea, Beth's mom made an appointment for her to see the doctor. *I don't know what is wrong with me,* she thought. Foods that she normally loved, like mayonnaise on her sandwich or spaghetti and meatballs, just made her run to the bathroom. It was the weirdest thing she had ever experienced. There was no fever or muscle ache, or headache.

The doctor diagnosed a viral infection and gave her antibiotics. He put her on a liquid diet for two weeks and announced that she would be cured. Glad to know the problem, she lived on soup and fruit juice for the next ten days waiting for the cure to take place. *How long before this feeling goes away?* she wondered.

Ten days later, there had been no change. Tracy had called several times to see how she was doing. It was Tracy that finally suggested that maybe she was pregnant. Beth was stunned. *Oh my God, how can this be?*

"Kyle and I have only been together twice, and I don't think the first time even counted! How unfair can that be? It isn't possible, it just isn't possible," said Beth with panic in her voice.

"Beth, I never told you this, but I got pregnant last year and had the same symptoms that you have. I went to the free clinic and had a pregnancy test. It didn't cost anything and I found out right then. I ended up having an abortion."

"No," said Beth, "it just can't be that. What would I do? It has to be something else." Beth was beginning to feel real panic, because in her heart she knew that, without a doubt, she was pregnant with Kyle's child.

Tracy told her where the free clinic was and that they were open the next afternoon.

It was the first week of December, a cold dreary overcast day, when Beth drove over to the free clinic after school and had a pregnancy test. *This is the scariest and most lonely feeling I have ever had.* Beth can't remember many details about the clinic, except that it was upstairs in a dumpy building and everything was dirty beige. It seemed that the walls, chairs, furniture, and people, everything was the same dirty beige color. She never could remember anything but beige, and the voice that announced that her test was positive. Placing her hands on her belly, she walked out of the beige place, scared, confused, and somewhat in awe of what she was carrying inside of her. *Kyle, I'm going to have your baby. I love him, or her, already. I am excited, and scared, but I know it will be okay. I need to talk to you. I know that we are only sixteen, but I know we can make this work.*

Finding the first phone booth, she put in her dime and called Kyle's house. He answered on the first ring. Shaking like a leaf, she told him where she was and the results of the test.

"Kyle, I'm pregnant. I just got out of the clinic and the test confirmed it. What a dreary place. I'm scared, what do we do?" Her voice was shaking.

"Oh Babe," he groaned, "are you okay?"

"Yeah, I'm shaking all over. I can't seem to stop." Tears were welling up in her eyes. She was fighting hard to maintain control.

"We will deal with it, don't worry. We'll have to tell our parents. I'll talk to mine tonight and we can discuss our options tomorrow, okay? I love you, Beth. Don't worry. Are you okay to drive?"

With hot tears streaming down her cheeks, she said, "I'm okay, really. I love you Kyle."

As she hung up the phone, she felt relieved that he would stand by her, although she had known he would. She stopped by Tracy's house on her way home to give her the news. Tracy lived nearby.

"I knew it," remarked Tracy with a smile that signified how romantic all this was in her mind. "What are you going to do?"

"I'll be a mom, I guess," said Beth, although still very overwhelmed, she found herself smiling too.

"Well, if you need anyone to talk to, I'm here for you. How do you feel? Are you okay with all this?" Tracy asked, putting her arm around Beth's shoulders.

"Scared. Yes and no. I don't know how to tell my parents. Kyle is going to tell his tonight. I'll probably wait until after I talk to him tomorrow before telling mine. Hey, I gotta go, no one knows where I am and all this took longer than I thought it would. I will call you tomorrow, okay?" With a hug, Tracy wished her luck and promised to talk to her the next day.

That night, as Beth lay in her bed, she placed her hands lovingly on her belly. "Don't worry little one," she whispered, "I am going to take good care of you." With fantasies of baby blankets and Kyle's gentle smile, reserved only for her and their baby, she fell into a deep dreamless sleep.

Promptly the next morning, which was Saturday, at seven AM, the phone rang. Beth woke up and answered it. It was Kyle's mom and she asked to speak with her mom. *I recognized her voice and I know she knew it was me.* Shaking, she went to wake up her mom and give her the phone. Beth got back into her bed knowing she would not have long to wait until she was called into her mom and dad's bedroom.

Beth can recall exactly the look on her mom's face. She aged that morning, not by a lot, but enough that Beth noticed. There was compassion and love, coupled with the look of panic and concern, maybe some disappointment, but there was no anger. Beth felt fear as she went into face both her parents with this earth-shattering news.

"Kyle's mom said that you are pregnant, honey, it that true?" asked her mom.

"Yes," a simple reply with downcast eyes.

"How do you know, are you sure?"

"Yes, I had a pregnancy test at the free clinic," replied Beth, taking a deep breath. *Beige, whole place was dirty beige,* she thought. All of a sudden it was cold in her parents bedroom. She started to shiver.

" Okay," said her dad as he ran his fingers through his hair. "Have you talked to Kyle about this?"

"Yes, when I told him last night, we decided that we want to have our baby."

"Is Kyle going to take care of you?" asked her dad. "You are both sixteen years old."

"We didn't really discuss any details, but I am sure that he will. We love each other very much, Dad."

"I think abortion is legal in this state, have you considered that as an option?" he asked. *No!* she thought, starting to feel real panic. Beth's heart constricted at the thought of aborting her baby. Without thinking, she laid her hands on her belly in a protective gesture. Kyle's family belonged to the Roman Catholic Church and she knew that he would never agree.

"No, we never even considered that." *Don't you worry little one, I will protect you.*

"I told Kyle's mom that I would call her back, I will discuss this with her too and see how they feel about it," said Beth's mom.

They will never agree, it is against everything they believe in. Beth took comfort from the thought.

Beth, still shivering, went in to take a long hot shower. *The worst is over, my parents know. We will make this work somehow, I know we will.* When she came out of the bathroom, her dad took her aside and told her that she better go in and talk to her mother. He told her that her mom was feeling like a failure as a mother, and was in tears. Beth ran into her mother's bathroom and hugged her mom, who was sobbing quietly.

"Oh Mom, please don't blame yourself. Kyle and I love each other. You are the best mother in the whole wide world." Beth hugged her tighter. Seeing her mother feel so much guilt, Beth felt tears start to well up in her own eyes and spill down onto her cheeks. *Please, I never meant to cause so much pain. Please, please Mom, don't cry*, Beth silently pleaded. "I am sorry if I have disappointed you, but please don't blame yourself." They hugged for what felt like an eternity, until both Beth and her mother could smile again.

Beth called Kyle later that day and told him that her parents knew about her pregnancy. One part of the conversation stands out as one of the turning points that lead to Beth's decision. *I am sure that Kyle has no idea how this one sentence affected the decision that would ultimately make such a dramatic impact in the course of our lives.*

As Beth relayed the details of the conversation that morning between her and her parents, she was thinking about how Kyle would have to get an after school job to help with the financial support of their child.

"My mom was so upset, she was in tears. She felt she had failed somehow as a mother. It broke my heart, Kyle, I never meant to hurt anyone."

"Was she okay after you talked to her?"

"Yeah, I think so. I think she was most upset at the impact that this will have on my life and my future. She only wants the best for me, and she knows how hard all of this will be." *Kyle, you will be there for me though, won't you? It is not like I will have to handle this alone.*

"My parents are the same way, their main concern is my well being and future." Then it came. "By the way, tryouts for the track team are a week from this coming Friday, so I will spending my time after school until about 5PM training for the tryouts. I won't be home until late, so don't try to call me until after that, okay?"

The color slowly drained from Beth's face. *What about our baby? You need to get a job, not join the track team. Don't you understand what we have going on here? This is a WE thing! I am experiencing morning sickness all of the time and I have our baby growing inside me. How can you be talking about joining the track team?*

With her voice trembling slightly, Beth replied, "I won't call until after five. I need to go now, okay?" Beth remembered the completely empty feeling that she felt as he discussed his plans for after school track practice and track meets. There was no indication that his life would change, while she knew that her life would change dramatically. It was that exact moment that she actually considered the possibility of an abortion.

Chapter Nine

Joseph and Laura Collins had been happily married for eighteen years. With two lovely daughters, and a nice home in an upper middle-class neighborhood, they had captured the American Dream. Joseph, at 6' tall with dark wavy hair and sky blue eyes, had rugged good looks marred only slightly by a bump in the middle of his nose that was living proof of it having once been broken. He was a determined man, who was very deliberate as he made his decisions in life. Carefully gathering all the facts, he pondered each decision in his methodical fashion. After making a decision, he never looked back. There was no point. He was satisfied that he had evaluated every option and with the data available, and was confident that he would have made the same decision again. Although the word of his eldest daughter's current situation left him momentarily paralyzed, by Sunday night he had formed a plan of action.

While lying in bed that night with his wife Laura, he outlined his plan of action for Monday morning. Laura, a lovely woman born from hearty German stock, had a slim petite figure, large brown eyes highlighted with flecks of green, and long fine straight auburn hair. She lay next to his warm body listening to his well thought out plan.

"I think that an abortion would probably be the best solution in the long run. But, before I even suggest it to Beth, I want to talk to a few doctors, physiologists, and anyone else who will talk to me. I don't know what the long-term ramifications would be, if any, but I know what being a mother at age sixteen will do to her. I don't want that for her, if we can help it," Beth's dad pointed out. There was sadness in his voice.

"I keep thinking about where she would go to school and what kind of people she would be exposed to. Beth is so proud and such an optimist. She really believes in all things that are good, almost to a fault. She has such energy and passion for everything that she gets involved with. I am so afraid that no matter what happens, she will lose some of the optimism that is part of youth and be changed somehow. I guess I know that she will be changed, and it makes me sad for her. She will get a very grown up picture of life and some of the ugliness that goes with it," Beth's mom said in a whispered sigh, with a hint of resignation in her voice that acknowledged her own realization of a truth that she did not want to face.

"You're right, she made a grown-up decision that resulted in consequences that no sixteen year old is prepared to face."

"I suppose that we should have seen this coming. I can't help feeling that we let her down somewhere along the line."

"I always thought that we had taught both of our girls higher moral standards. I don't even know what she sees in that boy. I don't even want to say his name. I certainly never expected this," Beth's dad sighed as he ran his fingers through his hair, a habit that had when he was upset over something.

"I believe she truly loves him, and I am sure that in her heart there are no moral issues to be resolved. I don't think that it is a matter of not having moral standards."

"Well, in any event, I will talk to as many people tomorrow as I can, and gather as much information as I can, and we will have to make a decision real soon. One thing is for sure, I don't want her seeing him anymore, not while she lives under my roof."

"I spoke with Kyle's parents, and we are all going to meet at their house on Thursday night to talk this through," said Beth's mom.

"I will have all of my information by then. Let's try to get a good night's sleep tonight. We are going to need our strength."

Beth lay in bed that same night, having momentarily forgotten her conversation with Kyle about his after school activities. She was somehow being absorbed into the glorious clan of motherhood by a magical osmosis.   She felt as though she was being welcomed into this private circle of extraordinary women, who have nurtured the world, kept mankind alive since the beginning of time, and were the exclusive producers of every great man or woman that ever walked our earth. It was as though there was this unseen bond among all women who had ever become mothers, and she was now being welcomed into the fold. *I can be a wonderful mother. I will be a wonderful mother. I know it's too soon to feel you move, little one, but I know you're there and I know I love you.* Beth smiled to herself as drifted into dreamless sleep, thinking of little toes and fingers, and was content.

***

Monday morning brought the usual flurry of activity, Beth and Susan getting ready for school, and their parents getting ready for work. On this last week before Christmas vacation, the streets were decorated with holiday cheer. Beth drove Susan to school each morning.

"Beth, are you okay?" asked Susan that morning while on the way to school. "Do you know what you're going to do or anything?"

"Well, it looks like I will be a mom. I don't know what I'll do about school and stuff; I'm not sure how that works. I haven't really thought things out that far in the future."

"Will you marry Kyle? Will you live at home, or with Kyle somewhere else?"

"I will eventually marry Kyle, I'm sure. I'll have to

live at home for now though, I know. We don't have any way to make a living to support ourselves, much less ourselves and a baby."

"Has Kyle asked you to marry him?" asked Susan.

"No, we really didn't talk about it."

"Well, I'll help you any way that I can, I can always baby-sit, you know. I think that would be great," remarked Susan, as they pulled next to the curb at Susan's school.

"You want me to pick you up after school?" asked Beth, as Susan was getting ready to shut the car door.

"Nah, I don't want to have to wait. I can walk home and be there waiting for you by the time you get home from school. See ya later," said Susan, as she slammed the car door shut.

Beth was preoccupied in her classes; she carried a secret, a special secret that made her smile. *I wonder if it shows on my face, the way I carry myself or the way I place my hands protectively across my belly.* She was happy, still with a lot of questions in her heart, but happy none-the-less. Her optimism carried her forth and she believed everything would be good.

***

Beth's dad went into his office that morning, but not to work. He immediately got on the phone to their family physician. He got referrals to local teenage mother support groups and counselors. He went to the local library and checked out books and magazines with relevant articles. He plunged into the subject of teenage pregnancy and plowed through the material that he acquired. He got a referral from their family doctor, who did not do abortions, to a doctor that did do them. He was obsessed with getting all of the facts to make the best possible decision for his daughter, whom he loved. He realized the importance of the decision that had to be made, and the long-term consequences. He had to be right. He could not afford to make a mistake. His daughter's life and her happiness depended on him being right. Intuitively certain that the right decision was just a matter of having all of the facts, he searched, not willing to miss even a single piece of data. He had to trust his instinct. It had been honed by many years of decision making.

Joseph Collins visited a home for teenage mothers. Although he knew he would never send his daughter to one, he had to know what they were like. He found them depressing, the young mothers dull and lifeless, nothing like his laughing and passionate daughter. These girls were already defeated by life. The adults that were supposed to be supportive for these girls had also seen too much of life's ugly side. They provided the basics, a roof over their heads, sub-standard food for their sustenance and donated clothing for their warmth, but little else. He could never imagine grouping his daughter with this stratum of society.

By Tuesday afternoon Joseph believed he had all of the data to make the best possible decision for his daughter. He had spoken with two separate physiologists, their family doctor, and the physician that was referred to him that did abortions. He had visited a home for teenage mothers and spoken with all of the counselors that were available at the home, called two separate pregnancy hotlines and read every article that was available at the library. He collected his data. He methodically evaluated the data. He proposed a decision that was based on that data.

"I believe that Beth should abort the baby," said Joseph to his wife Laura, with exhaustion showing on his face and reflected in his voice. "I then don't want her seeing Kyle until she is 18. After that, she is an adult and can make her own decisions. This is my recommendation. Although I will reserve the final decision until we meet with Kyle and his parents, but I honestly feel that this decision is in her best interest."

Laura slowly nodded her head knowing the extent of pain that they were about to cause their precious daughter. *Will she ever be able to laugh again from the very bottom of her heart? Will she ever be the same? Will she carry this, as we all will, or will she feel it like we are unable to because it is happening to her, her child, her body, and we can never really understand? Can I be there for her enough to allow her to heal completely? Will she ever forgive herself? Will she ever truly forgive us? How long will it take her to understand the consequences of having a baby when she is still a child herself? I know she thinks she is ready. Will she ever realize that she is not ready, and fault us for never giving her the chance to show the world that she is capable of motherhood? What if this damages her somehow and she is never able to have children? Would she be able to live with that? Would I be able to live with that? How will this affect Susan? Susan, we need to think about Susan, also. She does not understand what is happening. We need to be sure that we don't forget Susan and her needs. God, please give us guidance on this. Help us to guide our daughter, our precious daughter.*

***

Tuesday evening, Beth's parents sat with her. Her mom held her hand as her dad explained the extent of his research. Although he spoke calmly and lovingly to her, the flesh on the nape of her neck seemed to crawl with a dire expectation. She heard the word abortion and felt as though she was plunged into a cold Arctic Ocean current that numbed her deep into the hollows of her bones. She was drowning, and her heart was pounding so hard that it seemed as if each blow pushed her deeper and deeper into the silence of the ocean floor. She felt her breast swelling with a sob and struggled for control. Even one soft sob would bring on an uncontrollable wail. *No*, she thought, *Kyle will never agree. He can't agree. He has to show them that he will fight for me and for our baby. He has to show them that he won't abandon us, that he will stand by me and take care of us. He won't agree, I know he won't.*

"The law in this state gives an underage mother the right to make the decision," continued her father. "In order to get an abortion, you need to write a letter requesting an abortion stating why you want one. Your letter gets evaluated by a group of doctors and physiologists that decide if an abortion will be granted. This is a letter that you need to write and it takes several weeks to have it evaluated by the board.”

"And if I don't write the letter?" asked Beth in a hopeful voice.

"An abortion cannot be granted, and it is illegal for the doctor to do one."

"I need to talk to Kyle. He will never go for it, Dad. It is against everything that he believes in. He said that he would be there for me and help me support our baby. We never considered an abortion."

"Beth, this is not up to Kyle, this is your life we are talking about here." Her mom tightened the grip on her hand. *I need to remain in control,* thought Beth, *our baby's life is at risk here.* She could not afford to be sucked into a cloud of black despondency. She had to remain energized and clearheaded if she hoped to save their baby. Her father continued, "We are meeting with Kyle and his parents on Thursday night, we will reserve our final decision until then. I need you to think this through. Think of how this will affect your life and your future." *Kyle will stand by me. I know he will.*

***

"Do Mom and Dad want you to get an abortion?" asked Susan, as Beth got ready to go over to meet with Kyle and his parents.

"Yes, they think that would be the best thing for me. Kyle will never go for it, I know he won't. I don't want that either. Having a baby is a scary thought, but I know that together we can handle it. I will be a good mom and

Kyle will be a good dad. After we get out of school, we can see about getting our own place and really being a family. Dad will see. After he talks to Kyle, he will see."

"Well, I hope it goes okay for you. Good luck, Beth."

They rode over to Kyle's house in silence, each of them deep in their own thoughts. Beth did not even realize that they had arrived until her dad turned off the car. She looked up and saw where she was. They walked slowly to the door and rang the bell. Kyle's mother answered the door and invited them inside. They were shown to the living room; a chocolate brown plaid sofa was on one side against the cream colored wall looking out into the back yard. There was a wood coffee table, with a glass top, placed in front of the sofa. A light tan reclining chair faced the TV in one corner and a stuffed chair that matched the sofa sat in the other. It was a comfortable, well-used, living room. Kyle's dad rose from his reclining chair, turned down the TV and reached out to shake Beth's dad's hand. Kyle's dad gave Beth a look of compassion and love that she will always remember. *There is gentleness about him. I know he understands what I am feeling. There was no fault in his eyes, only compassion and a sadness that he was expressing to her, and I know that he was feeling for his own son.*

Beth was led to the sofa to sit next to her parents. When everyone was seated, Beth looked frantically for Kyle. She looked down the hall, expecting him to come out of his room to sit by her, to stand by her. He was not down the hall; he was not there. Kyle was not there. Mrs.

Montero asked Beth if she wanted some orange juice. Her throat was suddenly so tight that she was amazed to be able to speak at all.

"Yes, thank you," she said in a horse whisper. *Kyle, where are you? Why aren't you here? How could you let me endure this on my own? How could you abandon me this way? What about our baby, I need you here, I need you to tell them that you want us and you will stand beside us. WHERE ARE YOU? KYLE, WHERE ARE YOU?* Grief welled in her, black and cold. She heard "abortion" and "eighteen" and knew the decision had been made. These people, whom she depended on to stand by their beliefs, waffled and collapsed as soon as they had to apply that belief system to their own situation. Her stomach cramped painfully with guilt, failure, and sheer black despair.

Without knowing how she got there, Beth found herself standing in the kitchen with Kyle's mom and her mom. All three were in a tight embrace, all three sobbing tears, shed for a child they would never know, a child that would never be and the guilt that they all shared in making the decision that would haunt all of them for the rest of their lives.

Kyle, where were you? Why weren't you there? Don't you see that we had a chance? Now that chance is gone. I thought you loved me. You said you loved me, I believed in you. How could I have been so wrong about you? How? Beth now knew that Kyle was not going to be there for her, was not going to fight for their child.

That night when they got home, Beth wrote the letter.

Chapter Ten

Beth woke early that morning to a dark sky and drizzle. It was as if the whole world was mourning with her over the fate of what was to be. Her appointment at the hospital was set for eight AM. Afraid that thinking about the situation would paralyze her, she had become numb and listless in her feeble attempt not to feel the intense pain of her loss. As the time approached for them to leave, she began to have second thoughts. *Maybe I can do this alone. I don't need Kyle. I don't want to sweep this precious life from my belly. Maybe if Kyle sees that I have fought for our baby, he will forgive me for what I was about to do and come back to us.* Knowing that her thoughts were not rational, but stemmed from immense grief, she tried to maintain her numbness so she could not feel anything. *I* *have to get control of myself. Breathe.* She could feel the underlying panic start to flow to the surface. She was gasping with choking sobs, trying to tell her parents that she did not want to go thorough with this.

"Please," she pleaded, not seeming to be able to get enough air. "Please, I don't want to do this. I have changed my mind," she choked out between sobs. Seeing that she was on the verge of hysteria, her father lifted her up into his arms, stroking her hair as he did when she was a child, and carried her to the car.

The rest of her day was a blur. She has no recollection of her hospital room or any of the doctors or nurses. *Maybe this memory is just so painful that my own sub-conscious is protecting me from the pain.* Beth could never explain, or remember any details or feelings, other than being cold. She knows that she was cold, spent the day being cold and felt like she would spend her life being cold. The room was cold, the hands that touched her were cold, her heart was cold and when it was all over, her belly was cold. She knew she would never be warm again.

It may have been the next day or the day after, she wasn't sure, but she remembered that she had to talk to Kyle. *Will he ever forgive me? What about our love? I love him, I long for him, and I need him. I need him to be there for me. I need him to help me make some of this pain go away. I have to tell him how sorry I am. He has to know that I did not want this, I wanted us to be a family and be together always. Where was he when I needed him? I need to know why he was not there for us. I need him to tell me that he forgives me for what I have done. I have to talk to him.*

Beth drove to the corner store with a pocket of change. She could not call Kyle from her house because it was a long distance call and she was not to have any contact with him until they were both eighteen. Her parents could not know that she called him. She parked her car and walked the few feet to an enclosed phone booth. After getting inside, she closed the door to try to have some privacy, and shelter from the bitter cold December wind. She was trembling, both from anxiety and the cold, as she put her coins into the phone and dialed his number.

She was shaking almost uncontrollably when Kyle answered the phone on the third ring.

"Kyle, it's me, Beth," she said in a low trembling whisper.

She heard the phone drop as he said to someone else in the room, "You talk to her." She called his name into the receiver, waiting for him to answer her.

Ray picked up the phone and said, "Beth, its Ray. Kyle can't talk to you now. He says he just can't."

"Why not?" said Beth, shaking uncontrollably. Panic and tears were starting to overcome her.

"He won't say, he just says he can't talk to you." *I have to talk to him. I can't live like this. He has to talk to me.*

"Please Ray, tell him that I need to talk to him. Please. I am so sorry about everything and I have to tell him, please tell him how important this is."

"Beth, I am so sorry, but he won't come to the phone. I don't know why, but he refuses," said Ray, feeling awful for what she must be going through. "I am so sorry Beth." Beth could feel herself completely losing control. She started to sob uncontrollably.

"Oh my God, what have I done?" she wailed as her back slid down the glass wall of the phone booth to a squatting position. She did not feel she had the strength to stand on her own feet anymore. "What have I done?" She was hysterical now. She knew she was and couldn't get herself under control. The phone booth was in front of a busy market, and people were coming and going, several paused to watch her hysterically pleading into the phone, tears pouring down her cheeks. Ray stayed with her on the phone, listening to her sob, feeling her pain. When she was finally out of change, she told Ray that she had to go and thanked him for being there for her.

"You are my friend, Beth. I am sorry that you are going through all of this. Anytime you need to talk, you can always call me. I am so sorry about everything."

Beth sat in her car for close to an hour. She felt drained and exhausted. *I never realized how much pain a person could feel, how lonely, and desperate, and sad.* She had to have herself under control before she could go home. Knowing, without any doubt, that she had lost the splendor and wonder of the love that she held so dear in her heart, she dried her eyes, started her car and headed home.

Chapter Eleven

Their emails started out friendly and innocent enough. As the days progressed, they became more personal and intimate, adventurous and silly.

~

EMAIL
TO: beth0711@qmail.com
FROM: klm@qmail.com

Howdy,

I am using my cowboy lingo today, like it? Had a few minutes before I head out to work and wanted to drop you a quick hello. I am not much of a typist, so this won't be very long. Just wanted you to know that I am thinking about you and have been thinking about you a lot. Don't know if that is good or not, but it is true. I have this need to open up my heart and tell you

everything that I am feeling. I don't usually do that, I am a very closed and private person, but one of these days when I have a couple of hours, I will write a long rambling letter. So be warned! Write when you can, I love hearing from you, even if it is just to say goodnight.

Your bud always, k

~

~

EMAIL
TO: klm@qmail.com
FROM: beth0711@qmailcom

Hi,

Got your email. I have so many questions. Since I type all day, I can actually type faster than I write so I can squish a lot of questions into a small amount of time. So here goes - I am curious about your day, when do you get up in the morning? Do you drink coffee? Do you listen to the radio, talk radio, or an oldies station or something else? What do you do for your job? What time do you get home at night? Do you watch TV? What is your favorite show? Do you have a dog? Are you happy? I have at least million more, but I don't want your head to spin too fast when you read this so I will ask more on another day. Okay?

It was so nice to hear your voice the other day. I have missed you, Kyle, all of these years. It was like being home again. I have so much locked away in my heart that I want to tell you. So many feelings that I don't understand. It feels so natural to write to you. I guess old habits die-hard.

Well, I'll write more later. Better get some of this work done. It is piled up on my desk!

Always, b

~

Now, Beth lived for the mornings to see if she got an answer to her last email. When there was a reply, Beth was elated, when the inbox read "No New Mail" she slumped with disappointment. She checked every morning, religiously.

~

EMAIL
TO: klm@qmail.com
FROM: beth0711@qmailcom

Hi,

Thought of one more question for this inquiring mind.... Do you snore? One more that I just had to ask! Ha!   Miss you – b

~

EMAIL
TO: beth0711@qmail.com
FROM: klm@qmail.com
RE: zzzzzzzzzz's
Hey Babe,

It isn't too forward of me to call you that, is it? *Zzzzzzzzzzzzzzzz*, oops, guess I dozed off . . . Do I snore? What kind of question is that? I'm already getting a headache over all the questions that you asked me in your last email. I am going to need a year to answer all the other questions. But in answer to this one, NO, I don't snore!

Gotta run - miss you too. K

~

Beth giggled out loud over the reply to her last email. She realized that she was feeling again, feeling alive, feeling anticipation. She knew what happened so many years ago, why she forgave Kyle and how entwined their lives had been ever since.

Why did I ever let him back into my life? After the feelings of abandonment and the pain that I went through, how could I ever forgive him, why did I ever forgive him? Even at the young and tender age of sixteen, I had made a silent pact with myself never to depend on another man again. Always take charge. Never deal from a point of weakness; always be in the driver's seat. This is what helped me get on with my life. This is where the root of my strength comes from. It started from way back then and it is how I have lived my life. On my terms, at least outwardly.

With a cup of tea in hand, Beth took a moment to reflect back on her life at age seventeen. There had been real pain for him too. She did not realize the depth of his pain until later. By then, she had been able to put her own pain and loss aside, see his pain and offer understanding and forgiveness.

Chapter Twelve

How sad that so much of the richness in life, exotic colors and textures had faded to pale primary colors and mediocrity, before Beth had even reached her seventeenth birthday. She seemed to be just going through the motions of life. *I was almost surprised that the sun rose the next morning, as if nothing had changed. Then it rose the day after, and again the day after that. Am I the only one who realizes that the world has changed?* She wondered about Kyle; he was still paramount in her mind. *It's going to take some time to get over him,* she knew, *I wish he would talk to me. I hate not knowing what happened.*

The holiday season came and went. This was always Beth's favorite time of year. She loved the music, the festivities and the food. This year it seemed as though she didn't notice that it was all happening around her. Her parents worried about her. Outwardly she seemed fine, but the sparkle had faded, at times almost to the point of being non-existent.

"What do you say that we finally get that car of yours painted," remarked Beth's dad one evening. "Have you decided on a color yet?"

"Yeah," said Beth, with a hint of mischief in her voice. "I want to paint it pumpkin orange," she said smiling, "with the inside of the pick-up bed painted black."

"Orange?" said her dad as he tried to picture his daughter in a bright orange Ranchero pick-up, mis-reading the mischievous tone in her voice. He thought that she was pulling his leg. "No, really Beth, blue maybe? Or yellow?"

"Orange … really Dad. I think it will look really cool. And, I will never lose my car in a parking lot, or worry about it getting stolen. Who would steal a bright orange car? Orange. When can we get it painted? I have been saving my money, but I don't think I have enough yet."

"I think we can help you out with the rest. Okay, orange it is. You are sure about this, right?" Her dad was smiling warmly at her.

"Sure," Beth said, as she giggled

Within the week, Beth had her bright orange Ranchero, with the black truck bed. It was everything she had imagined, distinctive and unique. She laughed each time she looked out the window and saw it parked on the street, or opened the door to get inside.

Tracy had been a supportive and wonderful friend while Beth mourned her breakup with Kyle. She knew the pain that Beth had gone through. Beth spent many a night over at her house, talking teenage girl talk into the wee hours of the morning. Tracy thought that Kyle was a coward and a jerk and had Beth almost convinced that she was right. *If only I knew what happened, maybe it would be easier to let it go. It's not knowing that's the hard part. Kyle, what happened with us? How could we go from loving each other and planning on being parents together one minute, to you not being willing to talk to me the next? I just don't get it.*

"I know this guy, he is really cute and I told him about you. He goes to my new school and I want you to meet him, Beth," said Tracy.

"Oh, I don't know, Trace, I still miss Kyle."

"Will you forget that jerk?" she said sharply. "He is not good enough for you. Look what he did! Anyway, his name is Billy and plays drums in a band. I've been told that he's really good too. They're practicing tonight in Dennis' mom's garage and I told them that we would stop by and say hi." Dennis was Tracy's current boyfriend. *Am I ready for this? Heck, what's the big deal? I'm not obligated to anything. I'm just going to meet a friend of Tracy's. I can handle that. I need to get on with my life anyway.*

"Okay, sure. So, tell me about Billy." Tracy smiled a victorious smile as she started up the stairs to her room.

"Well, I don't know him very well, but he's

seventeen and a senior. He is really cute and one of Dennis' friends."

"I need to do my hair," said Beth, as she followed Tracy up the stairs. *I feel some anticipation at meeting someone new. Kyle . . . no, stop haunting me. I need some peace. I need to be over you.*

"Plug in the curlers, I need to use them too. Do you want to wear my black blouse?"

"Yeah. I love that shirt. I wish I'd bought myself one before they were all gone. Okay, curlers are plugged in." Beth picked up the mascara and begin touching up her makeup. She didn't wear much, a little mascara, a brush of blush across her cheeks and a touch of lipstick, usually a light plum or mauve. Tracy liked a little more makeup, eyeliner, heavy mascara, white eyeshadow and white lipstick She freshened her lipstick and they were ready to go.

Within the hour, they were in Beth's bright pumpkin chariot, on their way to Dennis' mom's house. Beth, in Tracy's black blouse, shiny fabric, elastic neckline and short puffed sleeves over the usual faded blue jeans and Tracy in tan cords with a blue and gold paisley patterned blouse, were singing along with the top ten hits on KHJ radio.

As they pulled up in front of Dennis' house, Beth could hear the band practicing in the garage. They sounded fairly good, not exceptional. It was a little hard to tell because the closed garage door muffled the sound.

"Let's go," called Tracy as she jumped out of the car and slammed the door shut. Beth locked Tracy's door and slowly got out of her side.

Why do I feel disloyal? What a stupid thought! Can't I give anyone else a chance? Or, will I always be thinking about Kyle? This IS really stupid. Kyle is just a guy and people breakup and move on all the time. I am no different. I will get over this, I know I will. Nobody dies of a broken heart.

Beth stood tall and put on her best smile and said, "So, Billy doesn't have a girl friend?" as they walked up to the house.

"No, and I think you'll really like him," Tracy replied. Tracy knocked on the front door and Dennis' mom answered. She looked tired.

"Oh hi Tracy, the guys are out in the garage, go on in," said his mom, as she opened the door. Dennis and his mom lived in a modest duplex with an attached one-car garage. She worked as a retail clerk at a local department store and was always struggling for money. Their home was furnished with second-hand furniture and was shabby and messy. Tracy had been involved with Dennis, who was a year younger, for about 6 months. Although Tracy thought they had a serious relationship, Dennis had been in trouble at school a couple of times and Beth did not think their relationship would last.

The garage was not very well lit, two double florescent lights overhead, but no windows, and the side door and the garage door were both closed. Dennis was there, playing an electric bass guitar. There was a lead guitarist, a keyboard player and the drummer.

Billy was about 5'10' tall, lean and well built. He

had sandy brown hair, blue eyes and a great smile. *He is very cute.* Beth smiled as Tracy introduced them. Billy was sitting behind a drum set, and the group had just finished playing "An Old Fashioned Love Song" by Three-Dog Night.

"You guys sounded pretty good," remarked Tracy. Actually, the music was not half bad, but they were badly in need of a lead singer. Steve, the lead guitarist was singing backup with Dennis, and Mike, the keyboard player, was singing lead. The vocals left a lot to be desired. The words were sung in a kind of talking, yelling voice, reminding Beth of a Bob Dylan style. Beth and Tracy kept any critical comments to themselves, and found a seat on some boxes stacked in a corner to listen.

"So, what do you think?" whispered Tracy.

"Well, they play pretty good, but I think they need to think about getting a singer."

"No, about Billy, what do you think about Billy. He's cute, isn't he?"

"Yeah, actually he is and he's great on the drums." They were playing another Three Dog Night song that Beth didn't know the words to.

"I told you, I knew you would like him. I think he's going to go over the Pizza Palace when they're done practicing. I told Dennis that we would go too."

"Okay. Any idea how long they're going to practice?" asked Beth. She noticed that Billy was watching her while he was playing the drums, as if he was playing just for her. They made eye contact, bright blue eyes, smiling blue eyes. She smiled back at him. *He is cute.*

Beth felt herself relaxing and getting into the music. She was feeling the rhythm of the drums. It was loud, and she felt surrounded by the music, the beat. She felt part of something, a connection, and it felt good.

"Don't know," replied Tracy. She was watching Dennis playing the bass guitar, bobbing her head to the rhythm of the music.

After a few more songs, the guys decided to call it a day and head over to the local pizza place. The Pizza Palace was a favorite hangout for all the kids that lived in the same condo complex as Tracy.

"Hey Beth, are you and Tracy going to join us at the Palace?" asked Billy.

"Yeah, I guess we are," replied Beth. Billy was putting his drum sticks is a small cloth bag that held a couple of other drum sticks and some other drum parts that Beth didn't recognize. The other guys were putting their instruments in their respective cases, unplugging equipment and mikes and turning off amps. They were able to leave everything setup, but it had to all be turned off.

"Cool, so I'll see you there," Billy replied with a grin. Tracy grabbed Beth's arm and started toward the door.

"I told Dennis that he could ride with us, I can sit on his lap."

"That ought to be cozy," giggled Beth. "Too bad I got new seats." Over the past couple of weeks, Beth had been working on the interior of her Ranchero. It now had orange shag carpet and white bucket seats. She was saving up to get a new muffler system; she wanted dual chrome side pipes. She had seen exactly what she wanted at a local muffler shop. They were louder than her stock muffler, but had a distinctive sound that said *power* when she pushed the accelerator.   After that, some chrome wheels and she was set.

Beth unlocked the doors and Dennis climbed in the passenger side and Tracy slid onto his lap. It was a tight fit, but the two didn't seem to notice, as they spent the entire eight minutes it took to get to the Pizza Palace making out with each other. Beth drove in silence, while listening to the radio, trying not to notice and trying not to remember what it was like being in Kyle's arms.

Grateful to be pulling into the parking lot, Beth saw that Billy and the rest of the guys were already there. Pizza had already been ordered and the guys had camped out at a couple of the tables in the back. Pitchers of coke were already on the tables.

"What took you guys so long?" asked Billy, in a teasing voice. He steered Beth toward one of the tables and slid in next to her when she sat down.

"Nothing, how did you get here so quick?"

"Steve drove, need I say more?"

"Why, is he a crazy driver or something?" asked Beth.

"Crazy driver, just crazy, period!"

"Oh." Beth smiled as she sipped her coke. *He is easy to talk to. Billy was smiling at her. He had the bluest eyes.*

Steve's girlfriend, Faye, showed up a few minutes after the rest arrived and was introduced to Beth. Faye was a slim girl with long strawberry blond hair, blue eyes and a very lively personality. She and Beth hit it off from the start. They found themselves frequently laughing at the antics of the guys. Someone put some money in the juke box and the music started playing so loud that Beth and Billy couldn't hear each other talk. Billy started singing along, then Mike and Steve. Faye, giggling, started singing too, and then Tracy and Beth also joined in. Pretty soon the whole gang was singing along to the music, laughing and joking with each other. It was an easy atmosphere. When the pizza arrived, the group was hungry and devoured the pie until there was nothing left. A couple of the other neighborhood kids came wondering, in to see if anyone else was there. Mike went home early. As people came and went, Billy and Beth sat and talked. They seemed to have a lot in common. Billy didn't know that Beth and Tracy sang together.

"What kind of music do you do?" asked Billy.

"Oh, James Taylor, some Beatles stuff, a little folk music, a variety really of mostly soft rock music with lots of harmony. We both play guitar for accompaniment, so we do music that we can play."

"What did you think of us today?"

"Honestly, the music was great, but I think you could use a lead singer."

"I know what you mean. Maybe you and Tracy should be our lead singers," said Billy jokingly.

"Yeah right, I don't think we really do the same kind of music, but you guys could sure use someone with a voice."

Beth glanced at her watch and realized that she should start thinking about getting home. She was having a good time and she really liked Billy. No sparks, but he was very good company, and cute, and had great eyes.

"I need to get Tracy and get going," said Beth.

"We'll be practicing again after school tomorrow, maybe you could come by again with Tracy."

"I'll see how much homework I have tomorrow, maybe I'll see you guys then."

***

"So, what did I tell you. He's cute isn't he? What did he say? What did you two talk about all evening? Did he ask you out?" Tracy was rambling on and on not letting Beth get a word in edgewise.

"Tracy!" Beth giggled. "Yes, he is nice, he is cute. He asked me to come by with you tomorrow and listen to them practice, if I can."

"Well, can you?" asked Tracy

"I don't know, depends on how much homework I have. I can call you tomorrow though, and let you know." They were just arriving at Tracy's house.

"I can't stay, I need to get home," said Beth.

"I know. I'll call you tomorrow, or you call me when you get home."

"Okay. Hey, I had fun tonight. Billy is really nice."

"I know. I thought you'd like him. Talk to you tomorrow." Tracy ran up the walk way to her front door and went inside.

***

Beth was deep in thought as she drove home that night. *Do I want him to call me? Yes, I think I do. I wonder if he will want to kiss me, I wonder how he kisses. I think I only thought about Kyle twice tonight. That's good. I hope he liked me. I think I will try to make it tomorrow. I'm actually looking forward to seeing Billy. It feels good too.*

The next morning, Beth found herself singing along with the radio as she got ready for school. It was a typical February morning, dreary overcast sky, chilly morning air with a hint of a promise of sunshine sometime before dusk. Beth felt great; she was looking forward to the day. After a short shower, hot rollers to give her hair some body and the usual jeans and blouse, she gathered up her books, yelled to Susan to hurry up and headed out the door. She was again delighted, as she spied her orange Ranchero with the orange shag carpet and white leather bucket seats. *All I need is the dual side pipes and she will look perfect,* Beth thought with a grin. Susan dashed out the door behind her; they both jumped into her car and headed off to school.

***

"So, are you coming over?" asked Tracy. "I have some interesting news. Bring your guitar when you come."

"I always bring my guitar, what news?"

"Well, are you sitting down? Dennis and the guys want us to sing lead for them in their band."

"What, are you kidding? We don't even do the same music. Billy was joking with me last night about us singing lead, but he was just kidding. Are you sure about this? How do you feel about this? Oh my God."

"Oh my God is right," Tracy blurted out. "Isn't this exciting? I think we could be great. Plus it will be so much fun with me and Dennis and you and Billy."

"Wait a minute, let's not get ahead of ourselves here. Billy and I are not an item, at least not yet. So are we still going over there tonight?"

"As soon as you can get here. Pick me up at my house. How soon do you think you can be here?"

"I just have to put some clothes away that my mom folded, grab my guitar and I will be there. I am so nervous."

"Me too," giggled Tracy.

As Beth placed the receiver back in the cradle, she thought about her phone call with Tracy. She discovered she was excited, as well as nervous.

Within the hour, Beth and Tracy were on their way over to meet Billy and the guys at Dennis' house. During the short ride over, both girls would talk at once, then seem to be deep in thought, anticipation most likely, and a slight case of nerves. Once they pulled up in front of Dennis' house, they shot each other a look saying, "Okay, here goes nothin'," and both girls burst into laughter simultaneously. They were still giggling when Dennis answered the door.

"Okay, the guys are waiting in the garage. We have

been practicing Fire and Rain by James Taylor. I know this is one of the songs that you guys know." Dennis opened the door and they all entered the garage.

Billy seemed to waiting just for her. His smile widened when she stepped into the room.

"You thought I was kidding yesterday when I suggested that you guys sing lead, didn't you?" Billy teased.

Beth smiled as she replied, "Yeah, I didn't have a clue that you were at all serious. I still don't think you were serious. Whose idea was this anyway? Not that I'm complaining."

"Well, I just mentioned that you said that we need a lead singer, and the idea just developed from there."

"Okay guys, here's the deal. You may not like the way we sing, or our style and we may not like your style, so this is a trial only, no hard feelings if it doesn't work out. Agreed?" asked Tracy.

"Agreed," nodded Dennis along with the rest of the guys.

They spent the first hour setting up microphones and adjusting volumes, tuning guitars to the same key and moving equipment to achieve both adequate room and best sound. They finally decided they were ready to make some music.

Billy counted it down and the music began. Tracy sang lead with Beth adding backup harmony. The guys seemed to understand their style and added a slow, muted, full electronic instrumental sound behind their voices and acoustic guitars. When the song was over, there was a moment of silence before they all began speaking at once. With excitement in the air and smiles all around, each member of their newly formed band felt the same feeling. A bonding. A blending. They felt the makings of something grand.

Tracy was the first to ask the question, "So, do want to keep us?"

"You guys sounded great," replied Steve. "My vote is yes."

"That is a yes from me too," echoed Mike.

"How can I say no to spending time with my babe?" asked Dennis with a smile.

"Well, I don't know," Billy said slowly, with downcast eyes. Everyone looked at him with surprise. *Billy?* thought Beth. Then he lifted just his eyes to look at everyone, to gauge their reactions and burst out laughing. "Okay, they can stay," he managed between fits of laughter. When everyone realized that he was kidding, there was easy laughter all around.

"Well, I suggest that we get busy and start picking some songs and working them through," suggested Tracy. Now the serious work began.

Working with Billy, Beth was thinking, *I really like him. We will be making music together, literally,* she was smiling to herself. *Kyle and I made music together, beautiful music. Will anyone ever steal my heart like he did?*

"Beth," Billy interrupted her thoughts, "looks like we will be seeing a lot of each other. I just want to tell you that I'm glad." *He has the most beautiful blue eyes, his whole face smiles.*

"I'm glad too." His smile was infectious and Beth found herself smiling back at him.

"Wanna join me for a pizza when were done?" asked Billy, hopefully.

"Tracy is riding with me, is Dennis going too?" *I think he is asking me out.*

"Hang on, I'll go ask him, why don't you ask Tracy if she can go too?"

***

Beth smiled to herself at the thought of Billy. She had not thought of him in so many years. *Sweet Billy. That is how it all started. Fond memories of Billy, but no regrets. I can't even remember exactly what he looked like, his face a blur, with bright blue eyes. He was very gentle with me, very understanding, always there. He never demanded anything from me. There was no intensity between us, no real heat. I grew to love him, but don't think I was in love with him. I never needed him like needing air, or warmth. I ended up treating him horribly. I wonder if he ever thinks of me, or remembers our time together. I wonder if he thinks well of me, I hope so. I actually still feel guilty over how I treated him. We were so young.*

Beth remembered the music most of all. *That's what Billy and I had in common, our music. The heat that I felt was from the blending of the music, the color and texture of the sounds that we created. What I thought was passion between Billy and I, was actually the effect of making music, not just making music, but creating a sound that was distinctly ours. We all looked forward to getting together to practice, experimenting with different sounds to make familiar songs sound unique. We even wrote a few of our own songs, nothing that was very good though.   We worked so hard at our music and were so dedicated. It was fun; we all became best friends.   I was consumed with something; it helped to fill the empty place in my heart and life. It helped to replace the passion that I needed to feel alive. Plus, I had my relationship with Billy. At night though, I still fell asleep with Kyle in my thoughts. I tried not to think of him, but it was of no use. His image was still so sharp and defined. He haunted me. I threw myself into my music and spent as much time as I could with Billy. I knew he was falling in love with me and I tried so hard to fall in love with him, too. Although I know I cared deeply for him, I can't remember the first time he kissed me or even how it felt when he held me. What I do remember so vividly, was what fate had in store for me next. By mid-March, on a beautiful spring Saturday afternoon, I was driving home from band practice to get ready for my date to go to the movies with Billy. Parked in front of the elementary school, down the block and across the street from our house, was a green VW. Sitting on the grass, watching our house was Kyle.*

Chapter Thirteen

"**W**hat are you doing here?" asked Beth. *Not the most tactful first thing I could have thought of to say, if I was able to think, heck, even if I was able to breathe. I felt breathless, lightheaded. There were a hundred emotions, maybe a thousand emotions hammering away at me at once, and all I could think of to say was 'What are you doing here?'*

Beth had made a left turn at the corner, parked her bright orange Ranchero next to his VW and walked over to where Kyle was sitting. She had a fleeting feeling of regret that her car was bright orange, because it was easy to see that she was parked at the school. No denying that it was her car. With her parents forbidding her from seeing Kyle, she risked losing the privilege of her car. Her dad used those keys to keep her on the straight and narrow. She was unconcerned with the consequence, only aware of the risk. After all, it was Kyle.

"Waiting for a chance to see you." He was looking down at the grass, watching his fingers playing with one blade then another. After a brief pause, he lifted his eyes to meet hers, searching her face for some indication of what she was thinking. "Watching your house, hoping you would eventually speak to me, maybe even someday forgive me." Another pause, then, "You look good Beth, really good." *He looked sad, it broke my heart.*

"Kyle, I forgave you a long time ago," Beth replied as she sat down next to him on the grass. "I cried, felt completely empty except for the heartache, but never blamed it on you. I didn't understand what happened and was so hurt when you wouldn't talk to me, but I never blamed you for my pain."

"Beth, I'm not the same without you. This has been the hardest three months of my life. I don't want to be without you. I need you in my life." He touched her hand. *I felt heat, so much heat from such a simple gesture. Did he feel it too?* "I know we're not supposed to see each other and I don't know what to do about that. I don't know if you want anything to do with me, but I want you in my life."

I think I have been holding my breath. Breathe, Beth. "I want you in my life too. Things can't be the same. I have been seeing someone for a couple of weeks. His name is Billy. It is not the same as with us, but I care for him. We are in a band together." Beth stopped, realizing that there was something she had to know. "There is something that I have to ask you." Kyle stiffened slightly, as if he knew what she was about to ask. "The night when my parents and I came to your house to discuss what we were going to do, where were you? Why weren't you there?"

Kyle looked down; he couldn't even look at her. For a moment, Beth thought he was in tears. In a whisper, unable to meet her gaze, he just said "I am so sorry Beth, I just couldn't be there. I was in my bedroom. I couldn't face you. There was nothing I could do or say that would have made any difference. I just stayed in my room, numb." Beth touched his cheek, gently, both to let him know that she understood and because she just wanted to feel his skin. When he looked at her, she realized that the depth of his pain had been not unlike hers. She read it in his eyes, knew it in her heart and loved him more at that moment than ever before.

She knew that she had better leave before someone noticed that her car was parked across the street next to Kyle's car. Although she wanted to touch him and hold him, she squeezed his hand and told him that he could keep in touch through Ray. Ray had called her a couple of times, just to see how she was doing. He had been a good friend to her, and she knew that he was still close to Kyle too.

Walking back to her car, Beth felt like she was walking on air. *Kyle looked like he was hurting inside too. It wasn't just me. I feel like I am finally complete again, someday I know we will be together. Is the ground still under my feet? I don't feel it!*

***

Susan tackled her as soon as she walked in the door.

"That was Kyle over there, wasn't it? Good thing Dad and Mom aren't home yet. You would have been busted! What did he say? What did he want? You have to tell me everything!"

"I will, I will!" said Beth, grinning from ear to ear. "He said that he wants me back and can't live without me."

"Wow! That's the most romantic thing I've ever heard. So what are you going to do? Are you going back to him? Do you still love him? What about Dad and Mom?"

"Well, I don't know what I'm going to do, honestly." Beth went into the kitchen, grabbed a glass from the dish rack, filled it with ice from the door in the refrigerator and starting pouring some sun tea. She had an old apple juice bottle that she put out on the side porch each morning, with a variety of tea bags and cold water, and let the sun make tea. Today she had put a bag of peppermint, two bags of Lipton, and had found a raspberry tea bag stuffed in the bottom of the glass miscellaneous tea bag jar that her mom kept in the back of the cupboard. "Do you want some iced tea?" Beth asked Susan. She added a spoon of sugar and stirred.

"No, I already have milk. I just made a sandwich." Susan started over to the dining room table that was part of the large well appointed kitchen, to finish her lunch. Beth followed her to the table with her tea, grabbing a banana on the way.

"I still love him. It'll be hard to really see him, but we'll keep in touch."

"What about Billy?" asked Susan, as she took a bite of her chicken sandwich.

"Billy is very special and I love spending time with him, but he isn't Kyle."

"Are you still going out with him tonight?"

"Yeah, we're going to the movies. He's going to get his mom's car."

"Are you going to tell him about Kyle?"

"No."

**

Beth was at her office on a Monday afternoon after getting back from the mountains. She and Jacen had stayed over on Sunday night so Beth was in the office by noon on Monday. She felt lucky to be able to have enough flexibility in her schedule to allow her to take those extra few hours. She dreaded when Jacen started back to school because it put a crimp in her style. Ethan was in sales, so his schedule was his own too.

Beth was delighted to find that Kyle had written her over the weekend.

~

EMAIL
TO: beth0711@qmail.com
FROM: kls@qmail.com
RE:

How was your weekend? I would really love to get a chance to go to the mountains too. I miss you out there. I miss hearing your voice. Do you have a voice mail where I can leave a message? I don't want to call you at work and don't think it is a good idea for you to call me at work. You can leave a message on my work voice mail though; I already gave you the number. I am the only one who has access.

I don't know if seeing each other would be a good idea. For now, I think we are safer just being email buddies. Well, I gotta go, write me soon. Miss you.
K

~

~

EMAIL
TO: kls@qmail.com
FROM: beth0711@qmail.com
RE:

Hey you! You can leave a message on my cell phone voice mail. I am the only one who has access to it. I love hearing your voice too. What do you think I am going to do to you if we have lunch in some public place somewhere? I know I have been naughty in the past (I have put you in some awful situations, I know, and I am so very sorry), but I promise to behave. Really. You can trust me. Honest. Anyway, I would love to see you. Leave me a message, I already left you one! Miss you too.

b

~

***

"Hi Susan, how are you doing?" Beth asked over the phone. She was at work and just felt this need to talk to her sister.

"Just okay, I guess," responded Susan.

"That doesn't sound very good, what's going on? What's the matter?"

"It's Michael, he hasn't called in two days. He said he would call yesterday, but I have not heard a thing. I hate this, he doesn't understand how hard it is for me, and how unhappy it makes me not to hear from him." Susan sighed.

"When he does call, what does he say when you ask him why he doesn't call when he says he will?"

"Oh, it is always something pretty important, like last time, his father-in-law was taken to the emergency room because he had a stroke or heart attack or something, and he couldn't get to a phone. I then feel so bad because I was ragging on him, and was such a bitch."

"Well, I guess I can see how he might have been otherwise engaged."

"I know," laughed Susan, "I know, he has a family and they have to come first and everything, but that doesn't make it any easier when I want to be there with him, be his family, be number one in his life and I simply am not. Then he will say something like, 'thank you for being so patient with me, you are the only reason I can endure all of this, because I know you are there for me, you are my peace.' What can I say? What I want to say is 'that is all fine and well for you, but what about me?' but that would make me look so horrible, but it really is so hard for me. He has no idea, he comes here and visits for a couple of weeks, then goes home to Indiana and still has his family and his life and I just fall apart. I feel like I am spending my life just waiting and only live the few weeks that he is here. And, he has not been here since Christmas, which is over six months ago. Anyway, I'm sorry, I'm talking your ear off!"

Susan and Michael had met while he was on a temporary job assignment in Washington State, where Susan lives. They started out as just friends, but there was a spark there and it soon developed into something more serious. They had to keep it a secret because they worked together.   One evening, over some wine, Michael was talking about a sister-in-law who was killed and Susan thought he was talking about his wife. Michael talked a lot about his two boys, but never mentioned a wife, so for the first four or five months, Susan thought he was widowed. She fell head over heels in love with him and was devastated when he finally confessed that he was married. He did not provide details, other than it was not a happy marriage. Susan had too much pride and was in too much shock to ask any questions. After about eight months, his contract was up and he returned to Indiana with promises that he would be back shortly. They had emailed and called each other every day since, at least Susan had. She was living on an emotional roller coaster, too.

"How are you doing?" Susan asked.

"Well, Ethan is still not hardly working so his commission checks have been terrible. He doesn't seem to care. I have been working my butt off to try to make ends meet. Kyle and I have been emailing back and forth. I want to see him. I know it has been a lot of years since we have seen each other, but there is some kind of connection there and I just feel like I owe it to myself to find out what it is. There are so many feelings buried deep inside of me. I just don't want to realize when I am old, that I should have explored these feelings and have it be too late, you know?"

"Just be careful, I don't want you be the one who gets hurt. It has been a long time since you guys were together, since you were kids. My God, you did have some adventures though. Remember the time when you guys were not supposed to be seeing each other and his VW wouldn't start and he was parked in front of our house?"

***

Yes, Beth did remember. She remembered every terrifying moment. Their parents were gone for the weekend leaving Beth and Susan at home. They were old enough, Beth was sixteen, almost seventeen and Susan was fourteen. They had spent an uneventful day at home on that Saturday in May. Billy had come over during the day and they played pool and listened to records. He had to leave early because he had to baby-sit his mom's dogs. Beth still gets irked when she remembers those damn dogs. Billy's mom didn't like her, and used any excuse to keep Billy unavailable to do things with her. She used to breed some kind of small dog, it took Beth a moment to remember what kind they were. Lhasa Apso. Yes, that's what they were. Anyway, when she had new puppies and somewhere to go, she would tell Billy that he had to stay home and baby-sit them. Billy was a very nice person and was not one to complain, especially to his mother, who seemed to run their household. So he just said okay and told Beth that he couldn't do anything that night because of the dogs.

"Fine," she said, and was thrilled when Ray called and asked if she was going to be home because Kyle had the VW and wanted to come over. "Yes, absolutely!"

Sometime in the early evening, Kyle drove up. He parked a couple of houses away so it wouldn't be obvious whom he was visiting.

"Hey Babe," said Kyle. Beth came bounding out the front door, bare-footed, wearing a yellow sundress, and ran up and gave him a big hug. He kissed her a quick hello as they walked arm and arm into the house. *God I've missed him.* Beth put a Beatles album on the stereo, and challenged Kyle to a game of pool. Since she had a table at home, she won her share of games. "Okay," said Kyle with a grin.

They played pool, teased each other, listened to music and drank sodas until about nine, when Kyle said he needed to go. By the time he actually got out the door, it was getting close to ten. Beth was cleaning up the family room, throwing away soda cans and putting the pool cues away, when someone knocked on the side door. She looked out the window and Kyle was standing there. With curiosity written all over her face, Beth opened the door.

"The VW won't start," Kyle stated, before Beth even had a chance to ask. He ran his hand through his hair.

What is it doing?" asked Beth, with genuine concern in her voice.

"It turns over, but doesn't seem to want to fire. Anyway, I've almost run the battery down."

"Well, we can't exactly call your dad, or even a tow truck for that matter. Shoot . . . . I could tow you home," Beth remarked, matter-of-factly.

"Are you nuts? It's over 30 miles and it's going on eleven o'clock at night, and anyway, have you ever even towed anything? It's not that easy, Beth. My God, what are you thinking?"

"I towed my dad in the Ranchero when we brought it home. It wasn't running, remember? I told you. It wasn't that bad. Have you ever been towed? Or, towed anything?"

"No. This is a long way, Beth"

"Okay, got any better ideas?"

"No."

"Well, unless you have a better idea, I'll grab a rope out of the garage and pull my Ranchero around front. We can do this, really."

"You are nuts . . no, WE are nuts." Kyle turned shaking his head and started back out the door to his disabled car. *She actually acts like she is looking forward to this,* thought Kyle incredulously.

With a rope, tripled for strength, tied to the trailer hitch on the back of the Ranchero and to the undercarriage on the front end of the VW, they started the long stretch between Long Beach and Anaheim.

"I'll start real slow so I don't jerk the rope, your job is to try to keep the tension constant and not to run into the back of my car! I'm gonna take Ball road and try to make as many of the lights as I can. We'll just take it slow and easy, okay? Ready?" Beth was smiling.

"Ready as I'll ever be. Just take it real easy. When we get about a block from my house, we can un-hook and I will push it the rest of the way home. I'll tell my dad that it stopped a couple of blocks from home and I pushed it, that's why I am so late."

"Okay, keep your lights on and the window down, and yell if you need anything."

Kyle finally caught a little of her confidence, broke a smile, shook his head and said, "Here goes nothin!"

They started off a little jerky, both getting the hang of the tow-er and tow-ee roles. Soon they had the starts and stops wired and the whole operation went fairly smoothly. Fortunately, at that time of night, there was little traffic and they did not meet up with any local police, a potential problem they hadn't considered.

Before long, they arrived at Kyle's street, a successful, although more than a little stressful, operation.

"I can't believe we made it," laughed Kyle, with relief written all over his face. His usual composure was a little strained back at Beth's house. He grabbed her and planted a big kiss on her lips. Forehead to forehead, he whispered, "You are nuts, but amazing. You still need to get home safe. It's really late. I can't call you, so please be extra careful. I still can't believe we made it," he smiled down at her. She smiled back looking deep into his eyes and kissed him.

Still smiling she whispered, "Gotta go."

Cars unhooked and the rope coiled in the bed of her Ranchero, she waved as Kyle started pushing the VW the last block home. She was tired, she realized, but happy. What an evening, couldn't wait to hit her bed!

***

"Did you know that silly VW broke down on us one other time? Did I ever tell you about that?" asked Beth.

"No," replied Susan.

"Oh my God, what a night that was! Kyle and I went to a football game. It wasn't at his school, but at another one and I didn't know where it was. So, I parked my car around the corner from his house, he met me there and we took his VW."

"What happened?" asked Susan.

***

It was a cool evening during football season. Kyle had invited Beth to go with him to a game that was away from his home school. She parked her car at a gas station that was about a mile from his house, on one side, next to a phone booth. Beth was wearing her favorite blue jeans, a light blue cotton sweater and a jean jacket, cropped at the waist. Kyle met her there; they got into the green VW and headed off to the game. They ate a couple of burgers at a local drive-through, on the way. It was a very fun night and Kyle's school won the game. *I feel like this is the way we are supposed to be. First of all, together, we do belong together, and second, carefree, holding hands, laughing, like it used to be. I am happy. I think Kyle is happy. This has been a perfect evening.* They walked, hand in hand, slow, in no hurry, just enjoying each other, out to the parking lot. They got in the car and sat in the front seats, deciding where to go next. Since it was just a few minutes after nine, they decided to find a restaurant for an ice-cream sundae before they headed back to where Beth was parked. Kyle put the key in the ignition; it turned over, but wouldn't start. He tried and tried, but no luck. They sat there, stunned, wondering what to do next. Kyle couldn't call his parents because there was no way to explain why Beth was there. Beth's parents were gone for the weekend, which was why Beth was able to go in the first place.

"So there we sat, looking at each other, wondering

what to do," explained Beth.

"What happened?" asked Susan, "What did you guys do?"

"There was a gas station about a block away; we decided to walk there and see if there was a mechanic, or at least a phone, or someone who could either help get the car started, help us push it there, or something. It was a little chilly, so Kyle had his arm around my shoulders as we walked to the local gas station. We explained our situation as best we could to the attendant, who went to talk to the mechanic. Kyle told the one guy that I needed to get to my car. This guy was really wacko. I don't remember if he was a mechanic, or an attendant, or was just hanging around. I do remember that he had only one front tooth and hair that stuck up all over his head, his beard was unshaven, but not like he was growing a beard, just like he hadn't shaved in a while, fingernails were caked with grease and he was so dirty. He may have been drunk, or at least drinking, had dirty hands and clothes, but . . . offered to drive me back to my car. I remember not wanting to be alone with this guy, and gave Kyle a look of panic. Fortunately, Kyle did not want me alone with this guy either and offered to go with me to drop me off at my car."

"So, you guys got in the car with this stranger?" asked Susan

"Worse than that, he had a pickup, but it didn't have any front seats. There might have been a driver's front seat, but no passenger seat, just a lawn chair where the seat should have been. Kyle sat in the chair and pulled me into his lap. That is how we drove, bouncing all over the place,

I was hitting my head on the roof of the truck cab. There were also no shocks, so we would bounce down the road, and the guy who was driving didn't even seem to notice. He drove like a maniac, looked like a maniac, and talked like a maniac. It was nuts. But, he drove us all the way back to my car, which was probably, oh, I don't know, seven to ten miles maybe. It was quite a distance away. He wouldn't take any gas money or anything, and saved our butts! I will never forget that crazy guy."

"Oh my God," laughed Susan. How did Kyle get the VW home?"

"They dropped me off at my car, then Kyle went back to the gas station and called his dad, and his dad came with the tow bar and towed it home. Yes, you're right, Sis, we did have some adventures. As a matter of fact, there was one other time that we almost got caught seeing each other. I had driven over to pick him up after school one afternoon, and we both needed to go to the library. The public library was just off the freeway, can't even remember which freeway now. Anyway, when we were done at the library, I let Kyle drive and we got back on the freeway to go to his house. We were driving along and all of sudden Kyle says 'Oh Shit!' I was singing along with the radio or something and I said 'What?' He says, very slowly, in his deliberate way, 'the truck just ahead of us getting off at the same offramp is my dad.' I looked ahead of us and sure enough, there was the pickup truck, with the camper that his dad drove to work. Of course, my bright orange Ranchero pickup, and by that time I had chrome dual side pipes, was hard to miss. And to top it off, Kyle was driving. Yikes! I remember asking 'should I duck?' What a stupid question, he was driving. It was obvious that I was somewhere around. Kyle gave me this look like 'Oh yeah, that will fool him' but instead said 'I'm going to stay real close to him and hope he can't really see me in the mirrors' and that's what we did. It was a tense couple of minutes, but he turned off and we went straight. We parked, caught our breath, then drove to a couple of blocks before Kyle's house and he walked the rest of the way."

"Did his dad ever say anything?" asked Susan.

"I asked Kyle, but he only said that he thought his dad gave him this look when he got home, but never said anything. I still wonder sometimes if he saw us behind him that day."

Chapter Fourteen

~

EMAIL
TO: klm@qmail.com
FROM: beth0711@qmailcom

Hi, - Hey, I have a funny story to tell you. I've been going to the classes that I need to get my financial advisor license and I am going nuts with the instructor. We meet in these classrooms, with tables and chairs that face a big white board that is all across the front of the room. It's a regular classroom. The instructor is a really nice guy, probably late 50's, balding gray hair, short, maybe 5'7" or so, belly that hangs a little over his pants. Just a regular looking guy, he's an attorney and looks the part. But, he has this habit of touching his face, forehead, nose, chin, all over his face while he is talking. The bad part is that when he writes on the board with the dry markers, it creates this black dust that gets all over his hands. Then when he talks, he touches his face, he gets these black streaks all over his face. Today, I really wanted to tell him because he looked so funny. He had a black streak that went from his upper lip to his nose. I really had to restrain myself not to laugh because he looked so comical, yet I felt bad because I didn't tell him. This was my second day, I have one more to go. Anyway, I wanted to share my day with you.

Been working hard, studying a lot, missing you. I want to see you. I promise I will be on my best behavior. Gotta go for now, write me soon. Love – b

~

~

EMAIL
TO: beth0711@qmail.com
FROM: klm@qmail.com
RE:
Hi Babe,

I'm assuming that you made it through all three days of your class. Sounds like a lot of work. Hope you were able restrain yourself, I know that's hard for you.

Hey, you think I don't want to see you because I am afraid that you will seduce me? Quite the opposite, believe me. I am afraid that I will seduce you and I don't think you will be able to live with the guilt. I just don't want you to get hurt. I know me, and I know us and I know what I will want if I see you. I have lived with guilt for a long time, but I think you would really have a problem with it.

Sorry to make this so short, but I gotta go. Will write more later.
Always – k

~

~

EMAIL
TO: klm@qmail.com
FROM: beth0711@qmail.com

Why is everyone always doing things for my own good? I am a big girl and can make my own decisions. I am sure that we can meet for lunch somewhere without ripping each other's clothes off. A nice lunch, in a public place, where we can just catch up and spend some time talking and hanging out. That is all I am asking for. I'm sure that you can handle it. What do you think? Is that asking too much? Let me know. Anyway, I just have a minute and wanted to drop a quick note. Love hearing from you. Brings a lot of raw emotion out from very well locked places. Sometimes I am not sure what to do with all of it. One thing I know is that I do love you, have always loved you and will always love you. After all of this time, I know that will never change. Oh God, are you running away at top speed? I said the 'L' word; hope that doesn't scare you too much. Anyway, gotta go for now. Write me soon. Miss you. L b.

~

~

EMAIL
TO: beth0711@qmail.com
FROM: klm@qmail.com
RE:
Hey,
I am not running . . . you think you could scare me away with the 'L' word? There isn't anything that you can say to scare me away. Public place, huh. Have to think about it, but sounds do-able. Sorry this is so short. Thinking of you, always - k

~

***

"Happy Birthday to you, Happy Birthday dear Beth," Ray sang into the phone. It had been ages since they had talked to each other. *It's wonderful to hear from him,* thought Beth.

"You are NEXT so don't get too carried away," laughed Beth. Beth's birthday was on the 11th and Ray's on the 22nd. Then you will be as old as me!"

"Neither of us look it."

"Or act it!"

"Think we will ever grow up?" asked Ray.

"Don't plan on it, how about you?"

"Nope."

I miss him in my life too. There were actually three of them that Beth missed. Ray, Kyle and Chris. The three were best friends and had been since high school.

Talking to no one in her office, she said out loud as she picked up the phone, "I have to call Susan."

"Hi Sis, Ray called me today to wish me a happy birthday," Beth commented when Susan answered the phone.

"He always calls me on my birthday too."

"It was really nice to hear from him. He sang to me, isn't that funny? Do you ever miss having all of us together? Remember how much fun we all use to have? Remember when we first met Chris?"

"Of course I remember, after all, I ended up marrying him, I should remember when we first met."

Beth remembered that weekend too, in great detail, for an entirely different reason.

***

It was the summer between eleventh and twelfth grade, Beth couldn't quite remember the month. She hated not being allowed to see Kyle. She missed him. Beth, Susan and a couple of other girl friends planned a camping trip, with motorcycles, out to the Anza Borrego desert. One of the other girls had a tent and camp stove. Beth couldn't help it if Kyle, Ray and Chris planned a camping trip on the same weekend, interestingly enough, also in the Anza Borrego desert. The girls, riding in two cars, met the guys, driving in Chris' family station wagon, en-route. They traveled in a caravan out to the desert to set up camp.

Beth and Susan had heard a lot about Chris from Kyle and Ray. He and Susan had actually written back and forth to each other a couple of times, but they hadn't had the chance to meet. Susan had been real excited to meet him; Beth was just looking forward to being with Kyle.

Chris and Susan hit it off. In a few years they would end up getting married and having three beautiful daughters. Beth and Kyle spent the afternoon on Beth's motorcycle, exploring the desert, trying to stay cool. By the time they arrived and chose a camp spot, set up camp and had a cold soda, it was well into Saturday afternoon. Details of the day are hazy, until it got dark. A campfire was lit and hot-dogs and marshmallows were the evening fare. *Best hot dogs I had ever tasted,* thought Beth, and she wolfed down two.

Evening turned into night and under a clear dark sky filled with stars, the group started getting ready to bunk down for the night.

My first time sleeping with anyone for a whole night. Beth was excited and a little apprehensive. In the back of her Ranchero pickup, she watched Kyle zip their sleeping bags together. Bringing both his pillow and hers, she placed them at the head of their newly made bed. He smiled at her. His first time too, she knew.

If I had not already been in love with him, I would

have been after that night. We did not make love, but cuddled under the stars, with nothing between the heavens and us. He held me in his arms, keeping me warm, nuzzling my neck, whispering to me, holding my hand. We talked, we kissed, we watched the moon come up. I dozed, waking up to him watching me sleep. He drifted off to sleep holding me tight, protected, loved. Even in his sleep, he didn't let me go. I never wanted the night to end. I almost didn't want to sleep, because I didn't want to miss any of our night together. We watched the sunrise, nestled limbs tangled under the covers. We could have been alone in the world. For that night, we didn't need anyone or anything but each other.

"How do I ever go back to my life?" Beth whispered into his neck, as the sunrise started turning into day.

"How do either of us go back?" sighed Kyle. "I love you Beth, nothing can ever change that. You have captured my heart and no matter what, always remember that, okay? Come on, we've got to get up."

"I know, but I don't want to." Her face was snuggled into his chest, arms holding him tight.

"I know, Babe, me neither."

And so it was. It was a perfect camping trip, a first for Beth, spending the night under the stars with Kyle, and Susan meeting Chris, whom she would marry in a couple of years.

Chapter Fifteen

Senior year in high school is usually memorable for everyone. It's the unofficial transformation to adulthood. Beth was on a limited day schedule, getting out at about 1:00 P.M. for the day. Her day would start around 7:30 A.M. First stop was Billy's house before school, after his mom left for work. She then ran in late to her biology class, always with some creative reason why she was late. At about 1:00 P. M. she headed to Anaheim to pick up Kyle from school and spend some time with him, then back to Long Beach to work by 4:00 P.M. and worked till 6:00 P.M. She was a busy girl. Although she did not see Kyle every day, she was at his school waiting for him several days a week.

"I'm interviewing for a new job tomorrow,"

remarked Beth, one afternoon while picking Kyle up from school.

"What kind of a job?" asked Kyle

"Well, it's an accounting firm. I heard that they are looking for someone, and called for an interview. The owner is supposed to be a real go-getter, and it's a very busy office." Her current job was in a construction office, doing filing and answering phones. "I would be actually doing accounting work, not just filing, and he said he would train me and everything. I'm excited, plus, the pay is better."

"That's great, Babe, I know you'll get it."

***

She did get the job. With resume in hand, she arrived for the interview, on time, dressed in business attire, dark blue slacks, white cotton blouse, red and blue patterned scarf and a blue blazer. He was very impressed with her, as she was with him. He was just eight years older than she was, and at age twenty-six, married with a nine-month-old son, he had the energy to become very successful. He was looking for clerical help that he could train to be a 'star' in his office. His name was Jim.

"I have a new job!" Beth exclaimed to Ray that night on the phone. "Can you call Kyle for me and let him know that I got it? I told him about it yesterday, but haven't talked to him since. Tell him I won't be able to go to his school as much because I start at three now, instead of four. I can skip my last class sometimes and still get over there for his lunchtime. I am really excited. My new boss, Jim, is going to teach me the business."

"That's great Beth. I'll call him for you as soon as we get off the phone."

Her new job started out great. Beth had a mind for numbers and she just naturally seemed to grasp the concepts of accounting. Jim was a good and patient teacher and the two meshed into an unbelievable team. He called her his "superstar" and she lived up to her name. She was working every day from 3:00 P.M. to 6:00 P.M., many days she would come in at 2:00 P.M. instead, just because she liked her work and wanted to do an extra good job.

Beth had been seeing Billy now for over a year and he was starting to get serious with her. Their relationship had finally become intimate and he was starting to talk about spending their lives together. Beth still had serious problems with his controlling mother. Even at age seventeen, she could sense problems in their future.

"Beth, I'm sorry but I can't get the car tonight, my mom says she might need to go somewhere and might need her car."

"Why don't you buy your own car, that way you wouldn't have to be dependent on the whims of your mom," replied Beth, with definite sarcasm in her voice. "I hate that you are so ruled by her, and I don't like always picking you up and having to drive everywhere." Billy had a job as an orderly at a nursing home. Beth hated that his job consisted of making beds (he had shown her how to do hospital corners, as if she would've been impressed), emptying bed-pans and being a go-fer. "You're working,

I'm sure we can find a car you can afford. Have you saved any money?"

"I have about four hundred dollars. Do you think I can buy something for that?"

"Yes, might need a little work, but let's at least start looking. I don't want to have to depend on your mom's car anymore. I hate this."

Beth thought a lot about Billy. He had been easy to have a relationship with. He was nice looking, never fought with her; she always got her own way, he was not demanding, but was affectionate, and was a pretty good drummer. He was the perfect boyfriend. He also was not going to college, had a job that Beth was ashamed of, was pushed around by his mother and had no car. She found that she was starting to push him around a little too, and did not respect the fact that he seemed to just take it. She didn't like the bitchy person that she sometimes became around him. It was unbecoming, and she could see herself getting really ugly to him and she didn't like herself when she was that way, but couldn't seem to help it.

***

"My mom said I could look for a car, but she didn't think I would be able to find anything for four-hundred dollars."

"You ASKED your mom if you could buy a car?" Beth asked incredulously. "You are eighteen, Billy, you don't have to ask your mom anymore. We will find you a car, one that you can afford, I promise." It had become a battle of wills between Beth and Billy's mom. She went down that day and bought the newspaper and started browsing the classified section, looking for cars in the four hundred-dollar range.

"Why don't you ask for a raise from that place you are working at?" asked Beth, later that evening. He had ridden his bike over to her house. There were only a couple cars in the paper for less than four hundred dollars. "There is a VW Bus in the paper for six hundred, we could make the guy an offer. My dad can go with us and check out the car."

"I would love a VW Bus. Would your dad really go?" asked Billy

"Of course. Lets go ask him, maybe we can see it today."

The engine ran, a little rough, but it ran. The body was straight but needed paint, interior was dirty and the whole car needed TLC. Billy was so excited. Beth's dad looked the bus over very carefully, making friends with the seller, as they considered the purchase. It had been sitting in the seller's back yard for months, being only started occasionally to keep the battery from going dead. Beth's dad could read his daughter's shining eyes and they gave him the go-ahead to try to negotiate a deal.

"This would be for my daughter's boyfriend here, it would be his first car. Although it does indeed run, a lot of work and some money would have to be put into the bus before it could be a safe vehicle. I'm sure you remember your first car," he said conspiratorially with a smile, "Billy here has three hundred dollars cash, would you be willing to let it go for that?"

A short pause then, "Can't let it for three, the very lowest I could go would be five hundred dollars. It would be a bargain at five and I know I won't have any problem selling it for that. I would like to help the kids out here, but five hundred is the best I can do," said the seller firmly.

"Okay, well, let us sleep on it and see what we can do. Can we give you a call tomorrow and let you know?" asked Beth's dad.

"Certainly, don't take too much time though, I don't think the bus will take long to sell."

"He is right, I don't think he will have any problem selling the bus for five hundred," remarked Beth's dad in the car on the way home. "Can you ask your parents for a hundred dollar loan? The engine sounded real good, the tires still had some decent rubber on them and if anything did go wrong, VW's are easy to work on and the parts are cheap."

"I'll ask my parents tonight," said Billy.

***

"Your mom said WHAT?" Beth screamed into the phone.

"She doesn't want me to get a bus because she is afraid that if I get in an accident, my legs will be crushed because there is nothing up front to protect me from the other car," said Billy, with patience in his voice.

"Billy, you are eighteen years old, old enough to decide what kind of car to buy! You don't need your mother's permission."

"I know, but it would cause real problems so I won't get the bus. It is not a big deal, really."

"That was a real nice bus; we could fix it up so cute."

"I know. How about a Volvo, my mom wants me to look for a Volvo."

Within the month, Billy had his Volvo. Beth, totally irked about it, hated the car. It was bright blue and old. She did have the last laugh, however, because after owning the car for less than a month, the transmission went out and the car sat in front of his house, not running, for as long as she could remember. That put them back to square one, though, as far as the car situation went. Beth had another idea.

"Have you decided what you want to do for a living?" Beth asked Billy one afternoon. He had just gotten off work. He did finally ask for a raise, after Beth bugged him incessantly. He was promoted in fact, to the guy in the nursing home that worked in the kitchen and delivered the meals on trays to the individual patients. *Cleaner work,* Beth thought, *but still, get real! I spend my day working with clients and being an integral part of their business. My boyfriend delivers food from the kitchen in a nursing home. He lets me berate him and push him around, just like his mom does to his dad, and he really thinks he is going to marry me? He needs to grow up and learn a trade, or go back to school, or something.*

"Well I have thought about being a plumber . . . ." *Okay, now we're getting somewhere,* thought Beth.

Plumbers make good money and it's honest work.

"I want you to join the service." She braced herself as she let the bomb drop. "My dad was in the Air Force. I know they are good, or any of the branches of the service. You can learn to be a plumber and get out with a trade." *And become a man in the process.*

By March, Billy was in basic training in the Air Force. Her only prerequisite was that he be available to fly home to take her to her high school prom. He was.

***

Beth had plenty on her plate. School every morning until 1:00 P.M., then she usually went to work early and worked until six in the evening. She had not been over to see Kyle much, but she knew that he had been seeing a girl named Dena. He was working at a local drug store making deliveries after school. She wrote to Billy, he wrote back and called her often, always collect.

Work was very demanding. She was handling more and more in the office, which gave her boss, the freedom to go out and meet with new clients. He had almost doubled his business in the six months or so that Beth had been working for him. He spoiled her, took her to lunch, bought her a new typewriter, and occasionally brought fresh flowers for her desk. She had already gotten two raises, and he told her that he was not paying her nearly enough. She loved her job, felt like an important part of the business and, most importantly, she was appreciated.

In April of her senior year of high school, her boss

Jim abruptly changed. He seemed distracted and withdrawn, not so much with her, just in general. He did not share his personal life with her, but she sensed that something was wrong. Although she did not pry, Beth let him know that if he needed anything, she was there. Two weeks of distraction was followed by frantic energy. Jim seemed to throw himself into his work and was coming in at 7:00 A.M. and working until well after she left each day at six. Beth could not figure out what was going on, he seemed obsessed with his business and making it grow. In early May there was a trade-show and Jim paid to have a booth, asking Beth to help him work it.

"This will be great exposure for us. We will be meeting with other businesses, large and small, who all need accounting services of one kind or another. I want you to work it with me. I want all of those business owners to meet the backbone of my office, my superstar." Beth was flattered.

"Of course I'll work it with you," she replied, smiling. *Sounded fun.*

The trade-show lasted three days, Wednesday, Thursday and Friday. It proved to be the hardest work that she had ever done. Beth must have talked with a million people, at least it seemed so. She spoke of the services they offered, answered questions, took names, handed out brochures, and smiled until her cheeks ached. Friday night, the promoters of the trade show were having a get-together, serving cocktails and hors d'oeuvre, to celebrate a successful show. Jim invited Beth to join him.

Beth was seventeen, almost eighteen, and used to

men flirting with her. Her auburn hair had been cut to flatter her facial features and green eyes. Although she was not a traffic stopping beauty, she was an attractive young lady, smart, with abundant energy. Jim kept close to her while at the party. She had worn black satin slacks that day, black sandals with heels and a gold metallic tunic top that shimmered when she moved. It was a very elegant outfit. Her hair was worn up that evening, with curled tendrils framing her face and long dangling gold and diamond earrings. He let her have one drink, a screwdriver, although she was underage. He had at least two that Beth counted, maybe three. Beth was receiving her share of attention from the men at the party, and was enjoying herself immensely.

When it was time to leave, both Jim and Beth said their good-byes and headed for the elevator. Laughing and feeling exuberant, Jim pulled her into the elevator and as the doors closed, he took her in his arms and kissed her. *Oh my God, what did he do that for?* thought Beth.

"I have wanted to do that all night. You look beautiful, Beth," Jim whispered, as he kissed her again. She didn't pull away, but looked at him puzzled, not knowing what to say. The elevator door opened and they were in the underground parking lot. *I don't think he had that much to drink. What's going on with him?*

"Let me walk you to your car." He slipped his arm around her shoulder. "Where are you parked?" As they reached her car, he asked, "Are you okay to drive?"

"Yes, I'm fine. I only had one drink. Are you okay?" she inquired, genuinely concerned, thinking maybe he was drunk or something.

"Yeah, I'll be fine. You be careful going home. I'll see you Monday at work. Thank you for spending the evening with me, Beth."

Driving home that evening, Beth was flattered, confused, not to mention a little nervous about going to work on Monday. She was a little excited about the possibility of a relationship with Jim. *He is married though, what about his wife. What did this kiss mean? Did I like it? Am I attracted to him?* That night, Beth lay in her bed, with just a lingering of the blur-of-the-edges effect of the screwdriver that she had earlier that evening. Her perception was not the razor sharp edge that she was use to. She seemed to be having trouble categorizing all of her feelings and putting them in nice neat places, like she liked things to be. *Like in accounting,* she thought, *where everything had a logical place, and fit like pieces of a puzzle.* With these unsettled feelings, she drifted off to a dreamless sleep.

***

Monday at school was torture. She was stressing about how it would go at her job that afternoon. When she got to work, Jim was not at the office. She let herself in with her key, made a pot of coffee and started putting the files away. She was in the back filing when he came in. He poked his head in the filing room, then went straight to his desk to drop the load of files he was carrying. After he was settled in his chair, he called her into his office.

"I want to apologize for . . ." he started, but was interrupted.

"Look, don't apologize to me," Beth stammered and put her hands up as if to ward off something ugly, "Say anything else but that, okay?"

"Oh, I am not apologizing for kissing you, I'm not sorry about that at all. I'm sorry that you got home late. I hope I didn't cause you any problems with your parents. I shouldn't have let you have a drink either. I'm sure your parents would not have approved of that at all."

"Come in here a minute, there are a few things that I think you should know." Beth walked into his office and sat on the couch. He came around his desk and sat on the chair next to the couch beside her.

"My wife and I have split up. I should have told you, I know you have been concerned that I have not been myself lately. With as much time as we spend together, you seem to know my moods better than my wife ever did. It may have been wrong the other night to kiss you, but honestly, it seemed like the most natural thing to do. You are an incredible person, and I would like to spend more time with you." *That explained a lot of things. But, how do I feel about Jim? He is mature, nice looking and a successful businessman. His kisses were nice, not the fireworks that I had with Kyle, but certainly nice. My future would be secure. That's important. Billy is off in the Air Force, future unknown. Kyle is working at a drug store, no college plans yet, future very iffy. It would be worth exploring a future with Jim. I am learning the business and we would be beneficial partners for each other.* Beth snapped out of her own thoughts as Jim leaned down and kissed her. She kissed him back, this time with enthusiasm. It was nice.

Chapter Sixteen

"**B**illy's coming home to take me to the prom," Beth remarked one afternoon at work. Jim had taken her to a movie, and they spent one afternoon at the beach since the night that he first kissed her. They had been busy at work; he was asking her opinion more and more often. They discussed the prom and both had agreed that it would not have been appropriate for him to take her. Plus, Billy had been planning on taking her all along. She had not told Billy about her relationship with Jim. She had only been in touch with Kyle a few times and knew he was taking Dena to his prom.

"Hi Beth." It was Billy on the phone.

"Are you here?" Beth asked with excitement in her

voice.

"Yes, I sure am and I can't wait to see you. Can I come over? Mom said I could use the car."

"Yeah! I will be here. Can't wait to see you either!" And she genuinely meant it.

Billy drove up in his mom's station wagon, in what seemed like just a few minutes. He looked great, and Beth was really glad to see him. When she saw his car pull to the curb in front of her house, she burst out the door and ran down the walk to see him. He jumped out of the car and grabbed her into a tight hug. She really had missed him. His blue eyes sparkled as he looked at her. Kissing her and laughing in her hair, they walked arm and arm back into the house. Beth wanted to know everything about being in the Air Force.

"What's boot camp like? What did you eat? What time did you get up in the morning? Are you going to be able to learn to be a plumber? Do you still want to?"

"Hold on a sec," Billy laughed, "let me catch my breath!"

"I want to know everything."

"So I see." Billy was still laughing. "I will tell you everything you want to know, I promise. Right now, I just want to relax and spend some time with you. I've missed you so much, Beth."

***

"So, what time do you want me to pick you up for the prom?" Billy asked over the phone the next day. The prom was on Friday and this was already Wednesday night.

"Have you ordered flowers yet? And are you going to rent a tux?"

"I thought I'd wear my military dress uniform," replied Billy.

"Great, you will look so handsome. I can't wait to see it on you." Beth was starting to get excited. "I bought the tickets today, so that's taken care of. Are we going to dinner before the prom, and did you get your mom's car?"

"No on my mom's car, we are going to have to take your car. I would love to take you to dinner, Beth, but I only brought thirty dollars home with me and only have twenty of that left."

"You only brought thirty dollars?" Beth was starting to feel bitchy. *I hate feeling like this, but I bought the tickets, went out and bought a new dress and will probably have to buy my own flowers and dinner too.*

"You did order our flowers, though, right?"

"No." Beth was starting to feel anger boiling up. She was fighting it though, this was her senior prom, after all, and she wanted to have a good time.

"Okay, I will order flowers, and I do want to go to dinner, so I'll pay for dinner too."

"I am so sorry Beth, I didn't plan this very well, did I? We'll have a good time, I promise. I will have someone drop me at your house on Friday about six or so, okay? Don't be angry with me, I will make it up to you. Really."

Beth looked stunning in an all white formal dress. It was ankle length, with an empire style bodice, short puffy sleeves and lace trim. The skirt fell in three tiers, one layered upon the other, each tier gathered adding fullness to the skirt. Her hair was up with baby's breath woven into her curls. A blood-red rose corsage added the finishing touch. Billy had on his dark blue Military dress uniform with a red rose bud boutonniere. They were a handsome couple. Beth's dad had offered to let them use his car.

Dinner was at a medium-priced restaurant and was very nice. Billy told her more about the military and boot camp. Beth was trying to have a good time, but she knew that she would eventually have to tell him about Jim, and she was still upset that he came home with only thirty dollars in his pocket. *This is supposed to be such an important night,* she thought. *The highlight of high school and I am feeling distracted and don't even really want to go.* She wanted to have a good time, but the time that she and Billy had spent apart, although it had only been a couple of months, had distanced their relationship to a point that Beth felt that it was over. Billy didn't seem to realize it, and she knew that she was going to hurt him deeply and she regretted it.

"..... missed you so much Beth," as he took her hand, "and I know that we are right for each other." Beth had been zoning out, thinking about a million other things, including breaking up with Billy. She missed what he said, catching only the tail end of his sentence. He was looking at her with such love in those adoring blue eyes, she wanted to get up and run. *Oh God,* she thought, *he wants to spend his life with me and I want to break up with him, I am going to break his heart. He deserves better than this, but I can't let him go back to Texas without telling him about Jim. Not tonight though, not tonight. We need to have a good time tonight. I will tell him tomorrow.*

The evening turned out to be very forgettable after all. *The room is beautiful, everyone is dressed up in beautiful clothes and I wanted this to be so perfect. But, my heart just isn't in it. I'm angry with Billy for not taking this more seriously, and at myself because I'm here letting him think that everything is fine between us, when it isn't.*

"Let's get out of here," shouted Beth over the loud dance music. She and Billy had danced a few dances and said hi to a couple of friends. It was about 10:00 P.M. and she just wanted to be out of the loud room.

"Okay," replied Billy and he took her hand. In the car he asked, "Do you want to go to a motel or something?" *He still didn't get it.*

"No," Beth said, with surprise in her voice. "Let's just go for a drive, we need to talk."

They drove up Pacific Coast Hwy, a scenic coastal route, past Newport Beach. It was about a thirty-mile drive. Beth explained what had happened between her and Jim, and told him that she wanted to honest with him. He parked the car in a parking lot overlooking the beach, let out a long sigh and looked at her with hurt eyes.

"Are you sleeping with him?"

"No, not yet. But I see the relationship heading in that direction. Billy, I am being honest here."

"You don't love me? I came back here ready as ask you to be my wife, Beth. I am really serious about you. I can't believe what you are telling me."

"God Billy, I really care for you, so much. But, I

am not ready to make a commitment to you, or anybody. I am so sorry; I would not have hurt you on purpose for the world. I want to still write to you and hope you will still write to me, but I need to see what is right for me in my life. Please try to understand."

"We better start for home. We have a long drive back." It was a long and quiet drive back to first drop Billy at his house, and then Beth drove her father's car home.

The next evening Beth had a date with Jim. He was picking her up and taking her to a movie. Beth had not heard from Billy until he showed up at her door at about five thirty, asking to talk to her. She told him she had plans and would be leaving in a few minutes. He was devastated when she left him crying on her front porch. Apparently her parents felt sorry for him and invited him in after she left. He spent the evening watching TV with her parents and Susan in their living room, finally riding his bike back to his mom's house at about 10PM that night. Billy's plane back to Texas left Sunday afternoon, the next day, at 2:00 P.M. He did not call her before he left.

They exchanged a few letters after that. He started dating and it didn't take him long to hook up with the girl that he would eventually marry. He never did pay her back for all the collect phone calls, but Beth ended up with several of his Moody Blues record albums.

***

The summer after graduation flew by. Beth turned eighteen and was a legal woman. She started spending most of her weekends at Jim's apartment. His ex-wife got their house, so he rented a small apartment in the neighboring town of Seal Beach. Beth helped decorate and paint, and between that and work, her life was full. Jim was hard working, but fun, very responsible, yet loved spontaneous adventures. They worked hard during the week, and on weekends went camping or fishing, or took Jim's son Kevin, now just over a year old, to a park. She had not heard from Kyle or Ray in several months. Chris was seeing Susan, but he had not heard from either of them either.

In late October, on a rainy dreary cold night, Beth and her dad were out in the garage working on her car. A van drove up and parked along the street and Kyle stumbled out. He stood in the driveway as Beth walked out of the garage.

"Kyle, hi. Are you okay?" He didn't look okay. "What's the matter?"

"Beth, I need to talk to you," Kyle mumbled as he started back towards his van with Beth following behind him. She climbed into the passenger seat as Kyle slid in behind the wheel. Beth could smell that he had been drinking. His eyes were red and bloodshot. *Something is very wrong,* she thought with alarm. Warm feelings came flooding over when she realized that he had been crying.

"Kyle, what's the matter?" she whispered as she put her arms around him and drew him close to her. He held onto her like she was a lifeline.

"Oh Beth, I have screwed up so bad and I am so sorry." He was trying not to cry and slurring his words as a result of the alcohol. "Dena, it's Dena, she's pregnant." He pulled away from her embrace and held his head in his hands, not looking at her. "We haven't told anyone, not her parents or mine or any of our friends. She's due in a couple of weeks. We're putting the baby up for adoption; all of the paperwork is done. She wanted to abort, Beth, but I just couldn't." He started crying in earnest. Beth, also in tears, realized how much pain he was in. "I don't love her, Beth," he sobbed. Beth pulled his limp body to hers and held him while he cried.

I am still in love with him. The realization came to her with a start. Gradually, his trembling stopped and he took a deep breath and let out a long sigh.

"I'm sorry for falling apart like that," he murmured. "I just started driving and ended up at your house. I had to see you, to tell you." Then he whispered, "To tell you that I am not in love with her, somehow that was important to me." *He's still in love with me too. He's in such pain; after this is all over, I'll tell him that I love him too. I want to be with him, to spend my life with him. I can't add to his burden now. It has always been him. When I hear a love song, I realize that it is him that I think of. It has always been Kyle.*

"Let me make you some coffee. You can't drive like this." She touched his cheek and felt the wetness from his tears.

"Yeah, I think I need some. Thank you," he replied with a smile.

***

Four weeks later, Ray called her. Kyle and Dena had a healthy baby girl and named her Jessica. She was born on Saturday morning. Kyle and Dena were married by a Justice of the Peace on Monday afternoon.

Chapter Seventeen

Beth said a hasty goodbye to Ray, hung up the phone and sat there in stunned silence. She could not believe what she heard. She must have missed something. He told her that he didn't love Dena, and that the baby was going up for adoption. *What happened? Why didn't I tell him that I still love him? Would it have made a difference? Kyle, you married her? How can that be? What about us?*

***

Beth did not hear from Kyle. She thought of him often. She missed him, but filled the emptiness in her with her work and Jim. Kyle was her past, Jim her future. Although Beth was only eighteen, she was a very together eighteen. She met many of Jim's friends, who accepted her warmly. He bragged about her to his business associates, clients and potential clients. She loved her work and was falling in love with him. With Jim, there was a whole package to consider. The business she was good at, and a vital part of, Jim, of course, was part of this equation, and Kevin, Jim's son. Jim drove an almost new car and was an exciting, successful man. The difference was that with Jim, Beth was considering a whole package, the man, the life, the future. It was so different from Kyle. The Kyle that Beth fell in love with stood all alone, no packaging, with future unknown. She had fallen in love the Kyle the person. Just him, nothing else to sweeten the pie or cloud the issues. She had a crystal clear view of Kyle, and had loved him with all her heart. It was not the same with Jim. There was no clarity. Jim the man could not be separated, in her mind, from Jim the business owner or Jim the father. She would not really see all of this for many years, although it would become clear, in retrospect.

Caught up in Jim's lifestyle and his life, she plunged in, full speed ahead, with her whole heart. She worked full time, even though she was getting paid only part-time wages. She pushed for the growth of the business, throwing out idea for idea and her enthusiasm matched his. She mistook her feeling of satisfaction as being love, and thought herself fulfilled. Jim encouraged her, spent time with her, sought her advice and told her he loved her. He was not ready, however, for a commitment. Having just come out of a very painful marriage, he was not ready to jump into anything too serious and kept her just barely at arm's length. She was close enough to believe that he wanted her as his life mate, but he was never actually able to face up to the commitment to make it so. She was okay though, telling herself that all he needed was time.

Beth had closed a door on one part of her life, shutting it away somewhere safe, under lock and key, where she couldn't easily get to it. Another door had opened and there was a distinct separation between her old life and her new life. The pain was put away, along with the happiness that she had felt. It was as if a whole wardrobe of feelings were locked in one closet. The feelings, like clothing, might be a variety of bright colors, flowers and butterflies, along with drab plaids or solids. When one closet was locked up tight, the other closet door was opened, revealing bright colors, sky and sunsets, along with drab paisley patterns or stripes. Both are closets, but containing a different, yet similar wardrobe. Beth did not analyze, she just lived completely in Jim's world, a world he had created. She pushed and pulled to make a place for herself in his life, but it always seemed to be his life. In her old wardrobe with Kyle, their world was completely their world. She did not have to make a place for herself, it was just there. Neither was complete without the other, so she belonged. She felt she was struggling to fit into her new wardrobe.

What confusion would occur if her old life and her new life were to collide? About two years after Kyle and Dena married, that is exactly what happened.

***

"I had no idea that you and Kyle ever even talked after he and Dena got married," remarked Susan. "Did he just call you? Or, did you call him? I thought you were happy with Jim and was surprised that you two never married."   Susan was feeling depressed after a fight between her and Michael and had called Beth for moral support. He had repeatedly promised to make the trip to see her, but still had not made the time. Beth tried to be supportive and wanted her sister to find happiness more than anything, but she just didn't see it happening and felt that Susan was going to get very hurt.

"No, actually, it was a real weird thing. I was around twenty or so, standing in the back of Jim's pick-up truck bending over picking up something, heck I can't remember what I was doing, but I was bending over and I heard someone whistle . . . ."

***

Wearing tight white jeans and a dark blue sweater, she was standing in the back of Jim's pickup truck, bent over when she heard a loud whistle. Beth made it a point to never look when someone whistled, but she stood up realizing that having her backside facing traffic was not very lady-like. She was embarrassed to see a pickup passing by, with a guy hanging out of the passenger side window. He was the one who whistled. She watched as the truck drove to the next available turn lane and made a U turn. Coming back on the other side of the street, she saw the driver look at her and she felt her heart stop as she realized that it was Kyle. He made another U-turn and pulled up behind Jim's truck.

He got out of the driver's side and walked up to her. She was still standing there in a state of shock as he said, "I would know that butt anywhere." He smiled at her. She smiled back and walked to the tailgate and jumped to the sidewalk.

"Hi," was all she seemed able to manage.

"How are you?" he inquired, looking deep into her eyes, it felt to her like he was looking into her soul.

"Doing okay, how about you?" *He is like my Kyle, but is now married and a dad. This is going to be hard to get used to. She felt the familiar tug at her heart. Quick check, everything locked up tight? Yes. Okay.*

"Been okay too."

The guy that was hanging out the window when they went by the first time came bounding out of the car. "Hey Kyle, are you going to introduce me? You actually know this foxy chick?" He whistled again. Kyle gave him a dirty look. Beth giggled.

"Beth, this is Tony. Tony, meet Beth."

"The pleasure is all mine," said Tony, as he made a dramatic sweeping bow to Beth. "So how come you never told me about her before, been keeping her for yourself, huh?" Tony was looking at Kyle with a mischievous grin. "So, lets take her with us."

"Where are you going and what are you doing here anyway?" asked Beth.

"My aunt lives in Long Beach," replied Tony, "and I needed to drop some stuff at her house and Kyle offered to drive me. Now we are going to the local pool hall to play a few games and have a beer or two. Wanna join us?"

Beth looked at Kyle; his expression said it all. *He was hoping to see me and wants me to go hang out with them.*

"Well, I have to get this stuff out of the back of the pickup . . . and if I had some help it would go quickly . . . then . .well, I have no other pressing plans for the evening," Beth said with a sly smile.

"Works for me," said Tony, and he started lifting boxes out of the pickup.

***

The closest pool bar was down in Belmont shore, a couple of miles away. Beth sat in the middle of Kyle's blue Datsun pickup; it had a bench seat. She was aware of how close she was sitting to Kyle. She was finding it hard to breathe. Tony was singing to the radio and laughing. *He is one of the happiest people that I have ever met,* she thought with a smile. Kyle was quiet and just drove.

Tony was medium height, with dark brown hair that was long to his shoulders. He was a little overweight, which made him seem round, somehow. His clothes were big, which gave him the appearance of being a little sloppy. His brown eyes were bright and full of laughter and mischief, and, he needed a shave. Beth liked him instantly. Before long, he had her laughing at his jokes and she felt like she had known him for years. Kyle was quiet and reserved, and looked amused at Tony's antics to keep Beth's attention. They split a pitcher of dark beer and played pool, loud music playing in the background. Beth felt at home in Kyle's company, although he had changed some. There was this sadness about him that had not been there before. He was almost withdrawn. She figured it must be the stress of a lot of responsibilities thrown on him all at once. When Tony declared that he needed to make a pit stop, Beth had a few minutes alone with Kyle.

"Everything okay with you?" she asked him, an edge of concern in her voice.

"Yeah, it's going alright," he smiled at her, a knowing smile acknowledging her concern.

"Kyle, I have to ask, what happened? When you came over that night you told me that . . ."

"I know, Beth, but Jessie was born over the weekend and by Monday, we just couldn't give her up."

"Well, I honestly wish you all the best," was all she could say. He took her hand and gave it a gentle squeeze. His hand was warm. The contact felt comfortable, familiar. She saw the same thought register in his mind, it was written all over his face; a brief moment of confusion, then acknowledgment, then regret. All in a split second, yet, Beth saw it as if it was written in black marker. Her response was a smile and he knew she had seen his conflict. Nothing had to be said.

"You know, I'm working at a print shop in Fullerton, you should come by sometime and say hi. We could have a cup of coffee or something."

"Yes, I would like that."

***

Two days later, she was up early and drove to Fullerton, a neighboring town. Kyle had given her directions and the address. She had spent the night at Jim's and did not have to be in the office that morning until ten.

Kyle was working in the back; there was a door that led out to an alley. She asked for him at the front counter and he came out front and led her to the back of the building.

"Just in time for a coffee break," he said grinning at her. "I didn't know if you would come. I bring in a special ground coffee that I buy at a local gourmet coffee shop. It's really good. How do you take it?"

"A little cream or milk, if you have it, or powered stuff will work if you don't have the real thing." *I have to get my nerves under control.* She was trembling and hoped it didn't show. He took her hand and led her from the coffeepot to the back of the building where the door to the alley was open. "Is this a good time to come by?" she asked. "I don't want to get you in trouble with your work."

"I can take my break whenever I want. I run the press, so while it's printing, as long as nothing goes wrong, there is not too much for me to do for a while."

"How long have you worked here? Do you like it?"

"I've been here for over a year and, yeah, I do like it. It is a decent job, for now anyway."

The office was part of a large industrial complex. It

was fairly new, Beth guessed the complex had been built within the past ten years, or so. The back door opened into an alley that was facing the back of another building. Kyle and Beth sat in the doorway, hip to hip, drinking gourmet coffee and enjoying the comfort of each other's company. Beth started to finally relax. He explained all about the printing press and Beth listened with interest, both just enjoying the company of the other. *I don't care what we talk about, or if we don't talk at all. I am content to just be here with him. He seems to feel the same way.* Beth did not stay long, she still had to go to work herself.

She started coming by for coffee several mornings a week. Beth looked forward to her mornings with Kyle. It seemed so natural to be with him. They talked, they touched, and they flirted. She met all the staff at the print shop; they seem to accept her as Kyle's friend. Tony came by one morning while she was there and seemed genuinely glad to see her. He asked when they were all going to get together to play pool again. Beth said that she was up for it. The date set, she realized that she was looking forward to an evening with both Kyle and Tony.

During the six months, or so, that she had been seeing Kyle for coffee a couple of mornings a week, Beth had been getting use to the rhythm of life with Jim. Jim kept his own life intact, still doing things with his friends, going out dancing on his own, and making his plans without consulting and sometimes even including her. It was like his life was divided into separate sections. She started out being part of the work section of his life. Then, he included her in one of his personal sections, not all of them, but one. She was his date when he needed, or wanted one. She spent several nights a week at his apartment but was not invited to move in. He had a group of friends he went dancing with; she was not included. He had a group of buddies that he went hunting and played poker with, and she was not included. He wanted her there frequently, but still kept her confined to just parts of his life.

Jim included her in his activities with Kevin, which she loved. On the weekends that he had Kevin with him, they would take him to the park or to a movie, and sometimes she stayed with him while Jim went out with his friends. She adored Kevin and he loved being with her, so she did not have a problem staying with him.

For the first six months or so that she and Jim started seeing each other, they just were dating and working together. Beth, as always, jumped into the relationship with both feet. Because it was a new relationship, she was trying to be patient and let the relationship develop. After six months, she wanted to be a bigger part of his life. She had all but abandoned her life, and her friends, and wanted to be all things in Jim's life. It was a frustrating year for her because she felt she was ready for marriage and wanted to be in all parts of Jim's life.

After Beth started seeing Kyle for coffee in the mornings, she had something else to fill all the empty parts in her relationship with Jim. She had Kyle. Although, she had only a very small part of his life, it filled her. She looked forward to the time they spent together and thought of him often. They would sit on the step facing the alley, hip to hip and not even need to talk. Contentment. Simple contentment.

Beth knew Kyle, she knew the kind of passion he was capable of, and deep fire that she knew still burned in his soul. She could see it brimming in his eyes. He kept all of his feelings buried deep, though. The once open heart that could express all that it felt, and wrote deep passionate letters of love to her, was locked up tight. He softened a bit here and there, but she knew that if ever he let his feelings free, that it would be all over for him. He was like a volcano that rumbled deep within. If he did not maintain control, he would blow and his passion would flow out like hot lava destroying everything he was trying so hard to build. Kyle also knew that the fault within his mountain, his weakness, was Beth.

They decided to meet at his work and she would follow him to a local pool hall to meet Tony. She was looking forward to spending another fun evening with them both.

She wore Gloria Vanderbilt jeans that day, with a deep plum velvet jacket and a cream silk shell underneath. Black boots with inch high heels completed her ensemble. She had brought a yellow cotton tank top to change into when they went to play pool, thinking it would be cooler and more comfortable. The day held the promise of warmth in the high eighties or low nineties, and the evening was predicted to be warm and balmy. During the day, her office was air-conditioned, so she was comfortable dressing up her outfit with her velvet jacket.

That evening she met Kyle at his work, changed in

the bathroom and followed him to the pool place. They parked across the street, in a residential area, her car at the curb behind his. She was now driving a Datsun 240Z, a sporty two-seater coupe, silver blue with black interior, and he still had his pickup. They walked side by side, laughing and flirting a little, into the building. Tony was already there and had ordered a pitcher of beer and reserved a table; he was practicing while he waited.

Tony greeted Beth and Kyle with a smile, giving Beth a slightly lecherous look of approval, his eyes lingering a little too long on her breasts. Kyle frowned and immediately challenged him to a game of pool. Beer flowed, laughter rang out, Kyle and Beth flirted, touched hands a little too often, and brushed hips moving from one side of the table to the other. She felt heat, desire and the effects of the beer. Their eyes met a little too often and held. His dark brooding eyes burned into hers. Her eyes bright, inviting, wanting him as she had so many times before. *Is it the beer?* she wondered. *Can Kyle know what I am thinking? Can he know how much I want to touch him? I feel like he is telling me with his eyes that he wants me too, is this just my imagination? Is it just me? Are we communicating with each other? Can Tony see this too?* Tony seemed oblivious to everything except the game at hand. She relaxed and enjoyed the evening. Kyle seemed more relaxed than usual, and Tony was just having fun. They all laughed, bantered back and forth, and played countless games of pool. At around ten, Tony announced that he needed to get on the road. They had not ordered a pitcher of beer for the last hour or so and Tony was feeling good enough to drive. Beth gave him a hug goodbye, and she and Kyle were alone.

"I'm not so sure I'm ready to drive yet," remarked Beth, with a very slight slur to her words.

"Come on," said Kyle and took her hand, "Lets go for a walk."

He led her down the residential street, about a block, to a park. He held her hand as they walked, and both Kyle and Beth were silent. *I wish we could just keep walking forever,* was her thought. The night was dark and moonless. There were just the few stars that are visible in the city. When you looked into the night city sky, it looked almost muddy. As they left the street and started into the park, the streetlights faded and the large park was very dark. Looking across the park on the other side, Beth saw the kids play area with swings.

"Hey, wanna swing?" she giggled, "I'll race you." And still laughing, she broke into a run toward the play area. Kyle started after her, but she had a head start because she had taken him by surprise. He finally caught up with her about half way across the park. It was very dark. He tackled her mid stride, breaking her fall with his arms and held her. They were both panting from the run.

"No," he said, "I don't want to swing." He looked at her, eyes open to watch, and kissed her. Long, desperate kisses. He looked at her, memorizing her face. Her body felt alive, every cell was reverberating. Her body molded into his. His hands slid under her shirt, his touch was hot and left a burning trail as he worked his way up her belly to her breasts. He moaned as he found the soft full breasts and cupped them, hands closing over her. Her moans matched his as he kissed her again, deeper, tongue probing her lips gently, but insistently. He slid her shirt up over her head, unbuckled and removed her bra. She lay back in the cool grass, Kyle above her as he pulled his shirt over his head. Her arms circled around his neck pulling him to her, skin touching skin, taut nipples pressing against his flesh. She felt his heat, his need for her. Arching her back, she pressed herself into him. Their bodies fit together like two puzzle pieces. He unbuttoned her jeans and felt her dampness. Her body screamed for his touch. His jeans, too, were unbuttoned and before she realized it, both her clothes and Kyle's were lying beside them. Nestled in the soft cool grass, nude, in the middle of the park, at about eleven at night, they made love. Sizzling, reckless, fervent, passionate love. Completely unaware that the world existed around them, for that span of time, there was only each other. Their lovemaking was familiar, yet different. For a brief time, Kyle had opened his heart, needing her like she was his sustenance. Then, when it was over, she watched as he closed himself up tight, locking her out, sadness washing over him, and she knew that they had to go.

They walked arm in arm back to their cars. She leaned her head against his shoulder as they walked, glad for his warmth as the night had cooled some. They didn't talk, didn't need to. Both were deep in their own thoughts.

"Are you okay to drive?" he asked her as they approached her car. Feeling completely sober, she leaned up and gently kissed his lips. He touched her cheek and for a tiny second, an almost incomprehensible span of time, he opened his heart and tucked away the memory of the kiss and the feel of her skin, then closed it again. She looked into his eyes and saw it all. In the time between one heartbeat and the next, she saw the memories he cherished, the passion kept leashed, the knowledge of what he lost and what could never be. Most of all, however, she saw the love for her that he still carried deep inside his heart.

***

"Naked, romping in the park, huh?" was Susan's reply. "I had no idea. I have a park story in my past too, maybe someday I'll get up the nerve to tell you," she giggled.

"How can you not tell me?" replied Beth, incredulously. "I am baring my soul to you, telling you everything. How can you keep your park story to yourself?"

"Well, I'll think about it. It is pretty embarrassing, though, yeah, have to think about this one."

Chapter Eighteen

*T*hat was so many years ago, yet I can remember the feel of the cool grass like it was yesterday. I have so many memories that are vivid and intense. We both cheated to be together back then, you on your wife and me on my boyfriend. We laughed, we made love, we enjoyed each other, and we talked. You always kept your wall around you, though. Sometimes you would let me in a little, but, the boy, my God, we were so young, the boy who gave me his heart back so very many years ago, was gone. I longed for the innocent boy who used to tell me that he loved me. He was long gone. In his place stood a man with a shell of steel around his heart, layers and layers of protection. Some of those layers may have been to protect me too, although, my heart always was open and vulnerable and *was often battered and bruised. To your credit, however, you never led me on, or made promises that you had no intention of keeping. I needed to experience our times together to the fullest. I couldn't afford to hold back, I think you understood that in me. For me, the horrible pain that I knew would eventually come was somewhere in the future. I knew it was there, but, since it was not that day, I could experience as much as possible, because after you were gone, my memories were all that I would have left. They had to be the best they could.*

We maintained our separate lives, yet, remained involved in some way with each other for well over a year before you walked away. Best friends and lovers, but neither of us would have been able to keep our separate lives intact, and remain involved with each other for much longer. Your marriage was starting to crumble, I knew it, yet did not have the strength to walk away from you. Over that last month or so that we were still seeing each other, I watched you withdraw, become distant with me. It was nothing that I could put my finger on, but it was there, nonetheless. I was not surprised when you told me you could not see me anymore.

For some reason, the sun was shinning. It should have been dark and dreary. It was a bright spring day, but it should have been cold and gloomy. I remember the sadness in your eyes. I came by for coffee, as usual, on a Monday morning. We drank a cup in silence; there was obviously something on your mind. I should have guessed what it was. You walked me to my car. I know this had to be hard for you too, but your mind was made up, there was no discussion. You simply told me that I had to walk away, and stay away. Do you remember that I wanted a kiss goodbye? You couldn't even give me that. You had such resolve and determination on your face. You had to salvage your marriage to Dena, and you couldn't with me in your life. I had to go. You chose her, again.

Chapter Nineteen

"**Y**ou had to be so devastated," replied Susan.

"You have no idea."

"So, what did you do?"

"What could I do? I left. I cried, I mourned, I felt empty and I went back to my own life and tried to fill in all my empty places. The worst part was that I had no one to talk to, or to go to for comfort. Obviously, I couldn't turn to Jim so I kept everything inside. I threw myself into work and that's about the time I started dancing."

"Didn't Jim notice that there was something wrong?" asked Susan.

"Ha! No. Jim was so into himself and his life. Although I was living with him by that time, he never even noticed, at least he never said anything. No, I don't think he had any idea. He was a very superficial guy, not a lot of depth there. He had been going out dancing with his friends for months and months and never included me. Maybe he was seeing someone else too. I know he always had phone numbers of different girls in his pockets. I would find them all the time. He said they were all just friends, but I suspect a few were more than that."

"I remember when you use to go dancing, as I recall you got to be pretty good. Didn't you even win a dance contest once?"

"Second place, I still have the trophy, it's up on a shelf at the cabin." Beth smiled into the phone, she and Susan had been talking for quite a while that morning. "Tom. He was one of the dance instructors at the place that I had started going to take disco lessons. He picked me out the first time I went there, and I got a lot of special attention. He started taking me with him to different clubs after dance class, and we would dance. He was great, so good looking, danced like a dream, and so confident that he made me look good too."

Beth remembered what it felt like to dance with him. It was like a high. Neither of them drank, they went to the clubs just for the dancing. Loud music, pulsing disco beat, strobe lights on the dance floor, beautiful people in their fine clothes and perfumed bodies. Sometimes they had a fog machine, and so it was like dancing in a cloud. He danced with her, taught her, held her, looked at her, flirted with her, both on the dance floor and off.

"We would dance and hand out his business card, and on the back was a coupon for a free dance lesson. So, it was both fun and business for him."

"So, what happened with him?" asked Susan.

"Well, he took my mind off Kyle. I loved the dancing, there was so much energy, and the exercise was great. I was in great shape and having a great time."

"So . . ."

"So, what?" asked Beth.

"So, you know what," laughed Susan.

"Okay, so about six months after we met, he finally talked me into going to bed with him.

"And?"

"And what?"

"I want details! And what happened with him?"

"Well, he was nice."

"Nice?" asked Susan. "I'll bet he would not think that was a compliment!"

"Okay, well, he was not bad, but there was no, I don't know even what to call it, fireworks, maybe. He went through the motions and I went through the motions and it was physically good, but there was no bond between us. After, I felt empty, regretful even. I didn't know what was wrong because I never felt that emptiness, or regret with Kyle. It's hard to try to explain."

"You didn't love him."

"No, I didn't. Thought maybe I was falling in love with him for a while, but it never really felt right. Had a lot of fun though."

"So, what happened?"

"Well, we danced together for over a year, I had a great time and I even was his partner for a while when he was teaching a dance class at a club. That was really fun, it was on Wednesday nights and we would go early and dance, and tell people that there was a class at ten. Then, he would teach the class and I was the person that he demonstrated all his moves with. He was the actual teacher, but I was his partner. I loved it. Then one day he told me he was getting married. He had been seeing this professional dancer, she was great, I had met her a few times, and they were getting married. It was okay though, our relationship wasn't going anywhere anyway."

"Did you keep on dancing?"

"Oh yeah, I still loved the dancing part. The part that I didn't like was the meat market element at the clubs. I didn't like going by myself, and being just another girl looking to be picked up. I wanted to dance and improve my dancing skills, so I hooked up with this guy, his name was Mark, who also just wanted to dance. We used to go dancing once or twice a week. God, I have not thought of Mark in years. He was such a good guy, probably eight years older than me and just a good guy. We never had anything romantic going on, although I suspect that if I would have given him any green lights, he would have made a move on me, but he was a great friend."

"Didn't I meet him once? I think I remember him from somewhere."

"Maybe so, we were friends for a bunch of years."

"You lost touch?"

"Yes. Then, about ten years ago I ran into him walking down in the shore one day. Jacen was about five, I think. He looked the same and we hugged and I was so glad to see him. Ethan was with me and I introduced them, we exchanged phone numbers and addresses. Mark had gotten married and had four little girls, and was as happy as can be. About a month later, I got an invitation for all of us to go to his youngest daughter's birthday party and I really wanted to go. Ethan threw such a fit and refused to go, and told me that if Jacen and I went that he would leave me."

"You're kidding! Why?"

"He didn't want anything to do with anyone that I knew in my past."

"But, you were just friends," offered Susan.

"I know, but, it didn't matter. This has always been a problem between us; he won't let me have any friends. We never socialize with anyone. Anyway, I didn't go, and I never heard from Mark again."

"That is so sad."

"Yes it is," Beth said, "you have no idea."

***

Beth had been living on and off with Jim for almost six years. He was still not ready for a committed relationship, and would not even talk about marriage. He said he loved her and she was his main squeeze. They had friends, went skiing, worked hard together and made plans that included them both.

Jim had finally been able to purchase a house for himself, and Beth helped him remodel and decorate. He then purchased a couple of rental houses, and she pitched in and worked along side him painting, doing plumbing repairs, landscaping and laying linoleum. Beth never shied away from hard work, but it seemed all the work was for Jim's benefit, nothing was in her name. Although Jim treated her as a full partner for the work side, the profit side was all his. Beth decided she needed to buy a house of her own and move out.

"I think that's a good idea," remarked Jim, when she mentioned that she wanted to start looking at property to buy.

"Do you want to go with me to look?" asked Beth.

"Well, maybe sometime, but I can't today. I have an appointment this afternoon and this evening I'm playing poker with the guys."

"Okay, well, maybe I'll drive around and look for some open houses, you know, check out some of the neighborhoods and see what the prices are."

"That sounds like a good idea. See what you can afford."

He doesn't even seem to care if I move out. He is almost encouraging me, like it's a challenge. Was I expecting him to be alarmed that I was venturing out on my own, to ask me to stay, maybe even finally want to marry me? Maybe I hoped he cared enough to want me to stay. Well, fine. I will move out. I will show him that I can make it on my own, because I can. I know I can.

The following week Jim offered to spend a couple of hours looking at places with her. He drove to a new condo complex that he had seen that was just a couple of miles from his house.

"I saw these one day on the way to see a client," Jim remarked. "They are close, new and look nice. I thought you might like to check them out."

"I don't think I want a condo," Beth replied. "I think I would rather have a house."

"I know you would, but can you afford one? I don't think so. Besides, they will accept a VA loan."

The condos were nice, but small and were still condos. Beth felt they were over priced, and she wanted to look around and see if she could get into a house.

"A VA loan is not important to me because I'm not a veteran and don't have a VA loan available," said Beth

"Yes, but I do," replied Jim. "I thought I could help you get in by letting you use my VA loan. You could live there and make the payments, and we could own the property fifty-fifty."

Lets see, thought Beth with her logical accounting mind, *I pay all the money, get to live there, of course, and only own fifty percent of my home? Why am I not jumping at this great deal? Here Jim is being so generous and trying to help me, and all he is asking is fifty percent? Such a deal!* Her sarcasm was turning to anger, then resolve, to do this herself and all on her own.

It took her a month of looking, widening the circle of her search, to find a new tract home in the City of Pomona. Coincidentally, it was near where Kyle had purchased his home with Dena. Beth signed the purchase agreement and gave a five hundred-dollar deposit.

I love this little house. All brand new, I get to pick the carpet and tile for countertops. My very own place. I can't wait to move in. Now all I have to do is qualify for the loan, and save my money for the rest of the down

payment. She was going for an FHA loan, so her down payment would be very low.

Ninety days later, her house was finished; she got loan approval, and only needed to close escrow for the house to be hers.

"I got loan approval today, and my house is finished," remarked Beth to Jim at dinner that evening. "I should be moving in about two weeks."

"Really?" asked Jim, he sounded surprised, and not exactly pleased. "You really want to do this? Move, I mean."

"Well, yes, I have been talking about this for three months. You have not even gone with me to see the house, or anything. I thought you wanted me out."

"I never wanted you out. I love you. You know that."

"You sure seemed like you wanted me out, you even asked me how long it would take to get through escrow, like you couldn't wait to be rid of me."

"You misunderstood. Please reconsider. I really don't want you to move out." He looked stricken, like he never thought this would really happen.

He didn't think I would ever figure out how to do this. He never believed I would qualify for the loan. I don't believe this; he was pushing me, knowing that I would fail and come crawling back to him, asking if I could stay. Beth could feel the anger pulsing though her.

"Why do you wait until I have one foot out the door to tell me this? You have been pushing me ever since I first mentioned that I wanted a place of my own. Actually pushing me, and now you tell me not to leave? I have put all of my money in this, gone through three months of escrow, gathering documentation to document every move of my life for the lender to finally get this approved, and now you tell me you don't want me to go?" *My God, I think he is going to cry.*

"Please don't go. I feel like I am losing you, and I realize how much I love you and want to spend the rest of my life with you," he said, his voice starting to tremble with emotion.

Is it really me that he wants? Or is his problem that I might actually be walking away from him? During our whole relationship, he has always made it seem like I was the lucky one to have him. I was always the one pushing to be a bigger part of his life, and he was always keeping me at arm's length. Have the tables turned a little? Is that what this is all about?

"I am not breaking up with you. You can come and visit me, or I can stay with you. I just feel the need to start establishing a life of my own, instead of living within yours. You understand that, don't you?"

Beth had never seen Jim cry before, and it disturbed her. That night he sobbed and begged her to stay. She held him and reassured him and told him that she loved him. But, she was unconvinced that his motives were pure, and had every intention of following through with her plan.

Four days later, loan documents were signed and Beth paid the rest of her down payment. Three days and the house would be hers and she could start moving in.

Chapter Twenty

Beth instantly recognized Kyle's voice.

"So, I understand you're my new neighbor," he said. It had been almost three years since she walked out of his life.

"Kyle . . . hi," her voice caught as she tried to hide her surprise. She had been sitting at her desk going over some tax returns when her phone rang. "How are you?"

"Still alive and kicking, how about you? How are you doing?"

"Well, as I guess you know, I bought a house and moved out of Jim's. I really love it. Pomona has such a small town feel, and the fall is really pretty there. With the mountains so close and everything, I am really enjoying it. Are you still working at the printing place?"

"No, the business closed so I was unemployed for a couple of months, and right now I am working at a convenience store, the night shift. Dena is working during the day and I take care of Jessie, then at night, she takes care of her while I go to work. It's a lousy job, but it's keeping the wolf away for the time being. You'll have to come by and say 'hi' one of these nights. I get there at six and work till two."

"Okay, I'd like that."

***

The convenience store was more of a liquor store than anything else, situated in a small strip shopping center in the older section of Ontario. She stopped in one day on her way home from the office. Kyle had gained a little weight around the middle, and his face had filled out some. He had aged since she had seen him last. His eyes showed fatigue and stress, and there was a dullness about them that had never been there before. He smiled when she strolled into the store. He was busy with customers, and seemed to be the only employee there. She looked around the store while waiting for a break in the action so she could say a quick hello. It seemed to take forever before there was no one in line to buy something.

"Is it always busy like this?" she asked, amazed. "Are you the only one here?"

"This time of day it's usually like this. I'll be the only one here until I get off at two. The other guy left at seven."

"This is a lot of work for one person."

"I know, I go home exhausted. But it's a job, until I can find something better."

She started to ask how he was doing, when a customer came up to the counter with a bottle of cheap wine, a package of toilet paper and a quart of milk. Then another came in and Kyle was busy for over thirty minutes before they could continue their conversation.

"Sorry it's so busy, it usually slows down around ten or so. Maybe you could stop in one of these days a little later."

"Okay, I still can't get over how busy this little place is. I will be back, not tonight though. What nights do you work?"

"Wednesday through Sunday."

"Okay, I'll be back."

What a depressing place to work. Hard work too, and standing on your feet. I couldn't do it. But, what choice does he have? With a family to feed and no education past high school, he's not looking at a real promising future. His eyes looked tired and sad. My heart hurts for him. These are hard times for him. I am glad he called me. I can at least be his friend. He knows I will always be that.

Two nights later, at ten, Beth stopped by the store. His face lit up when he saw her walk in. There was only one customer in the store, and Kyle rung up his purchase as he gestured for her to take a seat on a stool that was at the end of the counter. She sat, and realized they were alone.

"You're right, lots less people this late at night."

"The occasional drunk, most everyone else needs either a bottle to last them the night, or milk or something on their way home from work or where ever they have been. We see a little of everything here."

"Don't you worry about being robbed?" That was the first thing that Beth thought about, and was very uneasy about Kyle being here all by himself in the store.

"Yeah, actually I do worry. It would be so easy to do," replied Kyle. "I would just give them the money and pray."

"I don't like this shift. Can you change to a different shift?"

"This works out well because I can be home with Jesse during the day while Dena works. This is only temporary until I can find something else. Dena has a friend who works at an advertising agency, and they are looking for someone for a sales position. He's going to try to get me an interview. I've never done sales before, but after this, it could only be a step up. I'd be willing to give it a try."

"Advertising is a good business to be in, plus has to be a lot safer than what you are doing here."

"So, how do you like your new house?" asked Kyle. "Are you all settled in?"

"Well, I have almost no furniture," laughed Beth. "I never realized how much stuff you have to have to furnish a house." Kyle smiled. "I bought a water bed, it's a pine four-poster with a real dark stain. I love it. I didn't even have any sheets. I had to buy a refrigerator. I have been doing my laundry at Jim's house, but that's getting old. I need to find a used washer and dryer somewhere. Jim had some old sheets that I have up over the windows. I have no living room furniture or dining room table yet, and the outside needs to be landscaped or something. Right now it is just weeds, and no fence. I'm getting tired just thinking about all the stuff I have to do," Beth grinned.

"I know, I was in the same boat when I first bought my house. We needed everything."

"I did get an electric garage door opener installed last weekend. Jim gave it to me as a house warming present."

"You installed it yourself?"

"Yeah, and what a hassle that was! I think I still have some adjusting to do, but it works pretty well. My dad gave me some tips on the phone. You'll have to stop by one of these days and see for yourself. Just remember that I just moved in and still have lots to do."

"I'll take you up on that," replied Kyle.

***

And he did. Soon he and Beth were in a routine where she would stop by the store occasionally at night. Kyle would sometimes stop by her house on his way home from work. She would make him coffee, or have a snack ready for him. There was no awkwardness between them. The second night he stopped by, as he stepped inside the front door, he took her in his arms and kissed her hello. It was such a natural gesture that it took a second for Beth to realize what had taken place.

"I've wanted to do that since the first time you stopped by the store," whispered Kyle.

"Me too," Beth whispered back, smiling. That night they made love for the first time in several years. It still felt right, and, like every time she saw him, she hated the emptiness he left behind.

***

They started playing racket ball together at a public court on the evenings that he was off from work. To be more accurate, Kyle would stand in the center of the court and hit the ball from corner to corner, sending Beth running all over trying to return the volley. Kyle had been playing for years, and Beth was just learning. She always lost, and always came away from the court soaked, while Kyle had barely broken a sweat and spent the hour laughing at her. It was an easy time between them. They did not speak of Dena, or his home life. They did not speak of Jim, or Beth's relationship with him. They were best friends who enjoyed each other's company. They were lovers. Their passion for each other was like a hot ember that they both knew would always burn at the core of their souls.

Although it took over six months, Kyle did get the job at the advertising agency. As a junior member of the sales team, he got all the accounts to work that the senior members had either not had any luck with, or they were such small accounts that there was no money in them. Kyle used them to develop his skills and learn the business. Beth had started venturing out on her own, vowing to own her own accounting agency one-day. She went back to school to earn her CPA Certification.

Kyle was busy with his new job and becoming less and less available. Beth too was busy. Between her job, school, and working on her house, she had little time to spend with Kyle. Jim was becoming demanding of her time, and with Christmas approaching, he was dropping hints about his Christmas present to her. He had almost completely stopped going out dancing with his friends. Beth suspected that he had been dumped by some girl and was turning back to her for comfort. He said she was going to be so surprised by his Christmas present.   It was something she had wanted for a long time. He asked her what her ring size was. He told her that nice things came in small packages. He said that he had given a lot of thought before deciding on this present, and had been shopping several times to find exactly what he was looking for, exactly what he thought she wanted. He had piqued her curiosity and it sounded to her like he was planning on giving her a ring and proposing marriage.

At Christmas, Jim gave her a new stereo system for her house. She laughed with relief as she opened the box with the turntable in it. *Did I just imagine all of those hints?* she thought with amusement. *Or, did he simply change his mind?* Beth was glad, however. She realized that she did not want to marry him.

***

In mid-February, Kyle called her to tell her that he

was going on a ski trip to Mammoth, and wondered if she could get away and join him. *A whole weekend with him.* She could feel excitement start to drum inside of her at the prospect.

"I'll see what I can do. Are you sure you can stand me for a whole weekend?" she teased.

"I'm not sure actually . . . but I'd have to just make the best of it, I guess," he bantered back "I have done it before, you know."

"Done what before?"

"Put up with you for a whole weekend."

"Yes, I guess you have, and you even lived to tell about it!" she remarked easily. "Let me see if I can get away, and I'll call you back."

***

She took a bus as part of a group ski trip that was advertised at a local travel agency. She arrived early on Saturday morning and met Kyle at the main lodge at a Mammoth ski resort. She had her ski gear with her, and the rest of her luggage was being stored on the bus that brought her, and would be taken to her motel at the end of the day.

"Hey, you made it!" Kyle called to her as he saw her walk into the lodge. He had been obviously waiting for her. He was wearing a black ski cap, dark brown bib ski pants, with a cream wool sweater underneath.

"Finally!" she exclaimed and walked over where he was sitting. "The bus trip seemed to take forever." She had been anxious about the trip, but seemed to relax as soon as she saw him.

"Are you ready for the slopes?" he asked.

"Ready!"

The day was perfect. There had been a recent storm, so the snow was powdery and plentiful. The sky was clear blue and the sun was shinning. The temperature was a chilly 38 degrees. Although Beth had been skiing longer than Kyle had, their skill level was very close. They skied well together. There was an easy companionship between them, and they skied until late afternoon. Beth needed to be at her bus by five.

"I'll wait for you in the lobby, Babe," Kyle called to her as she was getting on the bus.

"I'll see you in a few minutes," she called over her shoulder as she was turning the corner inside the bus to go find a seat.

Arriving at the hotel lobby about half an hour later, she found Kyle sitting at the bar drinking a beer. There was some sort of a game on the TV that was situated up on the wall behind the bar. The hotel was a nice, modestly priced place, modest for Mammoth at least. Kyle had won the trip as part of a promotion at work. The lobby was a combination lobby and bar. It was decorated in traditional ski lodge style, with a large fireplace surrounded by plush couches. There were small tables spaced for privacy along the walls. The walls were covered with thick dark rich walnut stained wood paneling. With lights turned down, the room had a cozy romantic feel about it. Kyle led her to one of the couches, and asked her what she wanted to drink.

"Hot chocolate, I think," she replied. He smiled at her.

"I could have guessed that. I'll take your stuff up to the room for you. Enjoy your chocolate. I'll be back in a few minutes." There was an intensity about him. She was anticipating the evening. *It has been a long time since we spent a night together.* He grabbed her ski gear and duffel bag and headed up the stairs.

When Kyle returned, she was just finishing her hot chocolate, licking the last of the whipped cream from the spoon.

"Mmmm, that was delicious," she remarked.

"I'm going to take a shower, join me?" he asked with a sly smile.

"Ah, a shower sounds heavenly," she replied, with a sigh. He took her hand, gently pulling her up from the couch where she sat, leading her up the spiral staircase to the second floor where their room was located. The third step creaked quietly as he stepped, and again when she stepped there while being lead by the hand.

The room was small, but cozy, with a queen-size four poster bed covered with a handmade quilt. The dominant color in the quilt was dark, rich hunter green. It felt so good to get her snow boots and thick socks off her feet. The plush rich brown carpet felt good on her toes.

He unbuttoned the bib of his pants, and pulled the sweater and undershirt over his head, folding the sweater and throwing the shirt on the floor. He then removed his ski pants, folding those once, then laying both the pants and the sweater on a cedar chest at the end of the bed. In his green striped boxer shorts, he turned to her and gently helped her unzip the back of her sweater, slipping it off her shoulders, revealing silk long underwear. Helping her pull it over her head, he folded her silk top and sweater and set it next to his. She slipped off the rest of her ski outfit, hanging the bottoms on a furnished hanger in the open closet.

As Kyle walked into the bathroom, he pulled his boxer shorts off, dropping them to the floor. He reached in and turned on the shower to a nice warm spray. She joined him, noting that soap and shampoo were already on the edge of the tub.

"How warm do you like it?" he asked her.

"Hot, hot, ooh that's perfect." She had stuck her hand under the spray anticipating how nice it would feel splashing over her body.

She stepped into the tub and he stepped in behind her, pulling the shower door closed. With the spray on her back she faced him, putting her arms around his neck.

"Hot, just like you," he whispered, and leaned down to kiss her.

After Beth washed his back, he soaped himself up and rinsed off.

"Turn around and I'll get your back," he said as he was rubbing the soap to a rich lather. She turned and he rubbed and caressed her back, her thighs and washed down her legs. He rinsed her off and turned her around, lathering up her neck, chest, paying particular attention to her breasts, down her belly and the front of her thighs and legs. *What a luxury,* she thought, *to be washed from head to toe.*

She loved his touch.

Drying off with a thick, soft white towel, she rubbed her hair to get out the excess water. As she watched Kyle dry off, she wrapped the towel around her body. They walked out of the bathroom clad only in their towels. He took her hand and led her to the bed, eyes locked with hers. Gently, he lay next to her, looking down, eyes meeting eyes and tenderly kissed her lips. Her response was immediate. Fire. Heat. Longing. *My pulse is jumping,* she thought. She ran her fingers through the soft dark downy curls across his tight muscled chest, circling his neck, pulling his mouth down to hers. Their kisses were no longer tender, she felt her body instinctively press against his. Kyle tantalized her mouth using his teeth, biting her lower lip, tongue exploring the softness of her, feeling the warmth, the heat. A sound clawed up from her throat, a primitive hunger for him.

"I need you to touch me," Beth moaned as her body quaked. She eased off her towel, spilling ample breasts, and pushing her nipples hard against his body. He looked at her, smiled, and slid his hand over her breast. With a feather like touch, Kyle caressed her breasts, kissed her slender neck, gently teased her nipples feeling them grow hard with his touch. The combination of the scent of soap and her desire aroused him, overwhelmed him. He longed to ravish her, but wanted to go slow with her, make her wait, make her ache for him, as he ached for her.

Tearing his mouth from hers, he feasted on a pert nipple, biting gently with his teeth, then sucking, making her nipple harder, more sensitive. He buried his face in her breasts, kissing, touching, and caressing. She moaned louder, stirring his blood, inviting him to explore further. The brush of his fingertips along her belly, feeling smooth warm skin, found the dampness of her. With fingers exploring the heat of her, kisses soft as shadows, rich, sumptuous; her need for him became unbearable.

With his voice smoky with lust, he whispered, "I need to explore all of you, Beth," and moved his kisses again to her breasts, down her belly, down to taste the sweetness of her. He needed to touch her this way, gliding his tongue over the velvety petals of her. She opened like the bud of an exotic flower as his lips and tongue caressed her. Her moans thickened as she floated on delicate layers of silky sensations. Her desire rose to an aching need for him. She whispered his name, over and over, as she felt herself being driven to a powerful release. With breath quickening, hot blood pulsing, body trembling, she let go. Riding the sensation, her moans became urgent as she shuddered, desire peaking sharply, like a whiplash. He feasted on her. She arched herself against him, her muscles pulsating against his lips. He tasted her hot wetness, as deep ragged moans urged him to savor the depth of her. As the pulsating subsided, he felt her melt against him. His gentle kisses teasing her, loving her. He buried his face in the heat of her, wanting to taste the essence of her forever on his lips. She became aware of a delicious feeling of warmth, and a sweet tingling sensation coursing through her body. His feather light kisses overwhelmed her with pure joy. He wanted to love her again, slowly, pleasuring every inch of her. He took his time with her, caressing her, kissing her with lips and tongue, feeling her deepest places with gentle fingers. He had never wanted anyone like he wanted her, wanted to possess her, have her by his side, love her with his whole heart. Her desire started building again. Her breathing grew ragged. He sensed, as well as felt, the heat of her. Her skin became fragrant and silky smooth as her fervor intensified. Passion seemed to flow from every pore, as she approached the satin edge of her lust. He urged her higher, until she tumbled over the edge, feeling a falling sensation with long stretches of ecstasy, one tumbling over the other until she felt his warm body embrace hers. She pulled him to her and kissed him deeply, tasting the sweet honey of herself still on his lips. Her breathing was fast and shallow, and her green eyes were dark with the power of her passion.

"You okay?" he whispered, as he smiled at her.

"Yes, oh yes," she murmured, as she nestled her face in his neck, loving the scent of him. He held her close to him, arms wrapped protectively around her. She loved the warmth of his skin, the hairs on his chest tickled her skin. She felt his hardness pressing against her, raw need for her reflecting in his eyes. As her breathing started to calm, she savored every part of his body, running her hands over his chest, and down his thighs. Her very touch inflamed him. He felt both fire and thirst, and wanted her to quench them both. She kissed his neck, gently pulling on chest hairs. With a giggle, she kissed the skin at the spot that was next to the hair that she was tugging at. She teased, kissed and nibbled her way down, tongue playing with his belly button, delighted with his body. He slipped off his towel, exposing himself, hard and ready for her. He murmured a low groan of pure desire. She wanted to touch the hardness of him, caress him with her lips. First, she teased him with gentle feather light touches, tracing the length of him with the tip of her finger. Then she ran her tongue from the base of his throbbing shaft to the tip, making little circles around the velvety smooth cap of skin, moving her tongue down in bigger circles, until she had taken all of him in her mouth. She felt him grow even harder, as she caressed him with her lips and tongue, fingers wrapped lovingly around the base. As his need for her grew, she fed the hunger she had unleashed in him. As his breath grew ragged, his groans intensified until he growled, with a purely primitive release, and collapsed against her, his breath catching in his throat. Although he knew he could never get enough of her, he lay next to her, his hunger fulfilled, for now. His hand found hers, and he pulled her into his arms. He drank in the scent of her hair, the wonder of her, marveling at his passion for her, and hers for him.

"Can we do this every day?" she asked. He laughed, deep, rich, true laughter. "I wish we could stay here forever," she whispered.

"I do too, Beth," was all he could say.

***

That was the most romantic, passionate weekend I have ever had. After making love, I lay in his arms, all warm and cozy, with my face nestled in his neck. We cuddled, kissed, talked and slept. He held me all night, and the morning came too soon. With the morning came a change in Kyle. A very subtle change, but I noticed. He was holding back a little, nothing I could put a finger on, but he was withdrawing just the same. I knew the signs; I had seen them before. His self-protection was kicking in. I had gotten too close, once again. We both had to return to our own lives, the paths that we had chosen, or had been chosen for us. Those parallel roads that ran so close together that each time one of our paths made a small deviation, our roads intersected, and we would run on the same path together until one of us were pushed back to our own road again. I knew he was thinking about going home. He was getting himself mentally ready to return to reality, his reality. I could sense how hard it was going to be for him, because, for me, it seemed impossible.

Chapter Twenty-One

They agreed to meet at a sports bar, at about two in the afternoon on Thursday. Beth arrived at about ten minutes after two, and Kyle was already there. It had been fifteen years since she had last seen him.

I can't believe how nervous I am. I am actually trembling. Will I look old to him? What will he think when he finds out that I have to wear one pair of glasses to read and another pair to drive! Will he look old? Beth wore a pair of white stretch jeans with navy strapped heeled sandals, a sleeveless navy top with lace at the bodice and a navy linen blazer. A sharp, yet casual, outfit. She did not wear any jewelry, except a silver anklet.

She walked in and saw him immediately, sitting at a table facing the door. He was drinking a beer, and watching a game on the big screen TV. He looked up when she walked in, she saw he was smiling.

His hair was almost white, but he had hair. She smiled to herself when she saw that he was wearing glasses. He had a gray and white goatee, and was dressed in a pair of faded jeans and a gray polo shirt. His skin was tan and he still had freckles, she noticed. *He still looks like Kyle. I would know him anywhere,* she thought.

He pulled out a chair for her, looking her over as he invited her to have a seat.

"Hi," offered Beth, smiling, hoping her nervousness didn't show. "Have you been here long?" She took the offered chair and put her purse on the floor next to her.

"No, I actually just got here myself," replied Kyle.

"Good timing!"

"Would you like something to drink, or are you hungry or anything?" he asked her.

"How about an iced tea," Beth replied. He called over a waitress and ordered one for her.

"You look good," he remarked. "Real good."

"Thank you Kyle. So do you. Did you come straight from work?"

"Yeah."

"Is that what you usually wear to work?" she asked.

"No, today I was helping one of the other guys move his stuff from one office to another. That's why I am wearing jeans. I usually have to do the shirt and tie bit."

"I pictured you in a suit. I'll bet you prefer jeans, though."

"You KNOW that!"

The sports bar had a comfortable feel about it. The bar was on one side with neon beer signs hung tastefully throughout. The walls were warm wood paneling, with large TV screens placed strategically to afford a view from any barstool or table in the room. The tables were large enough to accommodate several occupants eating a meal in comfort, were solid dark stained wood with large homelike wood chairs. At two o'clock in the afternoon, Beth and Kyle were the only patrons.

"When did you start working for this company? I tried to call you a few years ago at the company you used to work for, but the phone number was out of service," asked Beth.

"Well, they got bought out and closed our office location. I did NOT want to relocate to Illinois, so I was let go."

"That had to be awful."

"It was. I was one of a million or so, at least it seemed like a million, guys out looking for a job."

"Do you like this company?"

"Actually, their focus is a little different; they promote mostly home improvement products and don't have the diversity that my previous company had, but it's working out okay. How about you? You finally got your own gig I see. Is it working out for you?"

"Being a business owner is not what it's cracked up to be. Instead of always knowing I will be paid, I am now paid last. I've been working really hard and I think in the long run, it will pay off. Plus, I make a lousy employee. It seems that I like to be in charge." She smiled.

He did not say anything. He just looked at her. Although there was silence, it was not uncomfortable. She looked into his eyes and saw what she knew was there. He still cared for her too. They stayed that way for several minutes, just looking into each other's eyes. Both seemed to be searching for the answer to the same question. He touched her hand, she felt his hand close around hers. She caressed the top of his hand with her index finger.

"It's really good to see you." He spoke in a hushed voice, full of emotion.

"I have missed you, Kyle." Their fingers interlaced with each other. Both content holding hands, he gave her hand a gentle squeeze, acknowledging her divulgence.

"How are your kids doing? I guess Jesse is all grown up by now," Beth inquired.

"She is. Out on her own, she's doing okay. Got a job and an apartment that she shares with a girlfriend. She's almost twenty-five now. I can't hardly believe it." He reached for his wallet opening it to the picture section. *Proud Daddy,* thought Beth. He flipped through the couple that he carried with him. The first one was a family photo featuring him in a suit, Dena, Jesse and his baby, Alexis. The photo was a few years old, Beth could tell because his hair had a lot more color. The second one was glamour shot with mother and daughter. Both Dena and Jesse looked beautiful.

"This is a very flattering picture," remarked Kyle. "Very flattering. This one too," as he flipped to the glamour shot of just Jesse. The next three were of Alex, one at age four, then about age nine, then a current one at age twelve. She was clearly his pride and joy. He lingered on each photo as he showed them to her.

"She is a swimmer, on a swim team. During the season, we have swim meets almost every weekend. She and I are very close." The pride in his voice was palpable.

"She's beautiful. I can tell how proud you are of her." He lingered a moment on her picture, closed his wallet and put it back in his pocket.

"How about you, Jacen must be thirteen."

"Fourteen," Beth interjected. "And doing really well. He's my constant companion. We are really close. I am a blessed mother. He is a really good kid. I guess we're both pretty lucky in the kid department."

"Yes, I guess you are right about that."

"How about Dena? You guys seem to have things worked out. You've have been married now, for what, twenty-five years or so?"

"We have completely separate lives. She's gone most of the time it seems. Her work requires her to travel. I think she prefers it that way. We don't talk, it's not a happy marriage."

"Why do you stay?"

"Oh, I have thought of divorce, but I have Alex to think about. On the other hand, I know she sees the unhappiness between her mom and me and I don't know which is worse; the example that we set by staying together, or the trauma she would experience if we split up." He took a long swallow of his beer, draining the glass. He called over the waitress. "How 'bout a Beck's dark this time."

"Another tall one?"

"Yes, make it a tall one," ordered Kyle. Turning back to Beth he remarked, "Sometimes I feel so bad when I see her pouring cereal for her dinner."

"Well, who cooks?"

"You are looking at the microwave king," Kyle replied, with a sarcastic smile. Her heart ached for him. "How about you? I gather things aren't great for you either or we probably wouldn't be sitting here."

"I suppose you're right about that. Well, things are not great. I work very hard and he doesn't. It seems like we fight all the time. I am unhappy a lot. He can be very controlling. I guess the marriage has not turned out the way I had always thought marriage should be. We can't seem to talk things out without the discussion becoming a finger pointing session, with hurt feelings on both sides. I really don't know what to do about it. I have the same issues with Jacen that you have with Alex. I hate the picture that we present to our kids, and this is such a critical time in their lives that I don't want to cause turmoil. Plus, I don't know, I guess I keep thinking that we will work everything out. But, in reality, he makes lots of promises to me, and does not keep any of them."

Beth realized that they were still holding hands when he gave her hand a gentle squeeze of understanding. The silence between them was not uncomfortable. He searched her face, as if he was memorizing every line, freckle, and expression. Smiling, she took her free hand and gently touched his cheek, trailing her fingers over his skin. He leaned toward her touch, eyes closing briefly, as if to savor the caress.

"Do you ever think of me?" asked Beth.

"Yes, Babe, I do," he whispered.

"There is something there between us, isn't there? It isn't just me, is it?"

"No, it's not just you. You are like this candle that stays lit deep inside me. It never goes out. And, believe me, I have tried to blow it out, throw water on it, break it in two, lock it up and forget about it, I have tried everything. It just stays lit. Always there, always lit." He brought her hand up to his lips and gently kissed the back of her hand. "Always lit."

"Me too. It's exactly that way for me too," Beth replied with wonder shadowing her voice. "Except, maybe I have not really tried to make it go away. I have used that flame as a source of strength numerous times in my life. I thought you felt the same, but never really knew for sure. I guess for me, my feelings for you and the feelings that I thought you had for me have always been like an anchor. Something that nobody can ever take away from me. It's one of the things that I feel make me special. God gave me this love so real and so pure, that it has lasted through time and distance, and has not faded or gone away. It has to be a gift."

"But the paths we have chosen make it impossible for us to be together."

"Not impossible. You know, some day in the not so distant future, our children will be out of the house, with lives of their own. Then what do we do? Don't you want someone to spend those years with, someone to grow old with, to do things with?"

"Yes, of course I do. But Beth, you would get bored with me. I am a boring guy. I know you. In your emails you talk about this adventure or that adventure. I am an old boring guy."

"I would not get bored with you," replied Beth, with a giggle. "Heck, you have kept me interested for thirty years, what makes you think I would get bored with you?"

"Yes, but we have not lived together day in and day out. I'm just a boring guy, believe me you would get bored and leave me and . ." his voice grew husky and in an intense whisper he continued, "I don't think I could take that." His expression was serious and somber. Beth realized that he sincerely believed what he had said. She wondered if there was any truth behind his feelings. She had never considered him boring, but she had not part of his life for a long, long time.

Beth took a sip of her iced tea, breaking the intensity of the moment. She smiled at him and brought his hand up to her cheek.

"I have missed you in my life," she said, looking directly at him.

"I do want a little kiss good-bye today," was his reply, as he started to get up. "I'll be right back."

"A big kiss good-bye," Beth smiled as she answered him. She watched him walk to the restroom, already missing his hand holding hers.

What am I getting myself into, dragging up all of these feelings, she thought. It felt to her like the raw emotions that result when things happen that are completely unexpected, and feelings materialize seemingly from nowhere. It's almost a panic while the struggle takes place to examine the feelings, and decide how to deal with them. The intensity during the process can be overwhelming, sometimes unbearable. Eventually, it all gets sorted out and the feelings are categorized, some are shut away, most likely the really painful ones, some are kept on the surface to re-live over and over, like the first time with a special lover. Some, like fear, are rationalized and re-categorized to some other emotion, but it all is a process. She found herself thinking, with anticipation, about kissing Kyle goodbye. She mentally pulled up her memories of his kisses and could almost anticipate what it would feel like. She wondered if she would experience the same deep tumbling head over heels, butterflies-in-her-stomach feeling that she felt on their first kiss. *I won't have long to wait,* she thought, amused.

Kyle returned after about five minutes. After he used the restroom, he had called his daughter Alex, to arrange to pick her up from her friend's house.

"I am going to have to go in a few minutes. I have to pick up Alex." He took a swallow of his beer, drinking it down to the last third of the glass. "Have I told you how good you look?" he smiled knowing he had, and folded her arm to link with his, laying his palm against hers, and caressed her fingers.

"Yes, you told me," Beth responded with a sideways smile. She closed her hand, making it as small as she could, and pressed it into his palm. He covered her closed hand in a protective, almost intimate gesture, eyes never leaving hers.

They stood, stepped away from the table, and walked together to the door. As they stepped outside, he slipped his arm around her shoulder, walking close to her. The feeling was so familiar, she felt that he had walked with her like that for the last seventeen years.

"Is that your Nissan?" she asked. She had parked next to the only Nissan in the parking lot, guessing that is was his.

"Yes, and how do you know what kind of car I have?" he asked with mock suspicion.

"You told me, silly, don't you remember?"

"No, I never told you."

"Yes you did, I asked you in an email."

"Well, how did you know that this Nissan was mine?"

"It was a no-brainer, like the only Nissan in the parking lot . . ." Beth laughed at him.

"Oh, well I guess that explains it then, doesn't it."

He walked over and unlocked his car. Putting the keys in the ignition, he started the car and turned on the air conditioning, closing the door behind him. He leaned against the fender of his car and took her hand, pulling her close to him. "I am claiming the kiss you promised me," Kyle declared.

His hands cupped her face and he gently leaned down and tenderly kissed her lips. As their lips touched, Beth felt a tidal wave of emotion hit her. She put her arms around his neck. He broke the kiss; eyes open looking at her. She realized that the same tidal wave had hit Kyle too, his expression was that of raw emotion. She leaned into him, pulling his lips back to hers. His response was like fire. He kissed her deep and long. The tumbling feeling started, she went with it, letting it carry her head long tumbling over and over, to touch the very depth of her soul. She felt heat, dizziness and that delicious butterfly feeling in the center of her. She felt breathless and amazed when their lips parted.

"My God, I could sure get used to this," he whispered to her, forehead touching forehead. He hugged her close to him, like he was making an impression to savor in his memory. A long sigh, then, "Drive carefully, Babe."

He turned her and walked her to her car, making sure she was in and the car was running before he turned to walk back to his car. He slipped into the front seat and with a quick glance back Kyle drove away.

Chapter Twenty-Two

Beth drove to pick up Jacen. She was on an emotional rollercoaster. The joy of Kyle and the heartache of Kyle. She wondered what would happen now. She longed to spend time with him, yet had her own life, and family, where she belonged. *Is that where I really belong?* she mused to herself. She replayed her conversation with Kyle over and over in her thoughts. What if she tried a relationship with him and it went bad, as Kyle predicted it would. She would then lose the reason she felt she was so special. Her special gift, the gift of true love, that she had relied on for strength so many times, what if she no longer had that? Where would her strength come from then? She knew that much of her intensity and sensitivity stemmed from her deep-seated belief that her love for Kyle was a

God-given gift, and that it would always be there. It was part of her, part of what has shaped her life, part of why she is who she is. What if it all was no longer there? Beth felt a stabbing jolt of panic as she tried to imagine how she would feel if there was just a large void in her, instead of a place brimming with love. How would she fill the void? Could she ever fill it? Or, would she forever feel the loss and the emptiness? On the other hand, what if Kyle was really the key to her happiness, no, their happiness? What if they were really meant to be together, and they both needed to take the paths they took to realize just how special the gift they have been given really is. Beth examined each of their lives and, for the first time, noticed the parallels between them. Their kids are almost the same ages, meaning that as far as their kids are concerned, their lives are in about the same place. Both kids will be growing up at about the same time. Both she and Kyle were established in their careers, and doing modestly well. Beth guessed they had similar spending patterns, both knew the money was there for the essentials; extras had to be budgeted for. Each had stuck with a marriage, trying to make things work, yet, serious problems still existed. *What if Kyle and I are destined to be together, but neither of us willing to step out of our own comfort level to make a change?* What if they wasted the precious gift of love that was so generously bestowed upon them? What if happiness for each of them was there all along, and all they had to do was just step up and take it, but neither was willing to take that first painful step?

Beth contemplated. There was one other essential

piece of information missing that was needed for her to analyze this equation in her life. How does Kyle feel? She doubted that he really knew. She pondered over recent emails and conversations they had, trying to get an idea of his perspective. He did say that she was his weakness. He admitted to trying to make his feelings for her go away, and he honestly felt that if they tried a relationship, that she would leave him and he didn't think he could bear the hurt he would feel if she did. *So, maybe I don't have a choice anyway.* Even if she was willing to leave her husband, and she was not convinced that's what she wanted, he might not be willing to leave his wife.

Time was both her friend and her enemy. The old saying "time will tell" was never more true. Yet, was every day that passed waiting for time to tell, a day that she and Kyle would never be able to recapture?

***

Jacen was waiting at the office for her, deeply involved in a Star War's role-play. The battle was on and he was winning when she walked in the door. The familiarity of the office, and the beaming smile that Jacen gave her when she walked in, was like a gentle balm that her soul was desperately in need of.

"Time to call it a day, Jacen," she commented. "Start winding up the battle, are you hungry?" Beth realized that she was starving and decided they should go out for dinner, as she didn't feel like cooking. Ethan was gone for a few days, so it was just her and Jacen.

"Yeah, I'm starving," responded Jacen as his fingers flew across the keyboard. His attention was fully on the battle at hand. "In a minute though, I'm winning," he smiled up at her with a quick glance, before resuming the all-important battle that was being fought in cyberspace. She smiled at his intensity and started the shut down process of the office. Most of it was already done, but she did want to wash out the coffee cups before she headed out the door. There were three of them in the sink.

~

EMAIL
TO: klm@qmail.com
FROM: beth0711@qmail.com
RE: Kisses

Hey,

How wonderful it was to see you. See, we kept our clothes on and everything. I knew, with a little bit of effort that we could do it. I have to tell you that my resolve almost went out the window when you kissed me good-bye. My knees went weak and I felt butterflies. You have always been able to do that to me, like no one else. It makes me long for more. I miss you too much already.

Please write to me soon. L b

~

Beth had to wait two days for a reply. She thought she would go nuts waiting to hear from him. The wait was worth it.

~

EMAIL
TO: beth0711@qmail.com
FROM: klm@qmail.com
RE: Kisses

Hi Babe,
**   Just got a minute. I felt the butterflies too. I have not felt like that in a long time. You always were the best kisser. That has not changed at all. Makes me want more too. We will have to think on that.**

~

***

Ethan was to be gone for a week on business, a rarity, but it gave Beth a chance to reflect a little on her life. Jacen had a birthday party to attend on Sunday afternoon, so Beth elected to stay in town for the weekend and not go out to her cabin in the mountains. On this Saturday morning, she woke up and looked around her home. She saw a home that reflected unhappiness. Neglect and disinterest surrounded her. She got up and started walking the house. The bathroom was badly in need of a good cleaning. There was mildew along the walls above the tile in the shower. A dirty towel was lying on the floor. Various bottles of shampoo, facial cleaners, and tile cleaner littered the counter tops, along with a tube of toothpaste and a toothbrush of unknown disposition. The toilet bowl was stained, and the mirror spotted with water spots and toothpaste spray, from numerous brushings over a long period of time. She picked up a bottle of conditioner, realizing it was empty, she tossed it in the trashcan that was almost full.

Walking out of the bathroom and back into her bedroom, she looked around at books and papers piled on top of the dresser. There were dirty clothes scattered around the room, and shoes out and also scattered. The covers on the bed were all askew and the sheets needed to be changed. Although she had just gotten out of the bed, it looked obvious to her that the bed was not made on a regular basis. A lightweight blanket was pushed into a pile at the end of the bed, partially touching the floor. There was a thick layer of dust on the furniture and visible dog hair on the well-worn light gray carpet that was stained, and in need of a good vacuuming.

With disgust, she started down the hall. She noted a dog chewy, a piece of rope, one of Jacen's shirts, a pencil, a rag, and several pennies lay in the short hallway between her bedroom and the kitchen and living room. Most of the dishes were done in the kitchen, just a couple sitting in the sink. There was mildew in all of the corners; the tile was dull and dirty. The kitchen sink needed a good scrubbing. The outside of the refrigerator and stove had food stains and drips that had accumulated over a period of time. Floors needed mopping and waxing, and the inside of the microwave was gross. Looking over the condition of her home, she realized that she was looking at a reflection of her life. It was not that she was naturally a bad housekeeper. The cabin in the mountains was kept clean, beds made, stuff picked up, cupboards well stocked, and floors mopped and waxed. It was a happy home and its condition reflected her contentment and happiness. She took pride in her little cabin, which represented so much to her, but her home was just the opposite.

As a working mother, she did not have time to keep a perfect home. She worked long hours during the week, and spent almost every weekend out at the cabin. She thought she could rationalize the condition of her home as a result of her long working hours. But she knew the truth. She had simply given up. She simply existed in her home, same as in her marriage. She mused that maybe she was trying to see how long the neglect would go on, before Ethan stepped up to do something about it. She was not sure that he even noticed the condition of their home. *I hate the way I live,* she realized.

By day's end, the house had been scrubbed from top to bottom. Bathroom and kitchen counters gleamed and chrome fixtures shone. The carpet had been vacuumed several times to get up all the dog hair. Furniture had been vacuumed, sheets changed, blankets washed and beds made. She even went out and purchased new pillows because the ones that were on the beds were so stained and ugly that couldn't stand to put clean pillowcases on them. Her home once again looked like a home. She vowed to keep her home looking this way, and would tell Ethan that from now on, he was to do his part. She never wanted to look around and see that she was living in such neglected conditions again. *I wonder what kind of a housekeeper Dena is. What does Kyle's home look like? Does it mirror the neglect that showed in my home? Or, has she managed to keep up the facade of a happy home?*

That night over a simple dinner of lamb chops, steamed broccoli, rice and sliced tomatoes, Beth told Jacen that she wanted to keep their home looking nice, and needed his help by keeping his things picked up and his room clean.

"The house looks really good, Mom," was Jacen's comment.

"I want to keep it looking like this, okay?"

They watched a movie, and by nine-thirty that night, Beth realized how exhausted she was. In bed that night, Beth's thoughts drifted to Kyle and Ethan. Looking for their similarities and differences. Both existed. At that moment, she found that she was not missing Ethan and wondered why. *Is it because Kyle is foremost in my mind? Or has the spark that I felt for Ethan actually died?* One thing she knew for sure, she would no longer live with such acute unhappiness. With all of her resolve, and the strength she knew she could draw from deep inside of her, she made several decisions as she lay there with exhaustion washing over her. First, that she would find happiness within herself, and never find herself living in conditions that reinforced unhappiness. She would keep the things around her clean and comfortable, to nurture a feeling of contentment. She needed to re-establish ties with friends that she had sorely neglected. Her friendships were a source of strength and laughter; both much needed elements in her life. Her second promise to herself was that she would no longer tolerate Ethan shirking his financial responsibilities. She was tired of the financial stress, and simply wouldn't take it any more.   No more empty promises. She wanted results.

Feeling content with her decision to take control back in her life, she wondered about the big question; what will she decide about her relationship with Kyle?   To exhausted to even think any more, her last thought was that *time would have to take care of the rest*, as she fell into a deep, dreamless sleep.

Chapter Twenty-Three

"**B**eth, the house looks great," Ethan commented when he got home on Sunday evening.

"Yes, it does. I spent all day Saturday cleaning and scrubbing. The house needs to stay looking like this. I can't live like a pig anymore."

"It wasn't that bad, Beth."

"Yes, it really was. It was awful, and it takes just a little bit of effort on everyone's part to make sure it never looks like that again."

Beth was in the kitchen making dinner when Ethan got home that evening. Her dinner menu included portabello mushroom ravioli pasta, a green salad with avocado and tomato, pesto sauce, warm crusty sourdough bread with dark rich vinegar and olive oil to dip it in, served with a glass of red Syrah wine. The table was set with bright yellow place mats, Blue Willow patterned dishes and a small vase of fresh flowers. The antique oak table had been dusted and oiled, and shone in the waning evening light. The room was warm and inviting.

After the grueling day yesterday, cleaning and scrubbing, today Beth spent the day going through cupboards, throwing away old packages of food, making lists of what was needed to restock the pantry, and grocery shopping. She made the purchases that she needed to replenish the larder. There was fresh fruit in the fruit bowl, and a full selection of Oreo's, Mothers Taffy Creams, and Fudge Cream cookies in the cookie jar. The breadbox had been cleaned out and restocked with a selection of breads. The butter dish was clean and held a new cube of butter. There was a selection of fruit juices in the cupboard, and ice cream in the freezer. Canned soup, a variety of cereal, several kinds of salsa, tortilla chips, condiments, crackers, canned fruit and several items that looked good from the isles of Trader Joe's specialty market were crammed into the small pantry. The refrigerator had fresh milk, eggs, cottage cheese, Brie cheese, and a selection of lunchmeats. Beth bought pasta, meats for dinner, and a variety of fresh vegetables and makings for healthy green salads. The potato bin had been cleaned out, and now held a five-pound bag of russets and a small net bag of red potatoes.

After dinner that evening, Jacen went into the living room to watch TV, and Beth and Ethan had a chance to talk.

"The house is clean," started Beth, "the pantry is

stocked, the laundry is done. It is really important to me that we keep our home clean and neat. We should be able to invite someone in at any time, and not be ashamed about how we live. I have had a couple of days to do some thinking and have realized several things. The first one is that I did not miss you while you were gone. Yes, I kept very busy, but, mostly because it seemed like I had so much less work to do."

"The really sad part is that I really missed you a lot," responded Ethan. "When I talked to you on the phone, it seemed like there was something going on. I had a feeling that you didn't miss me, so that's not a real surprise. I thought maybe you were going to give me my walking papers when I got back."

"I think that if we cannot get our act together with each other, I might not be willing to stay with you anymore. I don't want to live in a home that I cannot be proud of, and we still have the financial part, that for me is a real problem."

"Here we go again, it's all about money with you, isn't it?" replied Ethan sarcastically. "If I made a bunch of money, you wouldn't care what I did, would you? I should go out and rob a bank or something so I could just give you a bunch of money. I would be the greatest guy in the world then, wouldn't I?"

"It is not just the lack of money, Ethan, and you know that," Beth shot back sharply. "I am not asking for a big house, heck, I am not even asking you to provide anything for me. But, damn, you need to at least pay your own way. It is not fair to me that the burden of our financial situation is on my shoulders. What hurts me the most is that I feel that Jacen and I are just not important enough to you to make the effort it takes to provide some income for this family."

"I go to work and I try, but it is just never enough for you."

"You go to work, but you don't produce. Since you are on commission, it is not enough that you just show up at work. You have to produce in order to get paid. You have to make sales. If this job isn't working, then maybe you have to get another gig somewhere. I don't know what you need, only that you need to figure out what it takes for you to become productive."

"You definitely don't know what I need," Ethan responded in a tone meant to hurt.

"Okay, maybe I don't know what you need. So, tell me."

"You are always pushing me to change and nagging at me. You are not such an easy person to live with yourself, you know. There are a lot of things about you I would like to change, but I don't nag at you. I don't even tell you. I have accepted you just as you are. I'll bet you know even know what those things are."

"You're right, I have no idea. What changes do you want me to make? If you don't tell me, how can I fix them? I don't think I am that hard to live with, I really don't." Ethan laughed a short ugly mean-sounding laugh.

"I am not going to tell you what to change. If you can't figure it out . . ."

"What, am I supposed to be a mind reader?" Beth

asked sarcastically.

"No, but you should be tuned in enough to at least know what my needs are."

"Well, I guess I'm not. So, it seems like maybe you need to let me know."

"I am not going to tell you. If you can't figure it out, it must not be that important to you."

"That is so unfair, Ethan."

"So, now I am unfair too. Add that to my list of faults, my long list of faults. It must be nice to be perfect, Beth."

"Look, this is not getting us anywhere. I need to be able to tell you what I need to find happiness in this relationship. You should be able to tell me, too. We both need to be able to choose if want to make the changes necessary to make this relationship work. If not, maybe we need to go our separate ways. I am trying to tell you that I need to live in a home that I am proud of, and I need a mate that cares enough about his family to make it a priority to provide for them. You also need to know that I am serious this time. By having you gone for a week, I have realized that I could live without you if I had to. I am not saying that I want to, but there have to be some changes made in order for me to stay."

"Okay, so I will give up all of my other activities and devote myself one hundred percent to just working, so I can have money to give you," Ethan retorted.

"It is not me that you need to give your money too, it is the cell phone company for the phone that you use, the insurance company for your health insurance and car insurance, it is the mortgage company for the house that you live in, the electric. . .”

"Okay, okay, I get it," Ethan cut her off. "Just make me a list of my expenses so I know what I need to make to be able to stay living here." Ethan's voice was thick with irony.

"I hate when you put it in those terms," Beth replied. "You make me out to be this money-hungry bitch. I'm not. I don't ask you to provide anything for me. I have paid my way for long time, as I matter of fact, I have always paid my way. I am just not willing to pay your way anymore."

"Fine, but you realize that I won't be able to go to the mountains every weekend with you anymore."

"Is this to punish me? Take away the one thing that I get so much happiness from?" asked Beth.

"Not punishment, just reality. If I am working all the time, I won't have time anymore to do these kinds of things."

"Okay, fine, Jacen and I can go ourselves. I have certainly driven there many times alone." *I will not be bullied,* thought Beth. *Not this time.*

"You are going to drive yourself?"

"What do you think I did before I met you? Yes, I think I can manage to drive the trek to get to my mountain cabin. Jacen loves it there and I need to be able to get away and recharge, in order to keep the kind of work pace that I keep. Are you planning on working weekends too?"

"If I need to in order to make enough money to make you happy," replied Ethan. Beth sighed a long frustrated sigh.

*****

During her marriage to Ethan, they had not developed any friendships with other couples. Beth used to beg Ethan to accept invitations that were extended from other couples. She had always had lots of friends around her, and valued her friendships. Ethan was very much a loner, and never wanted to share his time with her with anyone else. He used to find fun and interesting things to do with her and Jacen on the weekends. In the beginning she did not miss her friendships that much. They were busy on one adventure or another. In the beginning, just going to the grocery store with Ethan could turn into an adventure. Pretty soon, other couples quit extending invitations, and it was not for many years that Beth finally realized that, as a couple, she and Ethan had no friends.

Beth had her sister Susan, but then she moved away, as did her parents and grandparents. Between her family, who she used to see several times a week, and her adventures with Ethan, she did not feel the lack of friendships. Then, her parents retired and moved up north to a beautiful home built on two acres of land, in a park-like setting. They had a second home built on the property for her grandparents. Then a year after that, Susan had moved up to Washington for a job promotion, and left Beth orphaned in Southern California. She still teases her parents, telling them that they waited until she was well established in her business. Then they picked up and moved, taking all of the family she had with them, leaving her orphaned. With her family living four hundred miles away, and Ethan no longer interested in planning adventures with her on the weekends, her life seemed suddenly very lonely.

Beth had two girl friends, which were a great source of strength for her. She met Sonja through a business contact. She and Sonja spent the first day they met chatting for well over an hour. Sonja was one of the sweetest, most giving people that Beth had ever met. Although she was seven or eight years younger than Beth, Sonja had a son that was a couple of years older than Jacen. She had been a single mom for years, and had done a fine job rearing her son. Sonja was a total contrast within herself. She worked in a man's world as a longshoreman, drove a big Ford 250 pickup, was tough and strong, yet had big expressive, always laughing, blue eyes, and a smile that totally lit up her face. Many times it seemed that her smile would light up an entire room. She was feminine, soft, always giggling, always chatting with anyone and everyone, outgoing, adventurous and fun. She was the thoughtful one, always showing up at the office with a loaf of cinnamon bread or cookies, because when she went to the bakery to get some for herself, she thought to buy extra for Beth. She might show up with lemons from her tree, or a box of blankets that she didn't need anymore but thought Beth might be able to use up at the cabin. She had been up to the cabin with Beth on a couple of occasions, and it never failed to be an adventure of one kind or another. Beth adored her, and whenever she felt even a little down, she knew she could always call Sonja and hang up the phone laughing and in a good mood.

Her other girlfriend, Anne, had led a very interesting life. While in her teens, her widowed father had decided to build a sailboat and take his two daughters cruising. In their driveway, a sixty-foot sailboat was built, and true to his word, the boat was launched and they took off for exotic ports and adventure. Anne had stayed with the sailing life in the charter business in the Caribbean, for over ten years, returning to get an office job and try to normalize her life. She had interesting stories to tell, was also single and had been burned in love, was fiercely independent, and always up for an adventure. She and Anne developed an instant friendship, and it seemed that everything that they ever planned automatically became a great escapade.

Beth remembers the first time that she invited Anne up to her mountain cabin. It was during the late spring, the day was warm and beautiful. Anne arrived at about noon and her first stop was to be the outhouse. This was a couple of years earlier, before Beth had the septic system installed and a real indoor bathroom. Beth had taken her bag into the house and was putting water on the stove for tea. A few minutes later, Jacen came into the house and said that Anne told him that there was a rattlesnake in the outhouse. Beth didn't realize at the time, that Anne meant that there was a rattlesnake with her in the outhouse. Beth spent the next few minutes getting out cups and putting in tea bags, waiting for Anne to come into the house. When she didn't come in, Beth looked out the window and saw that the outhouse door was closed.

"Jacen, where is Anne?" Beth called through the window.

"I told you mom, she is in the outhouse, there is a rattlesnake in there." Beth ran out the door to the outhouse.

"Anne?" she asked through the door.

"I was wondering if you were going to come out and help me with this," Anne replied.

"Jacen didn't say that you were IN the outhouse with the snake, only that there was a snake."

"Well, I am in here all right, the snake is on the concrete floor, right next to the door and I can't get past him."

"Are you okay?" Beth asked.

"Oh, I'm fine, but, I am standing on top of the outhouse seat and I can't reach the door to open it, and I don't have anything to shoo the snake out with."

"Okay, I'm going to go get a big stick, I'll be right back, don't go away," Beth replied with a giggle.

"Don't worry, I will be right here, I promise!"

When Beth returned with a stick, she opened the door and as promised, there lay a rattlesnake along the doorway, on the cool concrete. Beth wanted to pick him up with a stick and carry him off of her property, but as soon as she started to pick him up, he got very agitated and started coiling and rattling. She finally got him out of the outhouse, but he scurried behind the small building and up under the siding. She and Anne could hear the snake rattling, but couldn't see him.

"Can he get into the outhouse pit?" Anne asked.

"I don't know, I never looked before." Beth and Anne spent the next fifteen minutes examining the walls of the outhouse pit, looking for a rattlesnake, or a way for the snake to get into the pit.

"Isn't this lovely?" Anne offered.

"I really know how to spoil my guests, don't I?" Beth retorted back, laughing. After deciding that the snake couldn't get into the pit, they banged on the walls of the outhouse until the snake was silent, assuming that he scurried away. Ethan was getting water when all the excitement was happening, but heard all about it when he got back.

Beth always seemed to have an adventure of some kind when she got together with either of her girlfriends. When all three got together, it was sheer madness!

***

Beth knew she had two wonderful friends to turn to. Both loved to go to the cabin with her, so if Ethan didn't want to go, she would go with Jacen and invite Sonja or Anne whenever they were available. Ethan didn't like when she invited them up when he was there because he found both of them annoying, and they intruded on his privacy. She, on the other hand, loved having the company. *If Ethan wants to play that way, fine. He can stay home. Jacen and I will be just fine.* And she knew they would.

Chapter Twenty-Four

~

EMAIL
TO: klm@qmail.com
FROM: beth0711@qmail.com
RE:

Hey you, guess who. Yup, it's me. You have always been a good guesser. Ha! I have a couple of minutes before going to work out and wanted to drop you a note to say hi. You have been on my mind . . . as always. I haven't heard from you in a couple of days, where have you been?

Things have been busy here, working with a new client whose books have been a mess for the past three years. An accounting nightmare, but that is what I get paid the big bucks for! Yeah, I wish!
Anyway, just wanted to say hi. I miss you. Hope you

will write soon. L b

~

    Kyle had not written to her since the one email after they met that afternoon. It had been almost a week since she had heard from him, and she was beginning to panic. *Kyle, what is wrong? Why haven't you written?* Two days later she wrote.

~

EMAIL
TO: klm@qmail.com
FROM: beth0711@qmail.com
RE: Kisses

Hey, what is up with you? It has been over a week since I last heard from you. Are you okay? Kyle, talk to me! I miss hearing from you.
Beth

~

    Beth had a million emotions bombarding her all at once. She was working long hours with an especially difficult client. Her workload seemed enormous. At home, she was struggling with Ethan. She knew she had put her foot down, at last, and part of her wanted so bad for him to step up to the plate, and finally keep the promise that he made. She had to remain strong this time, and not buckle if he let her down once again. She was determined to get her life on track. She just wasn't real sure which track to choose.

Kyle had not written in over a week and Beth didn't know why. She was hurting inside, desperately willing him to write to her, tell her what was going on. *Does he not want anything to do with me after all? What did I do? Why doesn't he write? Please Kyle, just tell me what is in your heart. Please?*

Ethan sensed that something was different this time with Beth. She seemed preoccupied and distant. Her confession that she had not missed him while he was gone hurt him deeply. Something was different though, he just couldn't quite put his finger on it.

~

EMAIL
TO: klm@qmail.com
FROM: beth0711@qmail.com
RE:

Kyle, please talk to me. Are you okay? I don't know why you won't write me back. What did I do? You seemed happy to see me, then we kissed. I can't even describe the impact that one kiss from you had on me. It was like a whole lifetime of emotion came cascading over me. It left me breathless. It left me with a whole new set of questions about what I want in my life. I know you felt something too. Why won't you talk to me? Please write to me. I am going crazy. B

~

Beth was struggling to keep herself from falling apart. Working long hours was taking its toll on her physically, and emotionally she was a wreck. She was walking an emotional tightrope. To Ethan, she had given an ultimatum. Get your act together, or call it quits. She was trying to encourage him and help him get it together, while at the same time, she found herself keeping some distance between them. The distance was her safety net, in case Ethan once again broke his promise to her. She found herself also keeping emotionally distant from Ethan because of Kyle. She was feeling so many unsettling sensations that she was not sure what to believe about her own feelings. *I am an emotional mess!*

***

Time for a girl's night out. Beth put in a call to Sonja and Anne, and they decided to meet at a Marie Calendar's restaurant the next night at six. Beth couldn't wait. She needed the soothing laughter she knew she would get when the three of them got together.

Anne arrived in the parking lot at the same time as Beth. Sonja, bless her, was always late, and usually lost. Beth put in a call to her on her cell phone.

"Sonja, its Beth, are you on your way here? Anne and I just got here."

"Yes, I'm on my way. I got delayed a little, and then was not sure what the best way was to get there, but I should be there in a few minutes."

"Great, we're going to get a table, see you when

you get here."

Beth and Anne selected a booth in a corner of the restaurant. Since it was a weekday, there was no wait to be seated. Anne ordered coffee and Beth ordered hot tea, with cream. They decided to wait to order until Sonja arrived, but spent a few minutes looking over the menu so they would be ready when she got there.

After twenty minutes and still no Sonja, Beth decided to call her again.

"Sonja, where are you?"

"Sorry I'm so late, I got turned around and was going the wrong way, but I'm almost there. See you in five! Wait, I see the sign, see me? I am flashing my lights."

"Sonja, I am inside the restaurant."

"Look out the window, I am turning into the parking lot." Sure enough, Beth leaned over to the nearest window, there was Sonja's big truck turning into the parking lot.

"Yes, I see you," Beth replied into the cell phone.

"I'll be right in."

"She is here, finally," Beth said over the table to Anne, as she repositioned herself in the booth. Seconds later, like a hurricane arriving, Sonja came through the restaurant door. Walking fast, wall to wall smiles that lit up the room announcing her arrival, she started her greetings from three tables away. It was like she couldn't wait to say hi. Her usual exuberance was infectious and after hugs and greetings all around, Sonja flagged over a waitress and ordered a coffee.

"I have been up since five this morning and working since six. I need coffee just to keep me awake!" remarked Sonja, as she spooned several spoonfuls of sugar into the black liquid. Beth and Anne made quick eye contact, as they shared a brief moment of amusement at their friend's expense.

"Hey! I saw that look," she announced, with mock indignity. Beth and Anne both laughed a guilty laugh as she took the first sip of her coffee. "This should help wake me up."

The waitress was a good-natured red head, with mischievous green eyes. She would have fit in great with the girls at the table. She first looked at Sonja for her order.

"You two go ahead. I am not sure what I want yet," she replied as she nodded toward Beth to start.

"I'm going to have a chicken pot pie, with a salad and ranch dressing. And corn bread, lots of corn bread," Beth started.

"Oh, that sounds good," Sonja offered, "I'm really hungry, too."

"Is that what you want too?" the waitress asked.

"Anne, you go ahead, I'm not sure what I want yet."

"Well," Anne started, "I think I will have the pot pie too, same salad and ranch."

"Okay, well it's your turn now, have you decided yet?" the waitress turned to Sonja.

"Everything looks so good. I'm having a hard time deciding. Well, I'll take the pasta special, with salad and also ranch dressing. Can you bring some extra ranch on the side? And corn bread."

"Great, ladies, I'll be right back with your salads," replied the waitress, as she turned to walk away.

"Okay, girls. I have presents for us. Do you want them now, or after dinner?" said Beth, with a little air of mystery to her voice.

"Oh, now, I love presents!" said Sonja. Beth reached into her purse and brought out a small box. Opening it revealed three silver toe rings. One for each of them.

"They are so cute," Sonja exclaimed.

"I have never had a toe ring before," replied Anne.

"We each need to choose one, and no fighting," Beth responded with a grin.

One ring was a plain band with a small purple stone in the middle of it. The second was a single band with a silver filigree rope pattern in the middle, and the third was a single band with an S shaped pattern in the middle, with two small silver beads, one nestled in the each curve of the S shape.

"I want the purple one," Sonja was first to choose.

"I think I like the one with the S shape in the middle," was Anne's choice.

"That's perfect, because my favorite is the rope pattern one," replied Beth as she took them out of the box. "Now we need to try them on." Beth wore sandals that day anticipating the giving of the toe rings. Sonja was wearing jeans and tennis shoes.

"I hope my feet don't stink too much when I take these shoes off," she mumbled to herself as she pulled her foot up onto the booth seat.

"I'm wearing hose so I can't put mine on until I get home," replied Anne. She seemed relieved. Amidst laughter from all three of them, Sonja got her shoe and sock off and toe ring on.

"There, it looks beautiful," replied Sonja as all three of them were looking under the table admiring her foot. When the waitress arrived with the salads, Sonja showed off her new gift.

Later that evening, after entrees were eaten and they were deciding on pie, Beth told them how much she valued their friendships. *I sure needed this tonight,* thought Beth. *Whoever said that laughter was the best medicine was right.*

Chapter Twenty-Five

~

EMAIL
TO: klm@qmail.com
FROM: beth0711@qmail.com
RE:

Kyle, it has been almost two weeks since you have written to me. What happened? I need to hear from you. I don't know if you are getting my mail, if you don't want anything to do with me, if you are mad at me, did I look too old? What? Please let me keep my dignity and don't ask me to beg. Just tell me what is going on with you. The not knowing is killing me. After all we have been through with each other, I don't think it's too much to ask you to just talk to me. B

~

Beth was unhappy. It reflected in her work, she found it hard to concentrate. It reflected in her home life.

She was short with Jacen and distant with Ethan. She was unnecessarily critical with Ethan when he left a dirty dish in the sink, or the bed unmade. She had emotions raging within her and no release for them. She felt like she was drowning in her own little world and there wasn't anyone to throw her a life ring.

"Susan, it has been over two weeks since he has written to me," confessed Beth in a phone call to her sister. "I don't know what happened or why he won't write."

"Men are such jerks," Susan replied dryly. "They think they are communicating because they hear from us, and don't realize how badly we need to hear back from them."

"But, I have told him, have begged him to just write and tell me what is going on. You would think that if he did not want anything to do with me anymore, he would just write and tell me. Not just leave me with all these feelings and no place to put them."

"Michael has been a lot better at calling and writing lately. I told him that I need to hear from him at least once a day. I live for his calls. Sometimes I hate myself for being so needy, and accepting so little for myself. Here I am, a healthy forty-three year old woman in the prime of my life, and my happiness depends on getting a phone call or an email from my married boyfriend. He has still not made any commitments to become unmarried; we don't even talk about it. When I see him, you would think that it would be a perfect time to try to get some idea about where this relationship is going to go, but I don't want to spoil the precious time we have together so I don't even bring it up."

"What does he say?" inquired Beth.

"That he loves me and doesn't want to leave me, but he always does leave and it's the hardest thing in the world. He goes back to his life and I go back to no life, waiting for the next phone call, or email, or visit so I can live a few moments at a time, here and there. It is so hard."

"I understand completely, because I'm feeling the same way. I think I have been just existing with Ethan. For years I have lived from one broken promise from him to another. Each time I get my hopes up and wipe the slate clean and believe in him, but nothing changes because it doesn't have to change. I stay. He does small thoughtful things for me, like bringing me a jacket when he knows that I might not have one and might need one, or bringing home chocolate ice-cream when he knows that we don't have any. He might bring lunch by the office because he knows that I probably have not taken a lunch break. All of those things are supposed to make up for the broken promises. He thinks the broken promises shouldn't be held against him, because he does all of these other little things. He makes me feel like such a bitch when he does something nice for me. But at the end of the month, when I am struggling to keep the phones on, and taking call after call from creditors, I complain when his pay check won't even cover his health insurance premium. But, I stay. There is no penalty to him. He knows I always make it happen, somehow."

"It's not enough, though, is it?"

"No, I need a partner that I can lean on once in a while. That I know will pick up the slack and give me an occasional break.”

"God, Beth, how I know that feeling," replied Susan with a wistful tone in her voice.

***

On a Thursday, two weeks and two days later, Beth finally got a reply.

~

EMAIL
TO: beth0711@qmail.com
FROM: klm@qmail.com
RE:

Hey Babe,
Remember me? I am sorry that I have not written. Although I have been very busy, that is only part of the reason that I haven't written. I needed some time to sort things out in my mind. Seeing you brought back lots of feelings for me too. I see that I am hurting you and that's the one thing that I don't want to do. You deserve better than that. You have been on my mind. More than I thought you would be, and more than you should be. I needed the time to get a handle on my own feelings. I think we need to talk so there is a clear understanding of where each of us stands so I won't be hurting you any more. So, if you are still speaking to me, let me know what your thoughts are. k

~

EMAIL
TO: klm@qmail.com
FROM: beth0711@qmail.com
RE:

Hi,

Finally! Yes, I agree, we definitely need to talk. If for no other reason than just to put into perspective the expectations that each of us has with this thing. I guess I don't even know if there is a "this thing" between us. I am very confused, but very glad to finally hear from you. Of course I am still speaking to you. What a silly question! Things are tight for me at the office, but I can probably work around your schedule, just keep in touch with me, okay?

Jacen and I are probably going to start going to the mountains by ourselves. That's where we will be this weekend. Things are not going well at home. We will probably leave tomorrow afternoon and be gone the weekend, so check your schedule and let me know what your next week looks like. Please don't leave me hanging. Write me soon. b

~

Chapter Twenty-Six

"Look, you told me that you don't even like going to the cabin, so this will work out fine. Jacen and I can go by ourselves and you can do what you have been wanting to do on your weekends." Beth was in her office, sitting at her desk talking to Ethan on the phone. She was feeling better than she had in weeks because she finally heard from Kyle. Although Ethan had been going with her to the cabin each weekend, he constantly was complaining about having to go. He made her feel like he was making the ultimate sacrifice just by going with her. He also made it seem like she was not capable of driving there herself.

"I'll worry about you driving all that way by yourself, Beth," replied Ethan.

"Look, I drove here many times myself before I

ever met you."

"But, you are not used to driving the Cherokee." They had purchased their first Jeep Cherokee eight years earlier, and were so impressed with the vehicle that when they wore out the first one, they had bought a second, vowing to always own a Jeep.

"Ethan, you worry too much. I am a big girl and I have driven the Cherokee before. This is not such a big deal. This way, when you want to stay in town to do some of the things you have been missing out on, I won't be the one taking you away. Just think, when you decide to come to the mountains with us, it will be by choice, not obligation."

"Look, I really don't mind driving you there. That way you don't have to drive all that way, and I'll know you're safe," replied Ethan.

"So, you don't think I can safely drive Jacen and myself to the cabin? Is that what this is all about?" Beth could feel herself getting angry. "You have even told Jacen that 'I don't want to go either, but we have to do this for your mom' when Jacen has asked about going to the cabin. Now I give you an out, you just don't have to go, and you still are not happy. I don't get it. Look Ethan, I want to go alone, just Jacen and me. When you choose to join us, fine, we will welcome you. But I don't want you to come with us anymore because you feel obligated. I am tired of you throwing the fact that you give up your precious weekends for me in my face."

***

The drive up to the mountains was uneventful. Ethan called her several times on her cell phone. With the windows down and music blaring, Beth and Jacen sang along with the radio almost all the way there.

"Where are you guys now?" asked Ethan. His second call on the cell phone in the past twenty minutes.

"We are just at the freeway offramp for our turnoff," replied Beth. "We are doing just fine, you worry too much."

"Well, I am glad you are doing well. Will you call me when you get there?" Ethan asked. "There is something that I need to talk to you about."

"Sure, what is it?"

"It'll wait until you get there," Ethan replied.

"Okay, we will be there in about forty minutes, I will call you." *I wonder what's up?* thought Beth.

***

Beth and Jacen arrived forty-seven minutes later, opened up the house and unloaded the groceries. Beth put everything away, which just took a few minutes, then sat down at the desk to call Ethan and let him know that they had arrived safely.

"Hi, it's me. We are here!"

"Good. Was your trip alright?" asked Ethan.

"Excellent and uneventful. Jacen and I sang along with the radio all the way up. So, what did you want to talk to me about?"

"Beth, I just had my life crumble under me. I am sitting here in shock and in tears not knowing what to do. Beth, you, you of all people. You see, I know all about Kyle. I know how you have deceived me and lied to me. The thing that hurts me the most is that it took fifteen years for me to finally trust a woman. I would have put my hands in the fire for you. I would have never believed anyone if they told me that you were not being faithful. You are the woman who made me believe in women again. Then I do a little digging and find that you are cheating on me."

"Oh my God," Beth choked.

"I believe that you are not a deceitful person by nature. This couldn't have been easy for you. You must have been very unhappy to seek a relationship elsewhere." Beth could hear him struggling to control his emotions and not break down. "I don't think that I took your unhappiness seriously enough, and now I have lost you."

"No," Beth was now crying in earnest. "No, please," she pleaded. At that instant, Beth realized what she had put on the line. Did she want her marriage over? No, she didn't. The realization hit her like a bolt of lightening. "Ethan, I need to explain," she sobbed. "Please give me the chance to explain."

"What is there to explain?" Ethan managed, his voice tight with emotion. "You have been emailing to another man, declaring your love for him, practically begging him to write you back. I think that is the part that hurts the most. You are pursuing him. I was embarrassed for you when I read your emails. He doesn't even want you, Beth. He doesn't even want you. And there I sit, like a fool, loving you and wanting more than anything to be the man you want, and you throw me away."

Beth was hurting badly inside. She felt like she was carrying the weight of the world on her shoulders. She was having a hard time breathing, and her insides felt as though they were tied up in knots. Although, the idea of losing her marriage was devastating, what hurt the most was seeing what she had done to Ethan. She did love him, that she knew, and she had caused him enormous pain.

"Yes, I have been unhappy. I have tried to tell you that. Yes, I will admit that I was considering leaving you. But, now with the possibility of you actually leaving, I know that I don't want you to go."

"Why, because he doesn't want you? If he would have said that he was leaving his wife and wanted you, you would have been gone already. I knew there was something going on with you, I really did not think that you were having an affair though."

"I have not slept with him."

"Maybe not, but, I think you would have. You were heading in that direction."

"I know," Beth replied with a sign of resignation.

"Look, it is late and we are spending a fortune on cell minutes. I need some time to think things through and so do you. You need to decide what you want in your life Beth. I will do the same and we can talk when you get back."

"I'm afraid to hang up the phone. I'm afraid you will be gone if I do," Beth moaned.

"I will be here Beth. It's only because I truly do love you that I will be here. If you were anyone else, I would have been moved out by now, and would have never even looked back."

"Thank you for that," Beth whispered weakly. "I am so sorry that I hurt you and betrayed you." Hot tears were streaming down her cheeks. She knew she would not get much sleep that night.

"You try to get some sleep, we will talk more tomorrow."

"I don't think I will be able to sleep. I will call you tomorrow. I am so sorry Ethan."

"I know Beth. I know. Goodnight."

"Goodnight Ethan," Beth replied in a voice strained with emotion.

***

After hanging up the phone, Beth sat for a minute trying to grasp the turn of events that occurred this evening. She was in turmoil. The only thing that she could think about was the hurt in Ethan's voice. He had trusted her, he had believed in her. Other women had betrayed him in his life, but Beth was different. She had proved over and over that she was different. It took her years to build the trust that he had in her. She had worked hard to weave a delicate cord of trust between them. Finally after years of a perfect record, Ethan started weaving along with her, strengthening the bond, believing the trust they had developed. *Snap,* she thought, *just like that, the bond between us has been shattered. But I have worked so hard* to be a perfect wife. I couldn't let him see that I carry the terrible burden of a sin once committed. I had to be as perfect as possible so he wouldn't find the fault in me and take his love away.

Chapter Twenty-Seven

Sleep was impossible. Beth tossed and turned in her bed. *He must have read my emails, but how did he know what I wrote back?* She did not anticipate that Ethan would pry into her personal mail. Although she never told Ethan her password, in retrospect, she realized that it would not have been hard to guess. *Can things ever be the same between us again?*

Ethan was, by nature, not a trusting person. During the course of their marriage, he had badgered her about her friendships with men, telling her that there was no such thing as a friendship between a man and a woman. "The man always has another agenda," he would tell her. He criticized her for merely having a conversation with a man. She had changed how she dressed, how she carried herself, how she spoke with people. In order to make Ethan happy, she had developed a reserve about her that was really not her at all. "Beth, show some decorum," he would whisper sternly to her when she started to laugh to hard or allow any of the playfulness that was really her personality showing through.   Beth had spent fifteen years perfecting the persona that Ethan was happy with and that he trusted. *Is it really me that he loves? Does he even know who I really am? Do I know who I am anymore? Is part of my attraction to Kyle the simple fact that he never has tried to change me? I never had to watch what I said or whom I said it to. Kyle has this look of amusement that he used to give me if I got too silly. But he always accepted me and loved me for who I am. What happened to that passionate girl, with no patience, who loved burnt marshmallows, was always seeking the next adventure, was the eternal dreamer and believed in rainbows and true love? Did life get in my way? Did I simply grow up? Or, is that girl still in there somewhere?*

Not being able to sleep for a whole night gave Beth a lot of time to reflect on her life, and to try to come up with some answers to the questions that plagued her. She found that by sunrise, she had come to a few conclusions, but had many more questions swarming around in her brain.

Beth was not willing to throw away fifteen years of marriage.   There had been a lot of hurt between her and Ethan. *I went into this marriage with a deep dark secret. There is a part of my heart that will always belong to Kyle. I can never wholly belong to another man.* Beth felt that she had to compensate for the part of her that would always be locked away tight. She had to be perfect. She had to be everything that Ethan expected in a wife. He deserved the devotion of a whole person; somehow she had to deliver a whole person, even though she knew there would always be a small part missing. Ethan, however, could never know he was not getting it all, she had to be better than the rest. She had to make what she was able to give enough. She had to be perfect.

In reality, Beth has a dreamer's heart. She is an optimistic idealist. Her brain is always in motion. Ethan used to tease her, telling her that he could hear the cogs turning in her head. In her marriage to Ethan, she had taken on the responsibility for their family. She handled the money and made the decisions about their finances. She made sure there was always food on the table and a roof over their head.

Imagine what ideas I could have come up with if I was not saddled with all the responsibility of this family, she thought wistfully. The stress stifled her and made her cranky. Yet, she knew that Ethan could never have handled either the responsibility, or the stress. He simply was not equipped. *I know he does not possess the tools, and yet I fault him for it. I resent him for putting me in this position. Yet, am I underestimating him? Is it my fault for making it so easy for him to shirk the responsibilities? Am I fair to him when he tries to step in and take over part of the responsibilities or do I put him down for not doing it my way? Yet, is it my duty to delegate and manage? Shouldn't he just be able to come in and take some of this burden away from me, and do it well? Maybe he needs the same things that I do. Maybe he needs an anchor, a stable responsible mate and I have molded myself into the person that he wants and needs me to be. But is it really me? I need an anchor too. Someone to lean on, and depend on. Someone I can share all of my feelings with, someone who will not only allow me to soar, but who encourages me. I need someone who is not threatened by my strength, but complemented by it. Ethan, are you that person? Kyle, are you that person?*

***

Beth and Jacen left the mountain cabin at about three that afternoon. The weather was warm and balmy, but Beth did not notice. She was quiet and preoccupied. Jacen noticed that there was something wrong with his mom, but did not ask about it. He was just there for her, knowing she needed some space.

Beth needed to get home to Ethan and try to ease some of the hurt that they both were feeling. She had to fix this somehow. She needed him to understand what was in her heart. It was not like she had a choice about what was in her heart. She never planned this, nor did she have the power to change it or make it go away. What she felt in her heart for Kyle just was, simply put. It had been there for the past thirty years and she doubted it would ever go away. She could ignore it, deny it, or lock it away, but the reality was that it would always be a part of her.

Although Beth had no idea what to expect when she arrived home that evening, she was very surprised at what was waiting for her. The house had been cleaned, dinner was fixed and on the table with a candle burning and a glass of wine poured. Ethan had fixed pasta with Alfredo sauce and a green salad. Beth walked into the house and looked at the table with astonishment. With tears brimming in her eyes, she asked him why he was being so nice to her.

"Because, I thought you would be hungry when you got home," Ethan replied. "Plus, because I want you to know that you are loved." Ethan was smiling at her as she felt the hot tears silently rolling down her cheeks. "Please, sit and eat while it's hot," he commanded. "Jacen, be sure to go wash your hands first."

Dinner was very good, although, later Beth wouldn't be able to remember what it tasted like. She ate in silence, as much as she could, which was not a lot. Jacen ate his portion with gusto. He certainly was a growing boy with an appetite. She finished her wine and looked expectantly at Ethan.

"Jacen, your mom and I are going for a walk, we won't be gone long, okay?" Ethan grabbed a lightweight jacket for Beth and handed it to her as he gently eased her out the front door.

The evening had cooled off some. Beth was grateful for the jacket, although she could feel herself shivering as they walked side by side in silence. She was not shivering from the cold; she was just trembling inside, not knowing what was to come next. Ethan was the first to break the silence.

"Beth, first I want to tell you that no matter what else happens between us, I know you are a good person and I want to be there for you. I love you very much and I want to see you happy more than anything in the world. You deserve that. I have had some time to think about our relationship, and how unhappy you must be to seek a relationship elsewhere. I don't think I was willing to really look at what it must be like for you, but it's something that has now been thrown into my face and I am forced to take a long hard look at myself. I am not blaming you, Beth." Beth dropped her head in shame, tears cascading in rivulets down her face. "I know I have not been the husband you expected and you deserve more than I have given you. I am trying right now to take myself out of the role as husband and be an objective friend to you. No matter what happens between us as husband and wife, I will always be your friend because I know the quality of person you are inside."

"Why are you doing this?" Beth asked with an unsteady voice. She was trembling even more violently. "Why do you show me kindness when I have hurt you as I have? Are you willing to stay with me?"

Ethan sighed, "I don't know if I can stay, Beth. You are the only woman in my whole life that I had learned to trust. You had to earn that trust and you did. I would have never believed in a million years that you would have an affair. Not you. I don't know what to do. I don't know if I could ever trust you again. What kind of life could we have with me wondering where you are every time we are apart. I'm afraid I would not be a very nice guy to you. Could you live with that? Could I put you through that? Who is this person anyway? How long has this been going on? The things you told him, how important in your life he is, how much you have missed him. You were pursuing him. Practically begging him to write to you. I was embarrassed for you. I just don't know Beth, I just don't know."

"Ethan, I know I have hurt you, I never meant to, honest. Who is he? I'll tell you my secret, the part of me that I never share with anyone. The part of me that holds a hurt so painful that I keep it locked tight away, and the part of me that I don't understand, but it is all tied together and makes me who I am." Beth sighed a long emotional sigh, then she started. "When I was fifteen, I met Kyle at our mountain property. His family had bought property there too. We were so young, but there was something there, something very special and very real between us. We had no idea at the time, but we were to become so much a part of each other's lives, interwoven with love and tragedy, adventure and hurt, and incredible closeness and distance, all at the same time. Remember that I told you that I was pregnant at sixteen and had an abortion?"

"Yes, but you would never talk about it," replied Ethan. "I never understood why you could not confide in me, why you would never trust me with this part of your life. I knew it was a painful time, but I would have understood."

"Would you have? No, not if I told you all of it. Not if I told you what was really in my heart," replied Beth. Her crying had eased some and she felt a numbness take over as she started to relate her story to Ethan. "At first when I found out that I was pregnant, Kyle was going to be there for me. I really believed that he would. Then, my parents started talking about an abortion and Kyle shut me out. This was not what I wanted, but at fifteen, I had little power. Then, we had a meeting planned with him and his parents..."

"Kyle, you mean?" asked Ethan.

"Yes, we were going to his house to talk about what we were all going to do about the situation." Beth's voice started to shake again. She took a minute to catch her breath but the tears started again, and she found that she was sobbing uncontrollably. Ethan put his arms around her. "Kyle was not there," she choked out. "His parents were, my parents were and I was there, but Kyle was not. I felt so abandoned and so alone." Beth stood letting Ethan comfort her, her face buried in his chest, sobbing over a hurt that was so profound that even thirty years later, she found it so hard to face.

"My God, you must have been so devastated. Where was he? Why wasn't he there for you?" asked Ethan, trying to imagine the pain that she must have endured. Beth regained some of her composure as she continued with a tale Ethan would find both incredible and heart wrenching.

"Later he told me that he just couldn't face it."

"So he let you face it alone," Ethan responded angrily, shaking his head.

"We were so young, Ethan."

"I can't believe you are defending him after what he did that to you." Beth held up her hand to halt the direction that Ethan was taking the conversation.

"Anyway . . . it was that night that I consented to

the abortion. Our parents had agreed that Kyle and I were not to see each other until we were eighteen. I tried calling him after, you know, but he would not talk to me. He would not even get on the phone. I thought about killing myself, I was hurting so bad."

"And this is the jerk you were willing to throw me away over?" Ethan angrily interjected. "Why Beth? This guy isn't worthy of walking in your shadow."

"Look, this is hard enough for me as it is. Do you want to hear this or not?" Beth responded with an edge to her voice.

"Yes, sorry. I just get so angry that someone hurt you like that and . . ."

"Just hear me out, okay?" Beth replied.

"Okay, go on." They resumed walking as Beth continued her story.

"A couple of months later, Kyle walked back into my life. Don't you see that he had been hurting as much as I was? There was so much torment in his eyes. Although the pain will never go away, nor will the loss, there was forgiveness between us. We needed to forgive each other in order to be able to heal. Against our parents wishes, we continued seeing each other. It was very hard and we both were other seeing other people too. But, there was a bond between us. We just needed to be near each other to be content. I knew I had this terrible sin, like an ugly blotch, on my soul. But he did too, so I never had to explain, or keep it a secret, because although it was always between us, we understood it and had come to terms with it."

"Beth, you don't have a blotch on your soul," Ethan

offered.

"Yes, yes I do. I know it and I try each day to do something to make up for it. Although if I live to be a hundred, there will not have been enough days, or deeds to make up for taking the life that I took. I know that. I am so much more cognizant of that fact now that I am a mother. The realization of my actions so many years ago is so much more profound as I watch Jacen grow up. I have tried to make it up to God by being the best possible mother that I can to Jacen, just so He knows how sorry I am." Ethan noticed that Beth had stopped crying, but her voice had an almost emotionless quality to it, like she was speaking of someone else. *She has carried a heavy burden for a long time,* Ethan thought to himself.

"Beth, what else could you have done? In reality, how could you have been a good mother at age sixteen? You are much too hard on yourself. You need to forgive yourself."

"I have forgiven myself," Beth replied, "but I will make sure that I never forget."

"So what happened between you two?"

"He got another girl pregnant and ended up marrying her. I had just turned eighteen when it happened, he was almost nineteen."

"So, why now, all of a sudden is he back into your life? I don't understand."

"We stayed in touch during the first ten years of his marriage. It was on and off, but the feelings between us never went away."

"You lied to Jim all the time you were with him?"

Ethan asked incredulously.

"Jim and I were not married," Beth replied with a wave of her hand. "Not to mention that he dated and saw other woman. Our relationship was weird, and although I thought I wanted it to be exclusive, and I know that at times it was, I know that many times it was not."

"So, our whole marriage has been a lie? There has always been someone else in your life?" There was tightness in Ethan's voice as he spoke, trying to keep control of his emotions.

"No!" Beth almost shouted. "Ethan, I married you because you were the only man that I had ever met that I knew could make me forget about Kyle. You are the only other man that I have truly loved. I have not had any contact with Kyle during our marriage. I thought about him occasionally, but I was happy with you. I have been completely faithful to you in both body and spirit."

"You know, I drove by his house."

"You did?" Beth looked at him with a questioning expression.

"He even looks like me," Ethan whispered. "All these years I have been married to someone else's woman."

"No," Beth sobbed, seeing Ethan's pain. "No . . please try to understand. I never asked for these feelings. I am trying to be honest with you. I have tried so hard to be a perfect wife." Beth was crying in earnest now, struggling to be able to tell Ethan her feelings. She had to make him understand. "I am damaged goods, Ethan. I am a person with a terrible sin on my soul. I could never tell you. How could you have loved me? I never asked for my feelings for Kyle. They just are there, like a curse."

"Beth," Ethan grabbed her by her upper arms, Beth thought he was going to shake her, "you are not damaged goods."

"Yes."

"No. Beth, you are so worth loving. You are loving and giving and compassionate. Love is never a curse. Love can only be joy, not pain. This jerk is so unworthy of you, Beth. I am not saying that I am worthy, but he does not even want you. He would be willing to sleep with you, willing to demean you in the lowest possible way, to put you last on his list. To use you, but not want you. He has had time during all of these years to come for you if he really cared. Don't you see that? He has to know how you feel, and is willing to take advantage of your feelings for him. He is the lowest possible scum, not to mention that he is willing to cheat on his wife. Are those traits in a man to admire, Beth? I know I have a lot of faults and fall short in a lot of ways, but I would never have put you in that position. I would never have cheated on you and would never have used you. I see the good in you. I know the kind of person you are and I love you for it. You deserve to be loved, you deserve to be happy, you deserve so much more than the crumbs that he is willing to throw your way."

"Oh my God," Beth whispered, her eyes shining with fresh tears, "what have I done? Can you ever forgive me Ethan? Are we going to be able to get past this?"

"I don't know, Beth. Honestly, I don't know."

"Are you going to leave me?"

"If my uncles could see me now they would think I was such a pussy. If any their wives had done what you did, they would have done unspeakable things to the other guy. It would have been ugly, Beth. It is a good thing for you that they are not here. Look, I don't want to hurt his family, but I hate that he will get away with this without any consequence. You are the one who took all the risks; there is no consequence to him. You threw away your family, at least me, you threw away me over this guy. I don't know Beth. I just don't know if I can." Ethan could see her pain. It was so evident in her eyes, her face, in her whole aura.

He put his arms around her. He wanted to comfort her, make her pain go away. She had carried such a burden for so long. He found he wanted to carry some of it for her, lighten her load. For the first time since the day that he first met her, Ethan saw a crack in the exterior of strength that she always presented. *I have always depended on her strength,* he realized, *I have never given her the chance to be weak or vulnerable. I can understand why she would go looking elsewhere. I pushed her away, expecting too much from her. Always knowing that somehow she would succeed, she would carry the weight; she always has. I guess I can see why she turned to someone else to help lighten her load, she knew that I never had.* "Beth, I don't blame you for looking for someone else. I know that I have dumped a lot on your shoulders and have not taken responsibility for this family like I should. I'm sorry for that. I realize that in order for this relationship to ever have even a prayer of succeeding, that I have to step up to the plate and make some major changes. But why would you turn to him? Why to someone who does not even want you?"

"I was happy with him once. There are still very intense feelings between us. Yes, I have been very unhappy, I've told you that. I know he is in an unhappy marriage and we have been a source of comfort for each other in the past. I simply turned to what I know. A comfortable place, a familiar place."

Ethan nodded his head with understanding. "I would have understood, you know. I feel like we have not even had a real marriage. You hid a whole part of your life from me. You were not honest."

"Would you have understood? Really?" Beth sighed. "I don't think so. Would you have been willing to go to the cabin with me? All I wanted was for us to build memories of our own to replace, or at least build on, the memories that I already had. I wanted Jacen to experience the same magic of our valley that I experienced during my childhood. I wanted the beauty and peace to continue. I know you would have never even stepped foot on that property if you knew that I had loved someone else there. Yet, what you wouldn't have seen is that the valley represents love to me. A special place where I know that love can flourish and I needed you to be able to see that first hand. I think you did. We had some really nice times there, both with Jacen and also when we brought your other kids up for a weekend. I think they all benefited, they certainly remember the place and all seem to have good memories. Now we are able to take your grandkids with us and they too will benefit."

"You're right, I would have never gone with you had I known what had happened there. I don't think I can ever go again." Ethan instantly saw the look of fear that flashed across her face, then immediately it was replaced with hurt and acknowledgement.

"Please don't say that, please Ethan. Please help me build our memories, help me make them better than anything that ever happened in the past. Don't withdraw from me now. Please Ethan."

"What do you expect from me, Beth? I have feelings too; I'm only human after all. How much can you expect one man to take?" There was a touch of anger in his voice.

"I expect that you are either going to walk out of my life over this, or you are going to stay and try to make things work between us. If you walk, we all lose and I guess you were only in this marriage if it was easy.

"What marriage? We have not even had a marriage for the past fifteen years," Ethan shot back. Beth could hear the underlying venom as he spoke. She was not going to fight with him so she ignored the way it was said.

"Yes, we have had a marriage. Kyle was not a part of our lives or my thoughts. It was always you that I wanted. We started out so happy. I remember when you had that job where you were traveling all over the country for weeks at a time. I used to sit out on the front porch and wait for your car to pull up. I missed you so much. You were the only person on the planet that could have eased my loneliness. So I waited. You were the only man that I wanted. But, you got lazy and complacent, and here we are fifteen years later and I don't feel the same anymore. But, the truth is that I have stayed with you because I want to feel that way again. I want to long for you, to miss you when we are apart, to look forward to seeing you. This is what I need to feel."

"I still feel that way about you, Beth," Ethan choked out as he turned his head away trying to hide his tears from her. Seeing his tears brought a fresh wave of tears to her eyes.

Beth put her hand on his chin moving his face toward her so she could look into his eyes. "I need to feel that way too, Ethan," she said gently. "If you decide to stay with me we are going to have to forgive each other. We are going to have to listen to each other. I am going to have to earn your trust back and I know it will take a long time and I have to be prepared for you to never completely trust me again. You have to earn my respect back. You are going to have to take a look at our situation and take some of my burden, and carry it with strength. I need to respect you, Ethan, and that is going to take some work on your part. But, the good thing is that we no longer have any secrets between us. You know what I carry in my heart. You know my sins. It's actually a relief to me because I always feared that someone, someday, would say something about my past relationship with Kyle. There would be some reference to the cabin or something and I would have to try to explain and you would know that I have kept this from you for all of this time. So, we can start with a clean slate, if you are willing, and build from here. If you are willing."

"You can never see that guy again. Ever. I can't even say his name. He has to know that you know what a jerk he really is. He has to know that you deserve much more than he is willing to give you. Beth, I will be up front with you, this is going to really hard for me. I sincerely don't know if I can get past this. I was ready to pack and stay with my brother for a while, but I wanted to hear your side first."

"Are you still going to go?" Beth asked. Ethan detected a hint of fear in her voice.

"Not tonight."

"Please try to stay with me, Ethan. Try to make things work. I know this is major and I know that I have been wrong, but everyone makes mistakes and I made a big one. I did not sleep with him."

"You would have though. The relationship was heading in that direction."

"I can't deny that," Beth replied shamefully.

"I should have just not said anything and watched to see how far you would have gone. Instead I had to interfere and blow it for you."

"You may have saved me from doing something that I would have regretted."

"Maybe . . I would like to think that you would have regretted it. I also did it for Jacen. He is so close to you. Mothers are like saints to their sons and I can't destroy that illusion for him. He really does think you are a saint. It has to stay that way. I don't want him to ever know about this."

"Thank you Ethan, I don't want him to know either. I do have one question though. I presume that you read my emails, but how do you know what I wrote back?"

"I was searching all through your email and was able to hack into the system and see things that you had deleted plus emails that you had written. I know everything Beth, so there is no need to try to hide anything from me. You even told your sister how unhappy you were. She knew all along about this guy and nobody ever said a thing to me. They really played me for a fool."

"Ethan, that is not true. Yes, I admit, I confided in my sister about some of my feelings, but nobody has ever known the whole extent of my relationship with Kyle. I never told anyone. Susan knew how close we were when we were kids and she knew what I had been through and how badly I had been hurt. But, nobody ever knew that we continued to see each other after he married. Neither of us ever told anyone. Nobody played you for a fool."

"That isn't what it feels like on this end," Ethan said with a sigh. He put is arm around her shoulder. He could see that Beth was starting to get chilled. "Come on, we better start back." Beth put her arm around his waist and they walked arm in arm in silence, both deep in thought with their own demons, back to the house.

***

That night, Beth went to bed first. She was so tired that she couldn't keep her eyes open any longer. Ethan told her that he wanted to watch the late news and would be to bed in a little while. While Beth was struggling to fall asleep, she heard Ethan's gentle snoring from where he sat on the couch. He was still on the couch as the sky started to lighten with dawn. *I wonder if he will ever forgive me, really,* thought Beth with despair.

Chapter Twenty-Eight

The first item on Beth's agenda was to review her email and see if she could see what Ethan saw. She had saved all of Kyle's emails so she could read them over and over. With her password, Ethan could read all of the emails that Kyle wrote to her. She next checked the trash bin on her computer to see if there was anything still there. Yes, there it was, two emails from Susan, sent to the trash bin, but not completely deleted from there. Ethan had read those also. She checked her folders and was horrified to see that her **SENT** folder had 25 emails saved. These were the emails that she had sent. How did they get there? Why were they saved? *How could I have never noticed that my email system saves all of my outgoing mail?* Then she remembered. Ethan had originally set up this email account for her. *Of course he knew my password. How could I have been so stupid, so careless? I never thought he would pry.* Under the account options, there it was. The box was checked to save all outgoing email to the 'SENT' folder.

Beth opened the folder and re-read all of the email that she had sent Kyle and Susan. Things and feelings that came from the very core of her soul, things that were never meant for Ethan's eyes, feelings that came from a place in her that was very private, were all intermixed in emails that were sent to Kyle, and to Susan. By talking to Kyle and then seeing him, thirty years of emotions spilled out all at once. So much for one person to grasp. Beth never took the time to analyze her feelings, she just felt them. They came pouring out of her, tumbling over and over, and she wrote. It felt so natural to write to Kyle, anything and everything that she felt. She had spent two years in her youth writing to him every day. Telling him everything she felt back then. He knew her. He knew how she wrote. He knew her intensity, he knew her passion, and he understood her. Some of what she wrote came from her simply being unhappy. Some of what she wrote was an illusion, the remembrance of the relationship they once had. He knew they could never go back to that happy time in their lives, they were not even the same people they once were. He understood that she had taken a fragment of time, a happy time for both of them, and somehow managed to save it intact in her heart and then use it as a frame of reference to describe their relationship today. Although some of what she wrote was an illusion, he also knew that some of what she felt was very real. He knew, because he felt it too. He listened to her, read her words and took them to heart. The remarkable fact was that from the pages and pages that she wrote to him, he could read and grasp an understanding of her that was a true reflection of her feelings. *Oh my God,* she thought. *This is what Ethan read, all of this. He would not have understood the history, the time invested or where all the passion came from. He would not have gotten the same meaning from what I wrote that Kyle did. How could I have been so careless? No wonder he is so hurt.* Beth unchecked the box that saved all of her outgoing email, closed all of her folders and exited. She felt numb knowing the depth of pain she had caused Ethan. *Ethan, I have underestimated you. You are trying so hard to be understanding and work through this with me. I know how very hard this must be for you. I am so sorry that I have put you in this position. I am so sorry that I have hurt you. I hope that you can find it in your heart to forgive me. Forgive me for not being honest with you from the beginning. Forgive me for deceiving you. Forgive me for not trusting in you and your love for me. Forgive me, Ethan, please.*

Beth knew she had to let Kyle know what had happened. She had to make a choice; she had to let Kyle go, once and for all. *It's time to close that door, lock it and throw away the key.* The question was, could she do it?

Chapter Twenty-Nine

~

EMAIL
TO: klm@qmail.com
FROM: beth0711@qmail.com
RE

Dear Kyle,

This is the hardest thing that I have ever had to write to you. Ethan got into my email account and read the emails that you wrote to me, and the emails that I wrote to you. It has been a very tough time for us; I have caused a tremendous amount of hurt to people that I love. He is trying very hard to be understanding and work through this with me. I have realized that he is being there for me in a way that you never have been.

I know that you will be concerned that he will

want revenge. I have asked him not to involve your family. There is no reason to hurt any more people with this. He has agreed that there would be no benefit in telling Dena, so you can rest well about that. He understands that I am the one who called you and he knows that I am the one who was pursuing the relationship. That much was evident in the emails that I sent to you. He told me that he has your address and had driven by your house.

Truth be told, Ethan painted a picture of our relationship with completely different colors than I had ever seen. The portrait he painted is that of an unhappy, needy woman reaching out to a man who never really wanted her. A man who had years of opportunity to come for her, but didn't. A man who would have always put her second in his life, always. A man who would knowingly allow her to settle for second and let her jeopardize her family in the process. A man who could see, what she couldn't see, or wouldn't see, that he would walk away from her eventually, leaving her with nothing. A man who would put nothing on the line for her, and would walk away, without looking back, at the first hint that she may cause an inconvenience in his life. It was a very unflattering picture, Kyle. I deserve far better. I do.

The sad part is that I was willing to walk away from Ethan. A man who has always put me first and would never have allowed me to be put in the situation that you have. He thought enough of me to marry me and pledge his life to me. I underestimated his love for me, or took advantage of it. I never thought he would be willing to stand by me in a situation like this. I am very ashamed that I hurt him as I have. I am just glad that you and I did not act on the feelings that we both had. That would have been too much to for Ethan to forgive. I know it was just for lack of opportunity and Ethan knows that too.

This time it's me saying good-bye. Sometimes when we say good-bye, we know that it's just for a little while, and it is not really good-bye. This time however, it has to really be good-bye. Ethan deserves a wife who is devoted one hundred percent to him, and finally, after fifteen years, I am going to try to give him that.

Right now I am really hurting inside. There seems to be a million kinds of hurt churning around inside of me. Admittedly, one of them is loss. I guess it is the loss of the relationship that I thought we had that maybe was never really there. Was it there Kyle? Was it ever there? I know in my heart that you are a good man. I know you never wanted to cause pain either. I wish you happiness in your life. You deserve to be happy. Good-bye Kyle.

Beth

~

***

Beth did not read over her thoughts. She struggled only for a split second with her emotions, then hit the send button. It felt so final this time, so permanent. Letting out a long sigh, she realized she had been holding her breath. She was trying so hard to maintain her strength and not break down. Was her struggle really between Ethan and Kyle? No, she realized, Kyle was never really an option. He was never available to her anyway. Her struggle was letting go of the illusion of a special gift of true love that she had imagined had been bestowed upon her. She always thought she was special and that's why God had given her the gift of true love, a love so pure that it withstood the trials of both time and space. Fresh tears welled up in her eyes as she realized that she had just taken a giant step toward growing up. She was releasing forever an illusion, a dream. Although it was a beautiful illusion, it was an illusion, nonetheless. *I am not sure if I want to grow up, not sure if I want to let this go,* she thought to herself. As her inner struggle continued, her practical side interjected. *I guess since I am now in my middle forties, it's about time to finally accept what's real and what's an illusion and get on with what is really important, being a mother to Jacen and a wife to Ethan. They both deserve all of me.* She closed her email and walked away.

***

Being busy at work helped keep her mind off her personal life. It was only a temporary escape however. Ethan called her several times a day, just to say hello and make sure that she was doing okay. Things were different between them. There seem to be a conflict between what he was saying to her and how he was treating her. He was telling her that he was there for her, loved her and forgave her. Yet, he slept most nights on the couch, telling her that he just fell asleep there. He avoided touching her. She was trying so hard to give him the space and time he needed, and keep a positive attitude. She did not complain when he didn't make it to bed. She respected his distance from her, hoping that time would heal his hurt. Two days later, she was surprised to find an email from Kyle. Her heart jumped when she saw his name in her inbox.

~

EMAIL
TO: beth0711@qmail.com
FROM: klm@qmail.com
RE

Dear Beth,

I received your mail regarding Ethan getting into your email account. I don't have any idea how he could have read what you sent or how he got my name and address. He must be pretty damn bright when it comes to this computer stuff. Are you sure that he is not going to try to mess with me? Or cause problems for my family? We were trying to keep our families out of what you and I were doing, talking and whatnot. I hope you are right, I hope he keeps this in his end of town.

My main reason for writing, Beth, is to tell you how very sorry that I am for hurting you. I never meant for you to get hurt with any of this. It seems that

throughout our lives, I have hurt you so many times. Please believe me when I tell you that I've never meant to. You have been very important to me, you are a part of my life, a part of my past and nobody can ever take that away from us. You are still important to me, however, it seems that you and I are just not meant to be together. Something like this always happens, you would think that after all of these years we would see the writing on the wall.

I sincerely hope that you and Ethan can work through this and that you can finally find some happiness. You deserve that and so much more. I mean that from the bottom of my heart.

    Always,
    Kyle

~

***

He did care for me. I knew he did. Knowing that he did care for her was a small comfort. She still had a hollow feeling in her, an emptiness. *Ethan and Jacen. I need to fill that void by giving more to Ethan and Jacen. I can fill it. I know I can.*

***

"I hate that he got away with treating you like he did," volunteered Ethan, one evening after dinner. Jacen was in his room reading and Ethan and Beth were watching a movie together. "I feel like I just let someone walk on you and get away with it. I think I would feel better if I beat the shit out of him. What kind of husband am I to let someone get away with that?"

"Ethan, we can let it go," Beth nervously replied. "Just let it go."

"Does his wife even know what kind of a snake she's married to? She probably has no idea. She should know. She should have the choice of staying married to a snake, or finding someone who would treat her decently. I would never do something like that to you, Beth."

"I know, Ethan. More than ever I have realized. I am flattered that you feel the need to defend my honor, but I was guilty here too. I want to just walk away and put all of this behind us. Please?"

"I know you do. I do too. I just feel that it is unfinished."

"I finished it, Ethan. I said good-bye. I walked away. We need to concentrate on us now and leave the rest. Whatever the relationship between him and his wife is their problem, not ours. I don't want to make it ours. I have caused her enough pain already, I don't want to add any more bad deeds to my list, thank you very much!" She tried to put lightness in her voice to indicate that the subject could be closed now, that there was no more that needed discussion. They went back to watching the movie, but Beth felt the subject was still lingering in Ethan's mind.

***

"I sent him an email, Beth," Ethan remarked one evening, about a week later. "I just couldn't let it go. He had to know that you have someone who thinks enough of you to 'defend your honor', as you put it. He had to know that I was not going to let anyone treat you as he did and get away with it. He had to know that I would never put up with him hurting you again. You are far too good for him and important to me. I would never allow him to throw you crumbs again. If he were any kind of a man who cared for you at all, he would have been up front about all of this. He made it ugly by being deceitful. If he had wanted to make you happy, Beth, I would have stepped aside. I swear I would have. But he was willing to use you, willing to take advantage of the fact that I was not making you happy. Then, you took all the blame and he just hid behind you. He did not even contact me to take any of the blame; he just let you take it all. That is not a man in my eyes. I couldn't just let it go. I'm sorry, but I just couldn't."

"What did you say?" asked Beth. She was loved. She liked the feeling. He defended her; he stood up for her. She smiled at him.

"Do you want to read it?" he asked her.

"Yes." He turned and pulled his laptop out of his briefcase and opened it up.

~

EMAIL
TO: klm@qmail.com
FROM: Ethan@qmail.com

RE: YOU ARE TREADING ON THIN ICE

You are the scum of the earth and you are stepping on the wrong toes! Only a snake treats someone with the lack of respect that you showed my wife. You are a man without the balls to even take the responsibility for your actions. You, once again, left the situation up to her to handle. I feel sorry for your wife. I wonder if she knows just how low of a person you are. You are lower than a cockroach in my eyes, and I never want you to contact my wife again. There is no reason for you to ever see her or talk to her again. Ever. Have I made my position crystal clear?

~

Beth was touched by Ethan's actions. He wanted to be her knight in shinning armor. He wanted to defend her honor. No one had ever done that for her before, and she liked it. Her heart was healing. Although there was still tension between her and Ethan, she was really trying to make amends for her actions. She sincerely wanted things to work between them.

The weekend came and Ethan did not want to go to the mountains with her. "I just don't think I can ever go there again," was his comment when she asked if he would go with her. Her heart ached, but she needed the solitude away from the city and he encouraged her and Jacen to go. Jacen loved being there almost as much as she did.

The following week was another busy week at work for her. She threw herself into her work, setting up strategies for growth of her business. She volunteered to help with a couple of Taekwondo projects that were going on in her school. She was extra attentive to Jacen, and the areas of interest to him. Ethan was still distant with her. They had not made love in weeks and he was still sleeping mostly on the couch. The times that he did come to bed with her, there were always blankets between them, or he fell asleep fully clothed. She was giving him space, yet always letting him know that she was there for him whenever he was ready. There was still conflict in him though, she could see it. She wondered if they would ever really be able to put this behind them.

***

"Your friend sent an email back," Ethan mentioned one evening. It had been over two weeks since he sent his email to Kyle and Beth had not expected him to reply. Ethan was at the kitchen table finishing up some work and decided to check his email.

"What does he say?" Beth asked trying to sound casual.

"See for yourself. What a jerk he is."

~

EMAIL
TO: Ethan@qmail.com
FROM: klm@qmail.com
RE: YOU ARE TREADING ON THIN ICE
Yes, you have made yourself quite clear. There is no reason for any further contact.

~

The finality of it hit her with such force that she was unprepared for her own reaction. She felt as though someone had just punched her, full force, in the stomach. She couldn't breathe. What was she expecting? Did she think he would realize that he couldn't live without her and come for her? Did she think he would resist letting her go? Even a little? *He just turned and walked away. Just like that. He didn't even fight for me a little. What did I expect?* Did she hope that he would at least take some of the responsibility for what had happened, that he would try to take some of the blame? She was struggling to maintain her calm, trying to appear detached, although she was screaming inside.

"This is the guy you threw me away over," said Ethan, sarcastically. "He is really a jerk, Beth, really a jerk. Even after giving him every opportunity to take the blame, to try to protect you even a little, he didn't. He just turned away and left you holding the bag." Beth looked stricken. "He is a bigger asshole than I thought he was. It crossed my mind that maybe you two could have been happy, that maybe you were making the effort to be together and I blew any chance of happiness that you might have had. I actually felt bad, like maybe I should have not interfered. But, he simply does not want you, Beth. I'm sorry for you, this must hurt a lot. I feel bad for you that you have carried these feelings for all these years for someone who does not deserve to stand on the same planet as you, and cares so little. He is a jerk, Beth, a complete loser."

Beth read the email one last time, then turned away

to go do the dinner dishes. She tried to hold back the tears. One fat tear spilled from the corner of her eye and slid down her cheek to the corner of her mouth. It tasted salty.

Chapter Thirty

Life, of course, was still going on around her. Beth still had clients to deal with and tax season was just around the corner.   Jacen was getting ready for a Taekwondo tournament; he was planning on competing.

"I am going to need a new uniform, Mom," Jacen announced on the phone one afternoon just after getting home from school. "My old ones are getting too short and so I'll need a new one to compete in."

"Well, I suppose that can be arranged," Beth replied with a dramatic sigh as though the wants and needs of a teenage son were never-ending.

He was right. It seemed to Beth that he had grown inches over the past couple of months, he had finally caught up with her and was thrilled that he was now finally taller than she was. His favorite comment to her was, "Hey Mom, look up at me!" Then he would giggle. *He is growing up so fast,* she thought, *he is becoming a man. I wonder what kind of man he will be? He has had Ethan as a role model, which is been both a blessing and possibly a curse. Jacen treats me wonderfully, always taking care of my needs first. He will treat a girlfriend and eventually a wife the same way. That is good. I worry about his work ethic. He does not have any idea that up until recently, wives stayed home and took care of the household and the husband was the sole provider. Ethan has not provided the role model of a provider and Jacen has seen that. I can only give him the best that I have and the rest will have to be up to him,* Beth thought with resignation.

Beth liked the change of seasons. Fall was rapidly approaching winter and all the stores were decorated with the rust and gold, pumpkins and dried corn that depicted the time of year. There was a certain coziness that she loved, picturing herself in flannel jammies and fluffy slippers, sitting in front of a roaring fire with a cup of tea or chocolate, reading a good book. A quiet comfort went along with darkness approaching at four in the afternoon that Beth was looking forward to. She was hoping that the long snug evenings in a family setting would help Ethan ease out of his hurt.

"You left me again last night," Ethan remarked one morning as Beth was getting ready for work. Although the mornings were now decidedly cold, Beth felt a new chill tingle down her spine. "In my dreams," clarified Ethan.

"They are just dreams, Ethan. You have always had

them."

"Now I know why. All these years I have wondered why I always dream that you leave me. You never even look back. You never care for my feelings. Now I know."

"Ethan, please. These are dreams and you never before had any reason to have them."

"Yes I did. I have been married to someone else's woman for the past sixteen years. I must have known somehow in my mind."

"No," Beth whispered, "It was not like that. Please," she pleaded, "we don't have to go through all of this again."

"No, we don't," he said at last. He sounded tired. He seemed smaller somehow. Beth felt him throw up new walls, shutting her out. She had seen the look move across Ethan's face, the shadow of doubt, and the momentary possibility that he did not know her at all. The possibility that over the past sixteen years, the woman that he thought of as truthful and honest, maybe had never been. Maybe she had always been deceitful and unfaithful. Maybe he had just been a fool. In spite of the horror of what she saw, she was grateful when it passed and no more was said. No more stones thrown. With no more pride left in her, she felt drained.

The holidays came and went, almost without notice. Beth tried to keep the mood light and festive, but the underlying strain between them was invariably there. Ethan had only been to the cabin with her twice. Both times there had been a tension between them that was palpable.   Beth spent more time with Jacen. He sensed sadness in her that he did not understand, but did not say anything.   He told her that he loved her frequently, it warmed her heart that he was so sensitive and caring.

In mid January, Ethan had to attend a class that took him out of town for three days. He seemed hesitant to go. Beth knew that he simply did not trust her and would be miserable for the entire time that he was gone.   In his absence, she felt such a lifting of the burden of guilt that she lived with each day. It made her realize that her guilt was a reflection of Ethan's treatment of her. *Is this my punishment for the pain that I caused? How much longer can I live with this stress? Ethan had been so warm and understanding in the beginning. He said that he knew what had driven me to go look for love somewhere else. He had not blamed me entirely for my actions. He realized how unhappy I must have been to take such drastic steps. He said he knew that I was not a deceitful person and that I hated having to live a lie. He was right. I hated the lies, the deceit, but mostly I hated the direction that his and my relationship had gone. He vowed to take responsibility for this family. He promised to throw himself back into his work and start providing financially for this family again. He seemed so sincere and so much in love with me that I believed him. I believed that this time was different, this time he would really come through. Do I have the right to feel anger? Did I really hear from him what I thought I heard? Or, was I just in so much pain from the hurt that I had inflicted that I heard what I wanted to hear?*

Beth realized that he was not working more, in fact

he was working less. It was as if he was daring her to say something about it. She realized why her mountain cabin was such a haven for her and Jacen. There was no stress or strain when just she and Jacen were there alone. No conflict. She began to wonder if perhaps it might be better for both of them to live without this constant tension between them - to separate. She found it difficult to breath, just thinking about it. It had to be a relief for him also on the weekends that she was gone. Was she just a constant reminder of hurt and disillusion? She tried to imagine what her life would be like without Ethan. A small place with just her and Jacen. Would it be the same harmony that they felt on the weekends up at the cabin? Movies on the VCR in the evenings, homework at the kitchen table, Beth curled up on the couch with a book. It was tempting.

But, then he returned and life continued. A week gone, a month, chilly nights, nights alone. Beth kept busy with Anne and Sonja. She took Jacen to the movies, started involved projects at the cabin, read book after book and worked harder than ever. She kept a smile on her face and did not complain. She did not confide in Susan or Sonja or Anne. She kept her thoughts close to her heart, her heart that was silently grieving. Grief that she could share with no one. Grief for a special love lost. Grief for her marriage that was not working. Grief for the hurt she had caused. Grief for her loneliness, loneliness that was so acute at times that she did not think she could bear it another day.

Two weeks after Ethan returned from his business trip, Beth's mom called and invited her to fly up for a couple of days. Susan was planning on being in town and she was hoping that Beth would be available to visit.

"It would be so nice to see you," Beth's mom replied. *I think she senses something wrong,* Beth thought. "Susan is coming in on Thursday and leaving the following Monday afternoon. If you could work it into your schedule, it would be so wonderful."

"Let me run it by Ethan," Beth responded. "I'll call you back in the morning, okay?"

Ethan drove her to the airport. Conversation was polite and careful as they discussed topics of generalities.

"You should have really nice weather," Ethan offered.

"Yeah, Mom said it's been in the high thirties at night, but during the day it had been almost fifty. Which, by our standards is still cold so I packed a couple of sweaters."

"This is a pretty time of year up there."

"I like having real seasons, we don't get to experience that here. That's one of the downsides of living in Southern California. My parents sure love being away from the city."

Beth's parents had moved to a beautiful home on two acres of horse property in northern California after retiring. They were close enough to the city to have all the conveniences of city living, but far enough to have the quiet and peace of the country. Beth loved their new home, although she missed them terribly since they had moved. She was really looking forward to seeing Susan, whom she had only seen a couple of times since she had moved out of state.

Ethan pulled up to the terminal at the airport and he parked in the loading zone. Beth realized that he was not going to park and go up with her.

"You only have the one carry-on bag, right?" Ethan asked.

"Yes," Beth replied, "I can manage it okay, it will save you having to park and all that." Her voice sounded a little different, strained, as though she was trying hard to mask the hurt that she was feeling. If Ethan caught it, he didn't say anything. He had always walked her to her gate whenever she had flown anywhere. He got out and unloaded her bag for her. A quick embrace and a chaste kiss half on the lips, half on the cheek and he was ready to let her go.

"Have a good trip," he told her as he was turning away to close the car door that was still open from when he unloaded her luggage.

"I'll call you when I get there," she offered.

"Thanks, that way I won't worry. Bye." And he headed for the driver's side of the car, turning away from her. She pulled out the handle of her bag and pulled it behind her as she headed for the double doors that would take her to the gate, where her flight was to leave within the next hour or so. She was glad that she was reading a good Dean Koontz book because his books were so intense that it kept her mind from drifting to her own life. *Thank you Dean Koontz,* she thought, *I wonder if you know how instrumental you are in helping me keep my sanity.* The thought made her smile as she walked to her gate.

Northern California is beautiful in winter. Crisp,

clear, blue sky, the scent of burning wood lingering in the air from all the cozy fireplaces with roaring fires burning in living rooms, heating the homes in the country. Beth was glad she had brought a jacket on the flight because the air was noticeably colder than it was two hours ago when she left the airport in Los Angeles.

Susan was there to meet her. They saw each other immediately and embraced with a genuine hug. Energy was exchanged, Beth felt it immediately and it soothed her soul. She sensed that Susan felt it too, like the feeling of coming home. There was familiarity between them, the secrets that they each held plus the ones that they had shared with only each other. Smiling and chatty they drove through the country roads to their parents' snug home.

The weekend went quickly. Most of their time was spent in the company of one or both of their parents so there was little private time to discuss her relationship with Ethan, or Susan's relationship with Michael. Beth found that she didn't want to talk about it any more. Maybe it was still to too raw; the hurt she caused Ethan and the loss of Kyle. *How do you lose something that you never had?* Beth mused to herself. She wanted to talk of other things, so she avoided the opportunity to have time alone with Susan. She needed the routine of a happy family, time without stress, with laughter and people who were treasuring every minute that they spent with each other. Her family was good for her. They loved her, and were supportive. They knew she was hurting, but they did not pry, however, they let her know in subtle ways that if she wanted to talk, or needed anything, that they were there for her. She began to relax. She laughed a little easier and it was genuine. She did not need to keep her happy face on because it was real, the joy that she was feeling. Liberating. Her family, unknowingly, had strengthened her resolve to forgive herself, to make her happiness genuine, to discard her guilt and close this chapter in her life. Door closed . . . Ethan would find that he had a happy, loving wife again. He could choose to accept her and live with her without the disquietude that had developed between them, or not. She found that she could finally shed her unhappy skin, end her grieving and go on with her life. Liberating. Yes, very liberating.

Last night I had a dream. Something had scared me and I turned to Ethan for comfort. He was there for me, as he had always been. He was there to comfort and hold me. He had touched me, in my dream, reached out to hold me and make me feel loved and safe. I felt joy in my heart. He had finally come back to me and was ready to walk forward in life, hand in hand. I woke still clinging to the joy that I felt, knowing somehow that it was a message, a premonition that everything would work out fine.

When the plane landed at LAX, Beth gathered her rolling bag from the storage compartment above her seat. She had managed to come home with the same amount of luggage that she left with. This was not always the case when she traveled. With her black oversized purse slung over her shoulder and dragging a rose and teal tapestry rolling bag, Beth emerged from the long enclosed ramp between the plane and the airport gate. She expected Ethan to be there to pick her up and she realized that she was looking forward to seeing him. She spotted him immediately in the crowd that was greeting other travelers. He was wearing a pair of navy slacks and tan sweater. *He looks very handsome,* she thought. With his salt and pepper hair and well-trimmed mustache and beard, he was indeed a very distinguished looking man. It was as if she was seeing him for the first time, and she liked what she saw. She felt her step quicken when she spotted him, lighten, actually. He spotted her too. Smiling, he started making his way through the crowd toward her.

Without thinking about what she should say, or how she should be, she just acted. Standing her bag on end next to him, she threw her arms around his neck and held tight. She felt his body stiffen slightly, as if he was not expecting her embrace and was not sure he was ready for it. He paused ever so briefly then pressed his body hesitantly to hers. Suddenly, it was as if a dam in him finally gave way, and he held her tight, fiercely holding her against him. He buried his face in her hair, nuzzling her neck, drinking in the scent of her and the softness of her skin.

"God I have missed you, Beth," he whispered in her ear, his warm breath tickling her skin. Time seem to stand still as she clung to him, relishing the moment, preserving it into her memory, to be called up again at will. *I feel like I am home again,* she thought as he stepped from their embrace. His face softened as he looked at her then said with a smile, "Lets go home."

***

Both Ethan and Beth started picking up the pieces of their life together. One by one, the pieces were fitted into place. As with any difficult puzzle, sometimes a piece looks like a perfect fit, but when attempting to put it into place, it just doesn't quite fit. There were many times like that in the beginning. They finally began to talk to each other. Both avoided saying 'in other words, you mean this' as a way to cause pain, but instead actually listened to the words being said. Occasionally Beth would glimpse an expression of sadness in him, lasting only an instant. She knew it was like the touching of a nerve, a jolt that disappeared the moment he let it go. Letting go was very hard for him. He had to give up a part of himself in order to cross the bridge that would allow him to truly forgive her and go on with her as part of his life. It was a long road before he came to the bridge, the bridge that had to be crossed, a conscious decision made that he would brave the bridge because life with her continued on the other side.

Making love was a little awkward at first. Ethan seemed almost shy as he approached her after not having done it for so long. He was tender with her, kissing her deeply, stroking her body, paying attention to every inch of her skin. She was responsive and passionate. Her passion was for him and him only. They slept close to each other; she was no longer alone in her bed, but snuggled up close to Ethan's warm body.

Beth knew there were to be obstacles. The pain was not gone, but the healing process had finally started. She felt in her heart that she and Ethan would make it together. There were still other problems to resolve; problems that had developed over the past sixteen years and would not disappear overnight. Issues had to be discussed; feelings put on the table, compromises to be made. Beth knew she would have to give up a part of herself, as would Ethan, in order for them to function as an 'us'. She also realized how important it was for each of them to learn which parts of themselves that they were unwilling, or unable, to give up, that no matter what, had to be preserved. Their individualism is what will keep their relationship alive, interesting, succulent.

There are no more secrets between us. Our relationship has been put to the test, and we survived it. Talking is easier now, because it seems that more effort is made to try to honestly understand each other's perspective and point of view. In many ways I feel very foolish for what I did. Kyle walked out of my life and never looked back. Maybe things had to happen as they did for secrets to finally be told and a door to be opened that I thought contained a treasure, but in reality, contained nothing at all. Ethan and I need to build our own treasure together, a treasure we can count on, a treasure that will always be there for both of us.

Jacen is much more relaxed now. He sees his parents laughing with each other and touching again. He acts like he is embarrassed, but I can tell that he is secretly pleased.

Spring is a time of renewal. New green shoots sprout up from the ground, buds form and blossom into beautiful, colorful flowers. Our family seems to be in harmony with the universe, experiencing the same process of renewal, growth and color. Maybe a bit of my eternal optimism, my belief in love, is at work here. After all, that is the part of me that I choose to keep, that no matter what, had to be preserved, the individualism that keeps my relationships alive, interesting, succulent.

* 9 7 8 0 9 7 1 6 6 8 1 0 2 *